MATTER OF AVALON
VOLUME I
RETURN TO GAMALAOT

A NOVEL BY

E.J. Spencer

E.J. Spencer
MatterOfAvalon.com
EJSpencer@MatterOfAvalon.com

ISBN: 979-8-9930647-0-3

Cover design by E.J. Spencer

Printed in the United States of America.

Return to Gamalaot

Chapter I
The House Ragnell

In the dead of night, while all of house Ragnell slept, flames crackled fiercely from the narrow stone hallway. Savage and hungry, they lashed at the windows and doorways, roaring like some great beast, its breath hot and choking. In its wake, the desperate cries of terror were smothered, drowned beneath the sharp clatter of steel against steel, the heavy thud of boots that dragged through the smoke and ash. The voices that sought to break free were swallowed whole by whetted iron, their pleas cut short as blades ripped through soft, unprepared flesh.

"Gavain!" said a woman; her sharp cry tore from her lips as she sprang from the bed, her heart thundering in her chest. The stench of smoke choked her, thick and bitter, as it crawled into the room. She stumbled toward the bassinet across from the bed, hands shaking with fear and urgency. With a swift, desperate motion, she gathered the baby boy into her arms, pulling him close, murmuring soft, soothing words.

"I've got you. I've got you."

She turned her head sharply toward the door, straining to catch the ragged, shrill cries that seemed to hang in the air—distant yet painfully near, like something trying desperately to pull and tear into the room. Without a second thought, she darted for the narrow side door by the bed, her feet barely touching the floor as she moved, driven by a fear she had never known before.

"Hrethel? Hrethel, are you awake?"

"Yes, milady," a voice returned from the other side.

"Open the door! Quickly!"

The matronly nursemaid eased the door to her humble room open, and the woman with the babe in her arms stepped in.

"Milady!" Hrethel exclaimed, her arms wrapping around the woman in a warmth born of years spent in service and affection.

"Take him, Hrethel. Please."

"Of course," she replied, her hands gentle as she took the child, drawing him close against her breast. Her gaze, soft with a mother's own tenderness, swept over the boy before she spoke again, her voice low and assuring. "You're alright, milord. Everything is alright."

The woman then slipped back into her chamber, vanishing through the door quietly. Only a minute passed before she would return, but within that minute,

Hrethel cradled the baby gently, her movements a little frantic though still rhythmic, as if trying to soothe not just him, but herself. Her gaze lingered upon his small face, drawn to the deep, gleaming emerald of his eyes. In the deathly screaming of the night, those eyes glistened like distant stars, burning bright against the fear and darkness that pressed in around them.

"Good boy. Darling boy."

"Here," the woman said softly as she returned, her hands trembling just a touch as she wrapped the babe in a green sash, the fabric rich and comforting against his small form. She kissed his forehead, her lips lingering, and whispered, "This will keep you safe, my darling boy." Her gaze lifted then, locking onto Hrethel's round face, a well of concern deep within her eyes. "Take him away from here, Hrethel."

"But, milady!" Hrethel's voice cracked, a rush of panic rising in her chest.

"Hrethel," the woman said, her voice firmer now. "Find Lord Marius. He'll know what to do."

"The Archbishop," Hrethel's breath caught in her throat, and tears, like tiny shards of glass, began to sting in her eyes, refracting everything into a million pieces like looking through a broken window. She held the child tighter, the weight of this pressing heavily upon her. With a soft, almost imperceptible breath, she nestled him, her arms protectively thrown around him, her heart a storm of sadness and love. Without another word, without a glance back, she eased through the stone arch window, the cold night air rushing in as they slipped away. And there, in the stillness, her lady was left behind, alone to face what was to come.

Not after a moment's pause, the wooden door creaked open, and two shadowy figures emerged, painted by the pale moonlight that filtered into the small chamber. Cloaked in dark feathers that rustled with each movement, they walked with a quiet menace, their faces hidden behind cold obsidian masks, each shaped like the sharp, twisted beak of a raven. The room seemed to shrink beneath the weight of their presence, as if the very air held its breath.

"You're too late," she said coolly. "You and your bloody Talons have failed."

One of the cloaked figures took a slow step forward, silent. His sword, drawn and gleaming, dripping heavy drops of blood—dark as rubies—onto the floor, each drop landing with a dreadful thud.

"And you don't need that silly mask," she said defiantly. "I know it's you, son."

Hrethel ran with the swiftness of a rabbit and the quiet of a shadow, every step a careful dodge, every breath held tight. She slipped through the night, avoiding the watchful eyes of the feathered cloaks, their metal beaks glinting in the moon's cold light.

All around her, their dark forms swarmed the courtyard, moving amidst the screams and the crackling of burning wood. But Hrethel didn't stop for anything; she couldn't. She pressed forward, guided by the flickering flames and the pale glow of the moon, both fighting to light her way through the chaos. She moved faster, her heart pounding, until, with a sudden jolt, she collided with something solid; something cold and unmoving, like a wall of iron.

"Oh Gods!" she said, a sharp cry escaped her lips, a sound heavy with despair.

"Hrethel?" A voice, deep yet soothing, rumbled from above her.

Her eyes lifted, meeting the form of a man, massive as a mountain. "Sir Wiglaf?" Her voice cracked, and relief flooded her face. "Oh, thank Merlin!"

Before Hrethel loomed a behemoth of a man, a hulking figure that towered nearly nine feet tall, his fists the size of boulders, each one thick and mighty, his graying brown beard, braided with round, stately beads, hung heavy against his chest. His face was square and usually framed by a smile that could seemingly calm even the angriest of storms, but now, in the midst of the carnage, his face was a mask of cold severity, the warmth gone from his eyes, replaced by a grim reflection of the destruction that surrounded them. He stood like a wall of stone.

"Hrethel, this be…"

"Lord Gavain, yes."

"Thank Merlin," Wiglaf said. "And where be Elizabeth?"

Hrethel said nothing.

"Ah. Aye... We must haul ye two from this cursed place. The halls be swarming with Talons."

"We need the Archbishop!"

"He be here already," Wiglaf said.

"And he mustn't be bothered," said a slithering voice from behind them. "I'll take you back to the castle. You'll be safe there."

This voice, the one that cut through the dark, belonged to a tall, slender woman whose pale white skin gleamed in the dim light. Her eyes—sharp and yellow like a serpent's—peeked through the narrow slits of her eyelids, which themselves seemed to curve into a sly, unsettling grin. They gleamed with a strange, almost predatory eagerness. When she spoke, her voice was slow, a slithering drawl, each word twisting and curling around them.

Hrethel held Gavain just a little tighter.

"Aye, Miss Morrigan speaks true," Wiglaf said. "Ye'll be safe in her care, Miss Hrethel. I swear it on me life."

The thin woman stepped forward and extended her hand, her smile wide and toothy. "Come."

Despite feeling this knot of uncertainty tightening in her chest, Hrethel nodded and followed the woman. Wiglaf stood rooted, his eyes tracking their retreating forms as they slipped into the shadowed dark, swallowed by the night. The bray of a horse called out, its sound a comfort, grounding him. And so, with a steadying breath, he pushed forward, his nerves tempered. He crossed the threshold of the door ahead, not exactly knowing what gruesome sight he might be stepping into.

He entered the room to find two raven-cloaked men standing over a motionless body.

"Elizabeth!" Wiglaf shouted.

At that moment, more figures flooded into the room. The first to step through was a man with graying blonde hair, his presence commanding as he entered, clad in red and white armor that signaled like a bold flag. The weight of his uniform seemed to carry a history of battles fought and victories won, though his eyes, keen and calculating, betrayed none of the warmth one might expect from such a man. He moved with purpose, the sound of his footsteps deliberate.

"Arthur!" Wiglaf said with relief.

Behind him came two more, each a force to be reckoned with. First was Lady Guinevere, a woman Wiglaf knew well. She moved with a sharp, purposeful stride, her steps quick and urgent, though her face bore the weight of exhaustion. The lines of worry carved into her pale skin spoke of a life burdened by too much seeing, too much knowing. She wore a golden tunic trimmed in black, her fiery orange curls pulled tight into a bun, practical and unadorned, as though she had no time for vanity. Close behind her came Master Marius La Faye, Archbishop of Gamalaot, the most powerful wizard in Avalon. He entered with a quiet, measured grace, his steps soft but deliberate. His hair, long and white as snow, fell down his back, and his beard trailed just as far. His cloak, a deep navy blue, seemed to catch the starlight, shimmering faintly, as if spun from the night sky itself.

Of the two raven-cloaked men, one stepped forward, his mask gone, revealing the face beneath. A moment of recognition flashed in Arthur's eyes, and with it came a sudden, seething fury. His sword was drawn in an instant, its blade glowing with the alabaster light of Merlin's blessing, a brilliance that seemed to burn away the very shadows of the room. Without hesitation, he lunged toward the man, the air crackling with the weight of his rage. But the cloaked figure was no less swift. In a seamless motion, he drew his own blade, its edge gleaming cold and lethal, a perfect match for Arthur's fury. The clash was inevitable, the tension between them palpable.

"Mordred! How could you?!"

As the swords of Arthur and Mordred collided in a flurry of sparks, the second cloaked figure charged toward the others, a shadowy dagger raised. Before Wiglaf or Guinevere could even move for their weapons, the Archbishop raised his hand with a calm, decisive motion. In an instant, a surge of invisible yet overwhelming magic erupted from his palm, crackling through the air like a thunderclap. The assailant whipped backwards, his body slamming into the stone wall with a sickening thud. The force was so fierce it froze him in midair, shattering his bones like glass, before he crumpled to the ground, motionless.

Mordred continued to repel Arthur's sword strikes until he found an opening. With a swift motion, he held the tip of his blood-soaked blade to Arthur's throat. The men locked eyes with one another. Mordred pressed the tip a little harder, hard enough to draw just a tiny rivulet of blood that slid down his blade.

In the blink of an eye, another raven-cloaked figure materialized from the very air, as though she had stepped out of some vast nothingness. She moved silently, a ghost in the room, leaning in close to Mordred's ear, her whisper edged and urgent. The words that hit him changed the very aspect of his face. Mordred's grip on his sword loosened, and he slowly lowered it, his eyes clouded with a furious understanding. Without a word, this strange woman who had so easily appeared gripped his shoulder, and in an instant, they vanished—swallowed by the darkness, their forms dissolving into ethereal wisps, leaving no trace of them in their retreat.

Arthur slowly reached for his sword and readied himself to cleave the last remaining foe.

"Enough," commanded the Archbishop with a calm and kind voice no one dared challenge. "Wiglaf, please carry him back with you."

"Of course, Master La Faye, sir."

The old wizard smirked to himself, a look laced with apparent amusement. Wiglaf's knightly code, rigid as iron, seemed to forbid him from ever easing into informality whenever he was around him. With anyone else, he was perhaps too casual, but never with the Archbishop, despite a relatively constant pleading. Even so, it was likely the grim scene that had unfolded before them that reinforced Wiglaf's awkward formality. While the chaos had subsided, the bloody aftermath permeated; sorrow lingered in the air, demanding perhaps a certain distance, a formality that shielded all of them.

And so, Wiglaf seized the man from the ground, lifting him roughly over his broad shoulder, offering no tenderness. The assailant's pathetic whimpers rang out, and a cruel grin settled onto the giant's face.

It was just a terrible tragedy, one that would live on in infamy thereafter. The entirety of House Ragnell felled in a single night—everyone except little Gavain Laurent Ragnell, the most famous boy in all of Avalon.

Chapter 2
A New World

The fall of House Ragnell, that gruesome, grim tragedy, lay more than a decade behind Gavain now, and the world of Avalon had faded into something like a half-remembered dream, its features blurred and its language foreign. Under the stern but steady hand of the Archbishop, Hrethel had taken the boy in, and together they carved out a life far removed from the lands of myth and magic, across the icy reach of the North Atlantic and beyond The Veil. In the quiet, unassuming stretches of upper Michigan, the boy grew tall and sturdy, shedding his old name, his old life, for something safe and simple. He became Gavin Green, though he answered simply to Gav. His mother had taken to the name Ethel, wearing it with the same resolve that she brought to motherhood. To be the boy's mother was her foremost duty, a task she shouldered with every fiber of her being, pouring into it all the devotion and dedication she could muster. It was not a role she merely accepted; it was one she embraced wholly, as though the act of nurturing could mend the fractures of their past and anchor them firmly in this new, unassuming life.

And so, for Ethel, those ten years slipped by like sand through her fingers. One moment, Gav was a tiny, wide-eyed child, clinging to her skirts with shy curiosity; the next, he was a boy, and now, nearly twelve, he stood tall and broad-shouldered, teetering on the edge of manhood. Time, it seemed, had a way of racing ahead when she wasn't looking, and as the summer waned, a dread coiled in her chest, tight and unrelenting. She had been putting off this day for so many years now, refusing to pay it mind. No, today, she would be brave. Today, she would be joyful. It was a day to celebrate Gav, to pour out all the love she carried for him, to let it spill over and fill the spaces between them. What lay ahead could wait. It would have to. For now, she would hold fast to this day, to the sweetness of it, and let what will happen when it must.

"Gav! Gav, get up!" Her voice cut through the morning air, bright yet commanding, each word clipped with the precision of her thick English accent. The consonants snapped like whips, urgent and unyielding. "Gav! I said up!"

"Coming!" he said back from the top of the stairs, his voice tinged with the frustration of a boy wrestling with a stubborn shoe, trying to force it onto a foot that seemed to grow faster than his mother could keep up with.

Gav had reached that awkward age, the liminal space where the soft edges of childhood were beginning to slough away, revealing the raw, angular frame of a young man not yet grown. There was a promise in him, though, the kind of promise that might one day carry him onto a field under blazing lights, chasing something grand and fleeting. But what truly set Gavin apart wasn't his body—it was his eyes. They were sharp, like the edge of a blade, and a green so deep and intricate they shimmered with the complexity of a finely cut gemstone. They held something inscrutable, a mystery yet unraveled.

"Be down in a minute!"

To the average ear in their small Michigan town, the pair's conversations were a curious thing. Ethel's crisp, deliberate English clashed with Gav's slow, rolling Midwestern drawl, a peculiar blend that never failed to draw a bemused smile from neighbors and friends. It was a sound that marked them as different, a reminder of the life they'd left behind, even as they carved out a new one here, far from the shadows of Avalon.

"Gav!" Ethel called, her voice rising, her hand cupped halfway to her mouth like a makeshift trumpet. She turned slowly, only to find the boy standing right before her. "Oh! Sorry for shouting, dearie."

"It's all good, Mom!" Gav replied with a grin.

Ethel didn't hesitate. She pulled him into a fierce embrace, her fingers threading through the unruly tangle of his thick brown hair. "Happy birthday!" she said, her voice warm and rich with affection, a little breathless from the suddenness of it all.

"Thank you," he mumbled, his words muffled against her shoulder as he tried, with little success, to squirm free.

"I'm not done, boy!" she laughed, holding him tight for just a moment longer. "Just a little more!" Her voice was soft now, almost a whisper, as if she could press the memory of this moment into him, a keepsake to carry forward.

Gav sighed, a sound that carried both resignation and fondness, the smile never quite leaving his face. Normally, his mother's overprotectiveness might have chafed at him, like a sweater too tight around the neck. But today, it felt right. It felt fitting. It was his birthday, after all. And the love she wrapped around him felt nice.

"You all dressed, love?" Ethel asked, finally pulling away from him. Her eyes swept over him, scrutinizing every crease in his shirt, every wrinkle in his trousers, as though she could will perfection onto him with nothing more than a look.

"I think so, yeah."

"Well then—off to the car with you," she said, waving a hand dismissively, her tone suddenly urgent. "I'll be along soon."

"Where are we going?" he asked, his brow furrowing.

"Never you mind that! I said off!"

"Yes, Mom," Gav mumbled, turning toward the door, though not without a faint chuckle escaping him.

There was something in the way she spoke this morning, a coyness, a secrecy that wasn't entirely like her. And yet, it was still her—still kind, still tender.

Gav made for the door, stepping out into the crisp late-summer air. Kingston was a town that wore the seasons like a well-worn coat—blistering summers giving way to icy winters, the pendulum of change swinging steadily. But today, the breeze was gentle, carrying with it the warmth of summer without the suffocating weight of it. It was the kind of day that made him pause and take a breath.

Out on his porch, Mr. Sydney, his neighbor, was bent over his rose bushes, pruning shears in hand. The man's movements were deliberate, almost reverent, as though each snip were a small act of devotion.

"Morning, Gav," Mr. Sydney called, his voice as rich and deep as the soil beneath the bushes.

The sight of him always made Gav pause. The man was built broad and solid, with a posture that suggested years of hard work, yet his back curved with age or perhaps illness. His dark skin, smooth and marbled like onyx, was etched with small scars. Gav often wondered about the story behind them, whether they were the marks of a past accident or the toll of some war he never spoke of. Despite his imposing frame and the silent power that seemed to hang around him, Gav liked him. In fact, he'd grown quite fond of the man. And oddly enough, there was something else that tied them together, something that felt less like coincidence and more like fate: Mr. Sydney, just like his mother, spoke with an accent so thick and similar to hers.

"Morning, Mr. Sydney," Gav said, his voice light and easy.

"Where are you off to this morning, lad?" Mr. Sydney asked, his weathered hands stilling for a moment as he looked up from his roses.

"Mom's taking me somewhere," Gav replied with a shrug, the mystery of it all still wracking his brain.

"Oh, really? Where to?"

"She won't tell me!"

"Gracious me! You're so impatient!" Ethel's voice rang out. She appeared from the house just then, her figure framed by the doorway. She wore a large cerulean hat that matched the flow of her dress, the vibrant blue bright enough to turn heads.

"Mornin', Syd," she said.

"Morning to you, Miss Ethel."

Gav, watching the exchange, couldn't help but smile awkwardly to himself. There was something about the way the two of them spoke that made him feel like an outsider when he was with them—like they shared a secret.

"Well," Mr. Sydney said after a pause, his voice softening as he tipped his hat toward them, "the pair of you have fun, yeah?"

"Right, right," Ethel replied, her attention already shifting to the car. "Be seeing you, Syd."

"Take care now. Oh! And happy birthday, Gav!" Mr. Sydney called after them, his hands already moving back to the roses, though his gaze lingered on them for a moment longer.

Gav slid the seat back and folded himself into the cramped back compartment of the white Mini Cooper, the familiar scent of old leather and faintly floral air freshener wrapping around him.

"Buckled up?"

"Yes, mom."

"What's with that face, child?" Ethel's voice carried a hint of suspicion, though her focus was on guiding the car out of the driveway.

"Huh?" Gav chuckled, stretching his arms across the back of the seat. "I was just thinking how Mr. Sydney is always so nice to you."

"Is that right?" Ethel mused, her hands steady on the wheel as she backed the car onto the road. "Well, he certainly does seem to run into us a lot. I'd rather him be too friendly than not at all."

"Yeah," Gav agreed, his voice light but teasing. "I think maybe he likes you."

Ethel's grip on the steering wheel tightened just a touch, and Gav could see the faint reddening of her cheeks in the rearview mirror.

"What are you going on about, boy?" she said, trying to sound dismissive, though there was a note of uncertainty in her voice.

"He's always asking about you!" Gav pressed, his grin wide now.

"You're mad, child," Ethel scoffed, though there was a softness in her tone. "He's just being friendly. He asks about you, too, you know."

"I suppose so," Gav muttered, though a thought lingered. "Maybe he's just lonely."

"I would suppose he is," Ethel said with a sigh, her gaze fixed ahead, as though the thought had been on her mind longer than she'd care to admit. "Being so far away from home."

"So you know where he's from, mom?"

There was a pause, a beat of quiet in the car, before Ethel spoke again, her voice just a touch hesitant.

"I think he mentioned Norfolk or somewhere of the like," she said, her words measured, careful.

"Huh," Gav said idly, turning the thought over in his mind. "That in England?"

"Something like that," Ethel replied, her voice quavering just slightly. "A long way from here."

The brief conversation hung in the air, heavy and awkward, as if Mr. Sydney's life before Kingston was a story she didn't want him to know.

The car hummed along, the quiet settling in, casual and familiar. It wasn't an uncomfortable silence, but one that held a kind of peaceful ease, the kind Gav could sink into without thinking too much about it. His eyes wandered to the great green trees that lined the road, their branches swaying lightly in the breeze as they drove toward the city. His mind, however, was elsewhere. He couldn't help but wonder where his mom was taking him. Maybe it was to the electronics store in town, and he'd get to pick out a new game for his computer—something to keep him entertained for the next few weeks. Or perhaps, just maybe, she was planning a surprise party at the park, and all his friends would be waiting there with party hats on and presents in hand.

The trees transformed into brown and red brick buildings as the car turned corner after city corner, making its way deeper into downtown. Gav pressed his face to the window, his hair falling across his eyes. The streets passed by in a blur, but his attention was caught by something ahead—a large stone building, looming ever larger as they drove closer.

The building gleamed in the sunlight, its stone almost marble-like in its whiteness, standing tall and grand like something from a fairytale. The closer they got, the more it seemed to rise up from the earth itself, its walls strong and unyielding. It felt like the kind of place he might read about in stories—a castle or a temple, something meant to hold secrets or magic.

Gav squinted at it, his curiosity piqued.

"Where are we?"

"You'll see!"

The car came to a stop, and the pair stepped out, their shoes meeting the blacktop pavement beneath them. They approached the towering, shining white building that seemed to stretch up toward the sky, its walls smooth and radiant. Ethel led the way, her steps light as she pushed open the colossal double doors.

As they crossed the threshold, Gav was struck speechless by the sight before him. The floor beneath their feet gleamed with a mirror-like chrome, reflecting their movements in perfect clarity. The space around them was vast, open, and impossibly white, the kind of white that absorbed light rather than reflect it. Columns, tall and majestic, lined the wide, almost endless hall. The air felt charged with something—something that made the hairs on the back of his neck stand up.

At the far end of the passage, a sign looked over them, bold and colorful against the pristine backdrop: *Wonder World!*

Seeing the awe in her son's face, Ethel draped her arm around him, her face pulled into a delighted smile full of satisfaction. "Happy birthday!"

Gav, for a moment, was lost in the vastness of it all. His eyes darted around, trying to take it all in. There was this sense that something extraordinary was waiting just around the corner. The possibility of magic lingered in the air.

Ethel guided Gav over to the sign, and as they approached, a second set of doors came into view ahead, leading into a room that was noticeably darker; what lay behind obscured by shadows.

"Hi, Gav!" said a voice, bright and eager, startling him.

"Tommy?" Gav jumped in place, his eyes widening in surprise before breaking into a wide grin. "What're you doing here?"

"Your mom invited me!" Tommy said, his face lighting up with enthusiasm. "Oh! Hi, Miss Green!"

Gav's friend, Tommy, was a small boy—smaller than Gav by a good few inches. He was blonde and round, his body soft in a way that a child is. He was always fiddling with his thick, black-rimmed glasses, which seemed a little too big for his face, constantly slipping down the bridge of his nose.

"The pair of you go off and have fun!" Ethel said, her smile warm as she looked at the two of them.

"You sure, Mom?" Gav asked, hesitating for a moment, torn between the thrill of seeing his friend and a faint pang of guilt at leaving her behind.

"Yes!" Ethel replied, her tone playful but firm, her hands already waving them forward. "Off you go! Off!"

She gave them both a gentle pat, a shooing motion that was both affectionate and decisive. But Gav, unable to resist the pull of his mother's love, darted back toward her, throwing his arms around her for one last hug. Her hand, which had been ushering them away moments before, softened into a tousle of his hair.

"Go have fun, sweetheart," she whispered, pressing a kiss to his forehead, her voice tender. Then, with one last gentle nudge, she sent them on their way, toward the unknown adventure waiting just beyond the doors.

Chapter 3

A Kind of Real Magic

Outstretching before the boys was the *Caribbean Tunnel Tank*, a dark, almost otherworldly room that seemed to go on endlessly. A long hallway of curved glass walls surrounded them, filled with water that bubbled and glowed a soft, luminescent blue. It felt like stepping into another world entirely, a world where the familiar boundaries of reality were distorted. Perhaps it was like the ocean floor, where light dimmed to black and everything moved in floating quietness. Or maybe it was more like the vacuum of space—vast, terrifying, and full of endless mystery. Whatever it was, it was a place where time slowed and the water breathed with a life of its own.

The boys found an empty spot along the wall, claiming it as theirs. They leaned in close to the glass, their breath fogging it for a moment as they narrowed their eyes at the plaque that read: *Bamboo Shark*. They pressed their cheeks to the glass, peering into the watery depths, where a creature with a soft, ribbon-like body of purple and pink spots rested peacefully. Dark bands lined the length of its white form, and it bobbed gently in the water, moving subtly on its pectoral fins.

"I think he's sleeping," Tommy said, his voice hushed with a reverence that matched the quiet of the tank.

"Says he's nocturnal," Gav replied, his voice quiet as he read the plaque. They watched in silence for a moment longer, as if not wanting to disturb the peacefulness of the creature's slumber.

Suddenly, Tommy shot upright, eyes wide with excitement.

"Whoa, look!" he exclaimed, pointing toward a group of three spotted fish darting toward the surface of the water, their movements swift and purposeful. Gav's gaze followed Tommy's finger, and he bent closer to the glass to read the next plaque.

"Those are…Honeycomb Cowfish."

The fish moved swiftly and gracefully, their bodies slicing through the water with a determination that captivated them both. Each one was a work of art, their hexagonal scales glimmering like little shields of armor, shifting in color as they swam past the lights. The boys stood there for a long while, transfixed by their beauty.

They then bounced from wall to wall, their eyes darting from one marvel to the next; fish with iridescent scales, sturgeon gliding like ancient ghosts, and corals that bloomed in vibrant colors, each creature more fascinating than the last. They were swept up in the magic of it all, moving with a kind of wonder-fueled urgency, as if the whole world could slip away if they didn't keep pace. They laughed and pointed, caught in a shared excitement that seemed to echo through the bubbling water around them.

Eventually, they reached the end of the line, stepping out into an entirely new space—a wide open room flooded with bright white sunshine. The skylight above poured down its beams, bathing them in warmth.

Gav's eyes lit up as he spotted an open tank in the center of the room. Automatically, he bounded over to it, his heart racing with anticipation. He leaned over the side, gazing into the humming blue water below. There, darting gracefully along the bottom, was a wide, flat manta ray, its skin the soft, delicate color of peach blossoms. The creature moved with effortless beauty, its wings rippling through the water, soaring.

Gav rolled up his sleeve and plunged his arm into the cool, inviting water. His fingers brushed gently against the smooth, velvety skin of the manta ray, the sensation sending a thrill through his entire body. The manta seemed to respond, gliding closer to him, its enormous form a graceful blur in the blue pool.

"Gav! What're you doing?!" Tommy called out, his voice laced with both concern and disbelief.

"It's alright!" Gav grinned, nodding toward the monitor above them. "See?"

Tommy's eyes flicked up to the wide screen, which was cycling through pictures of manta rays—some gliding gracefully through the water, others being gently touched by people who had their arms submerged in the tank. The images made the whole thing seem normal, almost like they enjoyed being petted and touched.

"Wanna try?" Gav asked, his grin widening as he looked at his friend. "He's really slippery. Almost like bologna!"

"No way!" Tommy exclaimed, taking a quick step back, his face twisting into one of exaggerated horror.

Gav chuckled with amusement, letting his hand linger in the cool water just a little longer. The manta ray swam back around, its broad wings cutting through the water like rudders. It glided closer once more, brushing softly against his fingertips, the sensation like the smoothest silk—thin, slippery, and alive.

"Hey, Gav! Check this out!"

With a quick motion, Gav rolled up his damp sleeve and turned to Tommy, who stood before a pair of towering doors. Above them, a marquee of neon lights flickered and blazed, its colors so vivid that it was almost painful to look at directly. Bold, bright letters flashed with sizzling energy, spelling out: *Invention Dimension.*

A mischievous grin spread across their faces, as though they shared the same thought. Without a care, the two boys dashed through the doors, their laughter ringing out like bells. What lay before them was a world that stretched the very limits of earthly creation—a testament to human ingenuity. Devices of every kind filled the room, so many that Gav and Tommy could hardly take them all in at once.

At the far end of the chamber was a towering machine, its gears and wheels turning in an endless, hypnotic dance. It stood as a monument to perpetual motion, its presence both awe-inspiring and humbling.

In another corner, a maze of distorted mirrors created endless reflections, folding into one another in a surreal cascade of light and shadow. The boys felt dizzy, looking into the infinite paths that refracted before them.

Nearby, a station of sound beckoned, its bells, horns, and pulsing lights responding to the slightest touch. Each chime and buzz a symphony, playing a melody that seemed familiar and patriotic. And beside it stood an interactive telegraph station, its brass wires gleaming and buttons clicking rhythmically. Gav watched, fascinated, as blinking lights spelled out messages in Morse code, a secret language of beeps and clicks, of dashes and dots.

The entire room hummed with energy, each station a gateway into the boundless depths of human imagination. Time itself seemed to blur, the past, present, and future colliding in a whirlwind of discovery.

The boys stood silent for a moment, still, their breaths caught in their throats.

"Whoa," they said together, the word just slipping out. Before them rose a colossal dome of glass, its surface shimmering faintly. They moved toward it, their feet barely touching the ground, drawn to it like moths to some flickering flame.

At its heart, a brass rod stood tall, crowned by rings of tubing that coiled upward in a slow, deliberate spiral.

Unable to resist, Gav reached out and pressed his open palm against the surface of the glass. The moment his skin touched it, there was a flash—a sudden, crackling burst of energy. A bolt of plasma shot from the spiral rings, arcing through the air to strike the surface of Gav's hand. It was quick, intense, and utterly electrifying.

"Wow!" Tommy said, his voice tinged with wonder and nerves. He took a step back, watching as the plasma crackled and fizzed, leaving a bright, lingering trail of light.

Not one to back down from a challenge, Gav placed his other hand on the dome, grinning with reckless excitement. Instantly, a second bolt of plasma shot out from the center, again slamming against the glass with a crackling surge of energy.

Gav turned to Tommy, his eyes sparkling with the thrill of the moment. His smile was wide, inviting, daring him to join in on the fun.

Tommy drew a slow breath. Before him, the glass orb rose, vast and implacable. One step. Then another. His pinky grazed the surface—and the sphere answered. A spark leapt from its core, swift as a knife's flash, searing the space between them. Tommy's heart stuttered. Every nerve in his body howled as the air hummed with the promise of another strike.

But through the glass, Gav's face was framed clearly—unshaken, alight with that bold fire Tommy had always envied. Something tightened in his chest. Not fear now, but resolve, sharp and sudden.

There was no retreat. Not with Gav's eyes on him.

Tommy shut his own, steadied his breath, and laid his palm flat against the cold surface. No hesitation. Only the weight of the moment, and the pulsing energy beneath the glass.

The orb answered in an instant—a torrent of raw energy, plasma unspooling in a furious arc. It coiled around his fingers like lightning given form, searing the glass with a brilliance that nearly blinded them both. The air itself trembled, alive with the snap and hum of power. Heat licked at his skin, electric and close, as if the storm inside knew his touch.

His heart hammered—not with terror now, but with the wild, bright rush of victory.

"Alright!" Gav's voice burst through the charged air, laughter tangling with his words.

Tommy staggered back, breath ragged, the afterglow of energy still prickling in his veins. His cheeks burned, but his grin was unstoppable—wide and unchecked, brimming with the fierce joy of a thing dared and done. No fear. No regret. Only this: the pulse of triumph, hot and sweet in his chest.

Amidst the raucous laughing and shouting, Gav's stomach let out a thunderous growl—raw and insistent, a beast demanding to be fed. Before he could even feign dignity, Tommy's gut answered with a roar of its own, deep and echoing, as if in some primal call-and-response.

The two boys froze for a moment, standing square with one another. A mutual understanding passed between them. It was time for lunch.

They moved past wonders half-seen, marking them with a glance as they hunted for the way back. Their steps were steady but loose-limbed, the kind of gait that comes when hunger gnaws at focus. Gav led them onward, trusting stubbornness over sense.

Through the whirring clatter of *Automation Station,* where mechanical arms manipulated chess pieces with eerie precision. Past the *Simulation Wing,* its cockpits yawning open like metal mouths. Then into *HydroCity,* its miniature lakes glinting under artificial light, rivers carved in precise, tiny channels.

"This place is ginormous," Tommy muttered.

"Seriously."

And then—the lobby. Stark white, almost jarring after the riot of exhibits. A landing place. A sigh of relief. Beyond the polished floors, the cafeteria hummed: the clatter of trays, the murmur of families regrouping. The scent of something fried called out to them. Their stomachs roared in agreement.

The moment they stepped inside, their mothers came into view—Ethel's hand already lifting in a slow, easy wave, her smile an unspoken "eat!"

No need for prodding. The boys were already moving, drawn by the steam rising from the buffet line. Gav's gaze fixed on the mac and cheese—a molten cascade of gold, each noodle glistening. His stomach clenched in anticipation.

Tommy, beside him, zeroed in on the chicken strips. Their crusts cracked and peppered, still hot from the fryer, promising crunch with every bite.

They stacked their plates high enough to satisfy the fearless abandon of boys who'd earned every bite. Trays wobbling, they wove through the chatter and clatter of the cafeteria, past laughing families and scraping chairs, until they claimed a table near the back. Close enough to glance up and catch their mothers' smiles. Far enough to pretend, just for a moment, they were on their own.

The trays hit the table with a solid thunk. They grinned at each other, victorious.

"You having a good birthday so far?"

Gav nodded, maybe too fast. "I am!" But the words came out bright and brittle.

Tommy chewed slowly, then shrugged. "Not a bad way to end summer. You know, school starts next week."

"Ugh. Don't remind me." Gav's nose wrinkled—not at school itself, but at the shadow trailing behind it. The sidelines he knew too well. The practices he'd never join, the jerseys he'd never wear. His fingers drummed the table.

Gav's gaze flicked to his mother—her familiar silhouette, the way her shoulders angled toward him even as she laughed with Tommy's mother. She was protective of him. She loved him, yes. But it was a stifling love that worried too much, a love that never let him try the sort of sports other boys his age were playing.

He swallowed the old frustration like a mouthful of sand, looking at Tommy. He was grinning, happy, ketchup smeared on his cheek. Gav felt the knot in his chest loosen. However gilded the cage, at least he wasn't alone in it. · Tommy's grin was a flash of sunlight, and for a moment, the weight around Gav's chest eased.

With their plates cleaned, they plunged back into the museum's labyrinth, bellies full, legs restless. Every exhibit tugged at them: the whirring dance of robotic limbs, the whispered stories of lost cities carved in miniature. They'd linger, breath caught—then off again, pulled by the next wonder, the next marvel, two comets streaking through the halls.

Time bent around them. The sun dipped low, painting the polished floors gold, and suddenly the day had worn thin. At the exit, they hesitated. Feet aching, clothes rumpled, they traded a glance.

Gav hunched his shoulders against the evening chill, the museum's glow at his back. "Guess I'll see you Monday."

Tommy scuffed his shoe against the pavement. "Yeah. Monday."

Their fists met—brief, solid—then they turned toward separate cars. The lot stretched between them, asphalt still warm from the day's sun.

"You have fun, dearie?"

"Yes, mom."

As they drove home, Gav stared out the window, his eyes following the sinking oranges and pinks of the horizon, the colors bleeding together. The last remnants of daylight slowly slipped away, and with them, a sense of peace settled over him. It had been a good day, a great one, and he didn't realize how much he was savoring the moment until it was interrupted.

He was so lost in his own thoughts, he hadn't noticed his mother's quiet sobs at first, the soft sounds blending into the hum of the car's engine and the rhythm of the road. It wasn't until they pulled into their small driveway, the familiar surroundings of home rising before them, that Gav caught the faint tremor in her shoulders. His gaze shifted from the horizon to her face in the dim light, and that was when he saw it—the tear-streaked cheeks, her eyes red and swollen.

Gav opened his mouth to ask, but before he could say anything, his attention was pulled elsewhere.

In the thickening dusk, he saw the shadow first—large, looming, stretching unnaturally tall against the backdrop of the house. It was a silhouette that felt wrong, out of place. The figure grew nearer with each second, moving with a deliberate, heavy tread. A hulking man, impossibly large, his outline more like a mountain than a person, approached the car with a slow, purposeful gait. His footsteps were thunderous, and soon, Gav could hear the rapping of knuckles against the window, sharp and quick, demanding attention.

"Mom?" Gav asked, his voice small and shaky. His heart thudded in his chest, the unease pooling in his stomach.

Without a word, Ethel threw open the car door and hurriedly stepped out, her pace quick and almost frantic as she moved toward the house. The figure outside, towering and imposing, called out to her, his voice deep and gravelly.

"Hrethel! Wait! Hrethel!"

She didn't stop. She didn't even hesitate, her hand trembling as she reached for the door. "We'll talk inside. Gav, come quickly now!"

Gav, feeling his pulse quicken, scrambled out of the car and rushed to his mother's side, keeping his eyes fixed on the ground to avoid looking at the towering figure still standing by the vehicle. The man's shadow seemed to stretch across the yard like something wild, something meant to swallow everything in its path.

"Mom, what's going on? Who is that?"

She didn't answer at first, her eyes darting toward the figure before she looked at her son, her face set in a mask of determination. "Off to bed, Gav," she said sharply, her tone cutting through the air like a knife.

The edge in her voice told him everything he needed to know. She was done talking. She wasn't about to explain anything to him, not right now, not when this *thing* was in their house. He could feel the tension crackling in the air like static, and it was enough to send him up the stairs without a word.

As he reached the top, Gav pretended to slam his bedroom door for effect, making a show of the sound to cover his presence. But once the house was quiet, he crouched down low behind the banister, peering through the gaps to catch a glimpse of what was happening below.

There, in the dim light of the living room, stood the behemoth, his form like something out of a nightmare. The giant was monstrous in size, his broad shoulders filling the doorway as he spoke to his mother in a tone that sent a cold shiver down his spine.

His mother stood there, tense, her hands folded tightly in front of her. She was still trying to hold her composure, but the fear in her eyes was unmistakable.

Gav's breath caught in his throat. This wasn't just some random stranger. There was something more to this, something that had everything to do with his mother—and, now, with him.

Chapter 4
The Crossing Back

The man stood hunched in the doorway, his massive frame crowding the room, his head scraping against the ceiling. "Miss Hrethel," he rumbled, his voice deep and heavy.

Ethel stiffened at the sound of the name, her breath catching. "It's Ethel now!" she snapped. "How many times must I tell you that?"

The man's eyes widened slightly, and he smacked his forehead. "Ethel! Aye, that be it!" He flinched, shrinking before the fire in her voice. "I beg yer pardon, miss Ethel."

"That's all well and good," she said, her voice tightening with urgency. "Now would you kindly leave us?" She didn't back down, standing firm in the middle of the room, the fire in her eyes unmistakable.

But the man shifted, his large hands clenching at his sides. "Ethel," he began again, this time his voice lower, more insistent, "Ye know well why I be standing here."

Ethel's face hardened, the lines around her eyes tightening. "I do," she said quietly, her breath coming in ragged bursts, "and I don't care. You cannot have him, Wiglaf. You can't!"

"Ethel, see reason!" he roared, his voice heavy with frustration. "The lad be but eleven winters old, with no blade in hand, no training to speak of! How is he supposed to…"

"He's not supposed to do anything!" Ethel cried, her voice breaking. In a burst of anger, she stormed toward the giant, her fists crashing against his chest with a force that seemed barely able to make an impression on his massive form. "Wiglaf—Please just leave. He's safe here. Please! Please!"

"Mom!" Gav's voice cracked as he rushed down the stairs, his feet heavy against the wooden steps. He had no idea what was happening, but the fear and tension in the air were suffocating. His heart pounded in his chest, and he could feel the weight of the moment pressing down on him with each step. "Let her go!" he shouted, his voice carrying more bravado than he actually felt.

Gav froze mid-step, the true enormity of Wiglaf striking him like a physical blow. The man wasn't just large—he was a force of nature carved from living stone. His shoulders blocked out the light like fortress walls, his arms hung heavy at his sides, veins snaking through corded muscle.

A dry click sounded in Gav's throat as he tilted his head back, up, up—meeting eyes that gleamed like honed blades. For a heartbeat, he imagined the crunch of bones beneath those massive boots.

Then—a flicker. Almost imperceptible. The barest softening around those steel-edged eyes.

Gav planted his feet, holding his ground.

"Boy, I told you off to bed!" Ethel's voice lashed like a whip, raw with a wild, protective fear that made Gav's skin prickle.

"See!" Wiglaf's laughter boomed as he struck his chest with a fist that echoed like a thunderclap. "The lad's got the courage of a knight!"

Gav stood caught between them, pulse roaring in his ears. His mother's face had gone ashen, lips parted soundlessly. The air itself thickened.

Gav's voice cut through the tension—steady, but edged with something harder beneath. His shoes stayed rooted to the floor, knuckles whitening at his sides. No retreat. Not now.

"Mom." The word landed like a stone. "Who is this guy?" His gaze never left Wiglaf's face, even as his gut churned. "What's he doing in our house?"

Wiglaf's eyes softened as he looked at Ethel, who had retreated to her armchair, clutching her chest in a way that made her seem smaller, more fragile than Gav had ever seen her. Her shoulders shook with silent sobs, and for a moment, the giant man paused, his presence filling the room with an unsettling weight. Then, with a heavy sigh, he turned back to Gav.

"The king decreed it," Wiglaf began, his voice taking on a solemn tone. "The boy must return to Avalon."

Ethel stood up from the chair with a sudden, violent motion, as though she had been struck by something unseen. She didn't say a word, just turned on her heel and stormed out of the room, leaving the two of them alone in the heavy silence that followed.

Wiglaf didn't so much as blink at her sudden exit. His gaze settled on Gav like a weight—eyes alight with something between mirth and madness. His beard quivered as his smile stretched unnaturally wide, teeth glinting like a row of standing stones in firelight. The grin didn't fit his face. Didn't fit the room. Didn't fit the world as Gav knew it.

"By the wings of Merlin, ye've grown a mighty tall one, Gavain," he said with a deep laugh, his voice warm and comforting.

"Gavain?" Gav repeated, the name feeling foreign and strange.

"Oh... aye, right. Ye go by a new name now, don't ye?" Wiglaf said, scratching his chin and casting a sideways glance, as if the answer slipped from his mind. "What be it now? Yer name, I mean."

"Gav."

"Genius!" Wiglaf bellowed, his laughter roaring through the room like thunder on the far horizon. "Gav! A name fit for a knight, lad! A fine name indeed!" His grin spread wide, and for a heartbeat, Gav couldn't tell if the giant was joking or not. "The name's Wiglaf, boy!"

The silence stretched until Ethel returned, her movements urgent. Her trembling fingers worked the green sash around Gav's neck with frantic precision—each tug of the fabric like a silent plea. The moment the knot tightened, the weight of it seemed to anchor itself in Gav's chest, heavier than any cloth had a right to be.

"Don't you dare lose this," she whispered, the words fraying at the edges.

Gav's throat burned. "Mom—" His fingers skimmed the sash, searching for meaning, but her gaze flickered to Wiglaf and back, quick as a trapped bird. Suddenly, the room felt too small, the air thick with unspoken danger. He was standing in the eye of a hurricane, blind to the storm circling him.

Ethel stepped back, her spine rigid. When she lifted her chin at Wiglaf, her eyes were flint. "You will protect him." Not a request—a demand forged in some unbreakable part of her.

"Of course, my lady!" he boomed with a hearty smile. "Like he be blood of me blood, I swear it!"

Gav grabbed his mother's sleeve, his voice breaking. "What's happening?" The words tore loose, raw with fear. Around him, the world tilted—solid ground crumbling beneath questions with no answers.

Ethel crushed him against her chest, thinking that if she held tight enough, time itself might stop. But beneath the warmth pulsed a current of grief, a torrent of sorrow.

"I can't," she murmured into his hair, the words splintering. "I'm sorry. You must go."

Gav's hands fisted in her sweater. "I don't—" His voice cracked, hot tears betraying him.

"Look at me." She gripped his face, her thumbs smearing his tears. Not anger in her eyes—something fiercer. "Wiglaf is family. Whatever comes, he'll keep you safe." Her forehead pressed to his. "And he'll tell you... everything I can't."

Wiglaf, watching from afar, gave a solid nod, his eyes steely. "Aye, lad. I'll tell ye all once we set boots to the road."

Ethel cradled his face for a moment longer, like something precious, her touch feather-light yet impossibly heavy with all the words she couldn't say. "I love you," she breathed—as if it was all the strength she had left in the world. "Forgive me."

Her lips brushed his forehead, lingering. A farewell in the curve of her mouth, the tremor of her fingers.

Then she was stepping back, and the space between them yawned wide as a chasm. Gav stood paralyzed, the taste of salt on his lips, his mother's sorrow a living thing in the air between them. Something irreversible had clicked into place.

"I'm coming back," he choked out. The words were brittle, barely audible, but they burned with ferocity.

"Hrethel, ye should join us." Wiglaf's voice was heavy with understanding, but it did little to ease the tension leadening room. Ethel hesitated, her eyes flickering toward the floor, like she was lost in a battle between her own wants and something far greater than any of them.

"I can't. I can't watch as they…" She trailed off, her gaze briefly flicking back to Gav before quickly averting, as if the weight of whatever unspeakable truth lay behind those words was too much to bear.

Her voice cracked, and something in it—the fragility, the sheer exhaustion—sent a jolt of something deep into Gav's gut. But it wasn't compassion. It was anger. A fierce, boiling anger that roared to life inside of him.

Why? How could she let him go? How could she just give him away like this?

"I just can't do it," Ethel whispered, her words soft but filled with a finality that felt like a door slamming shut.

Wiglaf stood in silence for a moment, then nodded, the deep lines on his face softening just a fraction. "I understand. Come now, lad. We best be on our way."

But Gav didn't move. He stayed where he stood, his feet heavy like lead, his chest tight with emotions he didn't know how to process. The heat bubbling inside of him felt like it might explode at any second. Before he could speak up or say anything, his mother spoke again.

"Talk to Syd. He'll get you off now."

"Right," Wiglaf's palm struck Gav's shoulder—not cruel, but inexorable. The push carried the weight of destiny, a boundary crossed.

For Gav, every step stretched the tether to home thinner. The house shrank behind them, and with it, the life Gav knew.

Questions howled through him, fury and bewilderment twisting like wildfire in his gut. But the road ahead didn't care about storms. It only demanded forward.

"Mr. Sydney..." Gav muttered again under his breath. "He's part of this, too?"

Gav stumbled forward, his feet dragging as he glanced over his shoulder for one last glimpse of the life he knew. His mother stood in the doorway, her face pale and streaked with tears, her hand trembling as she reached out to him, her lips mouthing the words he couldn't quite hear.

"I'm sorry."

The night air sliced through Gav's thin jacket, settling cold in his bones. He kept his head down, hands jammed deep in his pockets, but nothing could loosen the knot in his gut. Each step dragged heavier.

Wiglaf loomed over him, shoulders blotting out the streetlamp's glow. The man's size shrank the world. His footsteps were slow, deliberate, the ground creaking under his weight.

"Cidolfus," he muttered, low and thick, "Open yer door, ye miserable wretch..."

Behind them, the world suddenly brightened. A flood of light surged from the back, so blinding it made their eyes squint and blink, like the sky had cracked open. Through the brilliance, a vague shape emerged—something, just barely, that looked like a van. From within that light, a voice broke through. Mr. Sydney's tone, soft but firm, reached them.

"No need to shout," Mr. Sydney called from the van. "Just get in."

Wiglaf wedged himself into the back, the metal groaning under his bulk, while Gav slid cautiously into the passenger seat.

Mr. Sydney studied him, frowning. "Gav," he said, voice steady but sharp. "You look dreadful."

He then shot a glance at Wiglaf. The big man gave a curt nod from side to side.

Mr. Sydney exhaled, heavy with knowing. "Right," he muttered, resolve hardening. "Long road ahead. Drink this." He shoved a thermos into Gav's hands. "For the nerves."

Gav clutched it, the heat seeping into his clammy skin. He sat motionless, the world's weight pressing down. The van hummed; the men muttered. An hour passed before he sipped. The warmth spread, but exhaustion dragged deeper. Traffic lights smeared into streaks. The voices of the men arguing frayed at the edges, then vanished.

When he woke, the sun glared high. The van stood still. Outside, Mr. Sydney and Wiglaf stared at the endless ocean. Gav creaked the door open and joined them.

"Good morning!" Wiglaf bellowed, his voice carrying on the salt-tinged breeze. He grinned wide, his teeth flashing in the sunlight. "Though I suppose it's more like 'good afternoon,' seein' as how the day's half gone already."

"Did you sleep well, Gav?" Mr. Sydney asked, his voice softer, gentler.

"Mostly, yeah," Gav replied, his voice still thick with sleep.

"Glad to hear it," Mr. Sydney said, nodding.

Wiglaf pointed toward the horizon, where a boat was making its way into the port. "Aye, Cidolfus. This be our ship?"

"Aye."

Gav frowned, his brow furrowing. "Is that your real name, Mr. Sydney?"

He chuckled, a low, warm sound. "Ha. You can call me whatever you like, Gav. But I must say, I've grown rather fond of hearing you say Mr. Sydney."

"Come, boy!" Wiglaf shouted, already striding toward the dock, his boots crunching on the gravel.

Gav hesitated, his eyes darting to Mr. Sydney. Then, in a sudden burst of motion, he threw his arms around the man, clinging to him tightly. Mr. Sydney stiffened for a moment before gently patting the boy's back.

"It's alright, boy," he murmured.

"Please take me back home, Mr. Sydney."

"Son, you are going home."

"What?" Gav pulled back, his eyes wide with confusion and a flicker of hope.

"Gav," Mr. Sydney said, his voice heavy with regret, "No, it's not my place to tell you. I'm sorry."

"Aye! Gav! Move yer feet, now!" Wiglaf's voice boomed from the shore, loud enough to make Gav jump, as though the man were standing right beside them.

"Safe travels, Gav," Mr. Sydney said, his voice steady but his eyes betraying a deeper emotion. "This isn't goodbye. Your mom and I will be here for you—always."

Gav released him, his arms falling to his sides. He turned and made his way down to the docks, his steps slow and deliberate.

The ship loomed before them, a towering beast of oak and cedar, its timbers weathered by salt from hundreds of journeys. A massive thwart ran down its center, lined with men whose hands gripped wide-bottomed oars, their muscles taut and ready. The air smelled of tar and sea, and the ship creaked as it swayed gently in the harbor, alive and waiting.

"Aye, she be a fine one, ain't she, Gav?!" Wiglaf roared, his voice carrying over the din of the docks. He slapped the boy on the back with such force that Gav stumbled forward, nearly pitching into the dark water below. Wiglaf caught him by the shoulder, laughing heartily. "So, listen here, boy," he growled, his voice turning stern. "We've got words to share, I know that. The men on this ship, well, they might not take kindly to ye."

"What? Why?" Gav asked, his voice small against the vastness of the ship and the sea.

"I'll get to that, lad," Wiglaf grunted, scratching his beard. "The long and short of it is, well... ye've become quite famous."

"Famous? Me, famous?" Gav's eyes widened, his voice tinged with disbelief.

"Very much so!" Wiglaf said, shifting his weight from one foot to the other, his boots scuffing against the wooden planks. "Let's board and get settled. I'll tell ye all while we sail to Gamalaot."

They climbed aboard, and just as Wiglaf had warned, Gav felt the weight of the crewmen's stares. Their eyes followed him, piercing and unforgiving, and their whispers cut through the air like daggers.

"That's him," one man muttered, his voice low and gruff.

"That's the Ragnell boy," said another, his tone laced with something Gav couldn't quite place.

Each look was charged with emotion—some men glared at him with contempt, their faces twisted in disgust, while others regarded him with a pity so profound it made his stomach churn. Gav kept his head down, his heart pounding in his chest.

"Gentlemen!" Wiglaf called out, his voice cheerful and booming, a courteous smile plastered across his face as they passed each sailor. But Gav noticed how Wiglaf's hand tightened on his shoulder, pulling him closer, shielding him as they made their way deeper into the ship. They finally reached a small cabin nestled within the hull, its walls rough-hewn and smelling of damp wood.

"Sit where ye will!" Wiglaf said, his voice too loud for the confined space. He wrestled off his heavy iron breastplate and dropped it to the floor with a resounding thud. "We've got a long stretch yet 'fore we reach Gamalaot."

"Wiglaf?" Gav said carefully, perched on the edge of a nearby cot. His voice was tentative and testing. "When you said I was famous, what did you mean exactly? The looks everyone gave me. They seemed angry."

"Ah, ye caught that, did ye?" Wiglaf said, settling into a chair that just barely resisted buckling beneath him. He leaned forward, his elbows resting on his knees, his expression uncharacteristically solemn. "Well, I reckon ye know naught of Avalon, nor Gamalaot, nor even House Ragnell, for that matter."

"No, I don't," Gav said, his irritation bubbling to the surface. "But I heard one of the crewmen say something about Ragnell. Who is he?"

Wiglaf hesitated, his gaze steady but his jaw working as though he were chewing on the words before he spoke them. "Well," he rumbled at last, "he's you."

"He's... me?" Gav's brow furrowed, and he scratched his head, his confusion deepening.

Wiglaf leaned even more forward, his voice lowering like he was sharing a secret. "Let me try to lay it all out for ye in one breath. Avalon be the name of our world. It runs alongside the others—continents, lands, and the like. Think of it like Europe or America! Ye followin' so far, boy?"

"Sort of," Gav said. "Avalon is like your country."

"In a manner of speakin', aye! But it's vast, lad, vast beyond reckonin'. I've never laid eyes on all of it meself. Only one I think might have is the Archbishop."

"So what's Gamalaot, then?" Gav asked, his curiosity piquing.

"The name of the Kingdom!" Wiglaf declared, his voice swelling with pride. "We are knights of the Round Table, and we fight in the name of King Uther and the order of Merlin."

Gav nodded along, though the words felt like they belonged to a storybook, not his life. King Uther? Didn't he mean Arthur? And Merlin? It was all too fantastical, too absurd. He pinched the skin on his arm, half-expecting to wake up in his bed, the sunlight streaming through the curtains. But the sting was real, and so was Wiglaf's earnest face.

"And lastly," Wiglaf said, his tone shifting, the lightness draining from his voice. He paused, his gaze dropping to the floor as though the weight of his next words required a moment of reverence. "Well, House Ragnell... they were a mighty clan within the walls of Gamalaot."

"And you said that I'm a Ragnell?" Gav asked, a flicker of excitement breaking through his confusion.

"Yes—Gavain Laurent Ragnell," Wiglaf said, his voice steady but heavy. "Ye be the last living soul of House Ragnell."

"Oh." Gav's face fell, the flicker of excitement snuffed out as a pit opened in his stomach. He felt like he was falling, though he sat perfectly still.

"It was a tragedy, lad. A bloody massacre. I should know. I was there."

"What?" Gav's voice was barely a whisper, his throat tight.

"I gave me all, boy. I truly did. But I was too late. We all were. In the end, we barely pulled ye from the flames."

Gav sat in silence, his mind reeling. He didn't know what to feel—anger, grief, disbelief—it all swirled together in a chaotic storm. Then, without thinking, he spoke. "It's okay, Wiglaf. I'm sure telling me this is just as hard as hearing it."

Wiglaf's face crumpled, and he leapt to his feet, pulling Gav into a crushing hug. His massive frame shook with sobs as he wailed, "Ya've got a kindness beyond yer years, young lord. Aye, ye're so much like yer mother, it strikes me heart."

"Wiglaf! I...can't...breathe!" Gav gasped, his voice muffled against the man's chest.

"Oh, aye! Forgive me!" Wiglaf released him, stepping back and wiping his eyes with the back of his hand. Gav coughed, sucking in air, his head spinning.

"So wait...how did they know I'm a Ragnell? I mean, I didn't even know,"

"I'd reckon it's in yer eyes," Wiglaf said, his voice still thick with emotion.

"My eyes?"

"Aye, lad. Those emeralds ye carry in yer head ain't common, not by a long shot. Them eyes be a dead giveaway 'round these parts."

"I see."

Gav went quiet. He hesitated before asking the next question, his fingers clutching the green sash around his neck. "And my mom. I mean, my mom back home...she isn't my..."

"Don't be gettin' it twisted!" Wiglaf growled, his voice sharp as steel. He stood tall, fists clenched, ready to defend. "Miss Hrethel—ah, Ethel, I mean—she did her utmost in raisin' ye as her own. That woman be yer mother, and ye best not be dwellin' too much on it! But to answer yer question, aye, she did not give birth to ye."

"Okay," Gav said softly, his fingers tightening around the sash.

"That scarf ye wear, that was a gift from yer mother. Yer birth mother, I mean. She swore it would shield ye from harm."

Gav didn't respond, but he raised the sash to his chin, feeling the soft satin against his skin. It was a small comfort, a tangible link to a past he couldn't remember.

"I'm certain ye've got a mountain of questions," Wiglaf said, his voice gentler now. "I may not be the best to answer them all, but know this—I'll give me all in tryin'."

"Thank you, Wiglaf," Gav said, his voice soft.

"Of course, boy!"

"I do have one other question right away."

"Strike me with it, lad."

"Back at the house, you said something about needing training. What exactly did you mean?"

"Ha!" Wiglaf's laugh thundered through the cabin, his usual fire returning. "That's the very reason I came to fetch ye!"

"Okay, well, what is it that I'm training for?"

Wiglaf grinned, his teeth flashing in the dim light. "Gav," he said, his voice brimming with pride, "Ye're a knight of the round table! Or ye will be soon enough!"

Chapter 5
Arrival in Avalon

The ship fought against the sea with a kind of strength that Gav had never seen before. He felt like he was in a dream or movie, like he was the protagonist in one of his adventure books that he'd read before bed. The waves—great, monstrous walls of water—rose up with a roar, breaking violently against the ship's battered sides, spitting froth and fury, their massive, foaming mouths snapping at the ship's weary hull. The wood screamed as the swell of water clawed at it, sharp as the teeth of some abhorrent creature lurking far below the surface.

Above, the sky hung heavy and gray, as if the heavens themselves were holding their breath. But on the farthest edge of the world, a sliver of white light shone through, small and distant.

"See that, boy?" Wiglaf pointed his meaty finger toward the ever-growing light in the distance. "We're nearly upon it!"

As the ship pulled into dock, the gray moroseness in the air above was beaten back by the beautiful shining sun. Gulls cawed as they soared suspended on the ocean breeze.

"Welcome to Avalon, me boy!"

Gav marveled at it all, standing frozen, eyes wide with wonder. Before him lay a city that seemed to have stepped out of the pages of a fairytale. The streets were alive with the pulse of the everyday—merchants peddling their wares, families moving in a lively procession from stall to stall. He marveled at the strange, old-world contraptions that filled the square—wooden carts creaking under their loads, horses tied to weathered posts, their hooves ringing on cobblestone. The people, draped in simple tunics of rich, bright hues, moved through the streets as if they belonged to a time long past. And though the distance blurred the details, Gav couldn't shake the unsettling sense that some of the creatures—both animal and human—were unlike any he had known. Their ears were sharp and pointed, their noses crooked, twisted into strange shapes that seemed more imagined than real.

"This be Carlisle," said Wiglaf with a step onto the dock. "It's but a stone's throw from Gamalaot now. But first, we make a stop."

Gav trailed along in a daze, his mind racing to keep up with the flood of wonder before him. His feet moved on instinct, matching the rhythm of Wiglaf's, but his eyes darted from one marvel to the next, never settling long enough on any one thing to take it all in. Every glance brought some new, strange delight—a peculiar statue, a brightly colored banner flapping in the wind, a creature that moved with a grace no animal from back home could match.

Gav kept pace with Wiglaf as best he could, silently listening to the man explain the town's history.

The city of Carlisle was a bustling vacation town nestled along the shores of the Aamir Sea—a stretch of water only known to Avalon, but somehow, as if by magic, connected and intersected with the North Atlantic. It was the deep blue of the Aamir, vast and endless, that gave it the name Jewel of Avalon. Its beauty called to all—young lovers chasing romance, retired nobles seeking rest and indulgence in their golden years.

This place was a town woven together with the hum of trade and the energy of travelers, drawn to its shores by the lure of its famous markets. Carlisle's claim to renown was its fierce, spirited bartering over the brightest of dyes and the finest silk-spun fabrics. The streets were alive with the chatter of merchants, their voices rising and falling in a rhythm that matched the ebb and flow of the sea beyond, each vendor eager to make the best deal, each customer hoping to walk away with a treasure.

"Look, mama! Look!"

Gav watched as a young boy tugged eagerly at his mother's dress, his bronze face lit with wonder. The wide brim of her hat cast a shadow across his features, leaving only the gleam of his eyes to catch the light of the gentle sun.

"How much?" The woman's voice was soft, but curious, as she held up a small silk elephant that shimmered with a thousand colors, changing with every flicker of the day's light.

Gav was transfixed, as if watching a scene in a movie.

The broad-shouldered man behind the stall squinted at the trinket, his thick arms crossed over his chest, and muttered a price. "That's, uh… fifteen besants, miss."

The man paused, a faint flush creeping up his neck. "Actually—just call it ten," he said, his voice softer now, as if the price had become something personal.

"I can pay the fifteen," the woman said, ever polite, though the warmth of her offer hung between them like an apology.

"I mean it, ma'am. Ten will do just nicely," the man replied, his hand outstretched with a finality that was as firm as the earth beneath their feet.

They exchanged smiles as gold changed hands and the little silk elephant moved into the boy's arms.

It was a nice moment, Gav thought. He scanned the rest of the market, noticing more moments just like this one.

Along the bustling oceanside market, life unfolded in a thousand small moments. Children pulled at their parents' sleeves, pleading for sparkling toys. Women huddled together, bargaining over scarves and gowns that shimmered like stars. Men, laughing, tossed a ball between them, their feet skimming the cool shallows of the sea.

"Gav, this way!" Wiglaf led them further into the stone-paved city. The ocean air smell waned and was soon replaced by the thick smoke of an iron forge.

"Where are we going?"

"Why, we've got to get ye kitted out, boy!"

"Kitted?" Gav muttered under his breath, his gaze flicking down to his cargo pants and striped green shirt, suddenly aware of how mismatched he felt in the midst of all the color and finery around him. He caught the eyes of those he passed—curious, lingering glances—and for a moment, it wasn't just his clothes he wondered about. *Were they studying his attire, or was it something deeper? Something in his eyes, perhaps, just like the sailors had?* Their whispers trailed behind him, soft but sharp, their gazes fixed and unblinking. A quiet discomfort settled in his chest, a strange weight pressing against him, as if he were a curiosity to them. He pondered it, silently, until Wiglaf's voice cut through the din, halting their movement with an unexpected sharpness.

"Morholt!" Wiglaf yelled. "Aye! Moreholt!"

"I'm coming! Hold on to yer trousers," said a low gravel voice.

Out from behind a small stone archway emerged a small bearded man holding a mallet. He was maybe an inch shorter than Gav.

"Is that a dwarf?!" Gav shouted without thought.

"Wiggy, who's the kid?"

Wiglaf stepped aside, giving the unruly dwarf a better look at the boy.

"Great Merlin's fang! Wiggy, is that?"

"Gav," Wiglaf looked down at the boy. "I'd like ye to meet me friend, Morholt."

The dwarf jumped from his forge and rushed over to the kid. To Gav's surprise, Morholt gripped him in a firm, quick hug before feeling the boy's biceps.

"He's a little scrawny," Morholt shot a look up to Wiglaf. "If he gets in with The Claws, you'll have to whip him to shape, Wiggy." Morholt then brought his attention back to Gav. "But looks at ye! Alive! Flesh and bone! This makes me happier than ye rightly sure know!"

"It's nice to meet you," said Gav softly.

"What's that?" Morholt shouted in Gav's face.

"I said it's nice to meet you!" Gav said again, this time with more strength behind his words.

"Keep that voice!" Morholt said, holding back a laugh. "That squeaky mouse nonsense ain't fitting for ye, son."

"Don't be rough on the lad," Wiglaf growled. "He's still findin' his feet, that's all."

"Feet or no, I still can't believes it. The young lord Ragnell, standing here all small and dumb before me. Alive no less." Morholt chipped his knuckles against Gav's chin. "It makes me happy, Wiggy."

"Morholt," said Gav, his voice striving to hold the same boldness as before. "Did you know my mother? My family?"

"Boy!" Morholt bellowed, his voice a trumpet in the dim forge. "I kitted the lot of 'em! Every Ragnell lad and lass for generations back! And afore me, me father did the same. And his father afore him. Aye, 'twas a tradition, like the turning of the seasons."

"Wow!" Gav's eyes widened, and he turned to Wiglaf, seeking some sign of truth in the man's weathered face.

"And I reckon that's why ye're here now, eh? That about right, Wiggy?"

"Sharp as ever, aye!" Wiglaf replied, his smile creasing his face like a well-worn map.

"Blow that smoke somewhere else," Morholt grumbled, waving a hand as he lumbered back to his forge, his bulk moving with the deliberate heft of a man who had spent a lifetime bending iron to his will. "So the boy be needin'…let's see here." The dwarf rummaged through his trunks, his hands moving with the practiced ease of a man who knew every nail and rivet in the box. He set aside a plain white tunic, its fabric sturdy and unadorned, a pair of beige trousers, and brown leather boots, their soles reinforced with steel plating that gleamed dully in the firelight.

Gav watched intently, his eyes following each item as it was laid out. The tunic, the trousers, the boots.

"Put these on!" Morholt barked, his voice like the clanging of a hammer on an anvil, his eyes fixed on some distant point. Without another word, he shuffled off to the adjoining room, his heavy boots thudding against the floor. "I got somethin' else for ye, but I'll be damned if I can lay hands on it straightaway."

Wiglaf gestured toward the back room with a nod, handing Gav the bundle of clothes Morholt had gathered. The boy took them, his fingers trembling slightly as he clutched the fabric. He slipped into the back room, the air thick with the scent of oil and iron, and began to dress. Or rather, he attempted to. The tunic hung loose on his narrow shoulders, the sleeves swallowing his arms whole. The trousers were worse—they pooled around his ankles, sagging hopelessly at his waist. Gav fumbled with them, his cheeks burning with frustration, until he remembered the long green sash his mother had left him. He wound it tightly around his waist, cinching the trousers as best he could. It was a precarious solution, but it would have to do.

When he emerged, he moved with the careful precision of a man crossing a frozen river. One misstep, one too-quick stride, and the trousers would surely tumble down around his ankles.

"It's a little big," Gav said, his voice steady despite the awkwardness of his gait.

"For the love of…" Morholt bellowed, emerging from the other room with a rusted box in his hands. He stopped short, squinting at the boy. "You really be a scrawny lad, ain't ye? Like a sapling bent in the wind! Ain't no meat on them bones, boy. Not a lick!" He shook his head, his beard bristling with disapproval, but there was a flicker of something softer in his eyes—he then cupped his hand around his mouth. "Moth! Moth, get in here, ye!" Morholt's voice boomed, shaking the very timbers of the forge. The room began to tremble, trunks and cabinets rattling as though possessed. Gav stiffened, his eyes darting around as the lids of chests flew open and slammed shut on their own. The cacophony of metal clattering and tools tumbling to the floor was deafening.

"Moth!" Morholt roared again, his voice cutting through the chaos. "Quit tryin' to scare the boy, ye daft sprite!"

In a sudden burst of shimmering light, a small figure materialized, floating midair with a grin that could only be described as impish. At first glance, it appeared to be a man—a tiny, whimsical man—but the longer Gav stared, the more the creature's form seemed to shift and blur. It was small, no taller than a child's doll, and clad in a patchwork of leaves in colors both natural and impossible—vivid purples, shimmering blues, and hues that shifted like the surface of a prism. The figure orbited Gav's head, its long, golden hair trailing behind it like the luminous tail of a comet.

"I didn't know ye lived with a fairy!" Wiglaf said, his voice tinged with awe.

"Can't get the nasty bugger to leave!" Morholt grumbled, crossing his arms over his broad chest. "Been here longer than the forge, he has."

"This was my house first!" Moth declared, their voice a deep, resonant bass that seemed to vibrate the very air. They took a swig from a tiny tankard, and as they hiccuped, their voice shifted to a high, squeaky pitch. "Back before the ocean swallowed up the swamp, or monkeys learned to talk! Long before any of you three babes even—" The fairy stopped abruptly, their gaze locking onto Gav's. "Ah! You're…you're the boy!" they boomed, their voice oscillating back to its deep timbre before rising again to a shrill squeak. "The chosen one! The chosen one! Off to play The Christmas Game! The chosen one! The chosen one!"

Moth began to dance gleefully in the air, their tiny form bobbing and weaving as they chanted.

"Moth, ye stupid drunk!" Morholt bellowed, hurling a leather boot at the frolicking fairy. "Can ye just fix 'im up?"

Moth took another long pull from their tankard, then floated high above Gav's head. With a mischievous grin, they sprayed a cloud of ale into the air, which transformed into a glittering rain of pixie dust as it fell. The ill-fitting clothes on Gav's body shimmered and shifted, shrinking and molding themselves perfectly to his frame.

"Thank you, Moth," Gav said, his voice filled with wonder as he looked down at his now perfectly fitted attire.

The fairy drifted back down, hovering mere inches from Gav's nose. They winked at him, their eyes sparkling with mischief, before spitting another cloud of ale directly into his face. And with that, they vanished, leaving behind only the faint scent of ale and the echo of their laughter.

"Right sorry about him," Morholt grumbled, his back still turned as he carefully retrieved a folded cloth from one of his many trunks. "He's dreadfully mannered, that one. Ain't got a lick of sense when it comes to proper behavior."

"And that's comin' from a dwarf, boy!" Wiglaf chimed in, his chest puffed out with mock pride, a grin spreading across his weathered face.

"Come off it, Wiggy!" Morholt shot back, though there was no real heat in his words. The two men fell into their familiar rhythm of playful bickering, their voices a comforting backdrop to the forge's steady hum.

Gav, however, barely heard them. His attention was wholly consumed by the marvel of his newly fitted clothes. He ran his hands over the fabric, now snug and perfectly tailored to his frame, and felt a giddiness rise in his chest like a bubbling spring. He had just seen a fairy—a real, honest-to-goodness fairy—and watched it perform magic. Actual magic! And not just any magic, but magic that had touched him, transformed his clothes, and left him standing there in awe.

And then there was Morholt, the gruff dwarf who had hugged him not ten minutes ago. A dwarf! Gav's mind reeled at the thought. He glanced up at Wiglaf, the towering figure beside him, his presence as solid and unshakable as the mountains themselves. *How could any of this be real? How could he, a boy from a quiet town in Michigan, suddenly find himself in the company of such extraordinary beings?*

For a moment, the world seemed to shimmer around him, as though the veil between the ordinary and the magical had been lifted, and he was standing in a place where anything was possible. The forge, the fairy, the dwarf, the giant of a man—it was all too much, and yet it felt right, as though he had stepped into a story that had been waiting for him all along.

Gav's heart swelled with a strange, unnameable joy. He didn't know what lay ahead, but for the first time in what felt like forever, he felt alive—truly, wonderfully alive.

"Sorry for the wait," Morholt said as he returned to Gav, holding something wrapped in fine burgundy cloth. He thrust it toward the boy with a gruff nod. "Go on. She's yers."

Gav took the bundle, his hands nearly buckling under its unexpected weight. The cloth was soft, but the object inside felt dense, solid, and pulsing with a kind of latent energy. He glanced up at Wiglaf, who stood beside him, his grin widening.

"Open it."

Gav's fingers fumbled slightly as he unwrapped the cloth, and as the fabric fell away, a brilliant flash of metal caught the light. The blade gleamed like liquid silver, its surface almost blinding. It was thin and straight, its edge razor-sharp and true, and it seemed to radiate a soft warmth in his hands, as though it carried something ancient and powerful.

"Her name is Galatine," Morholt said, his voice low and reverent. "Forged her for ye ages ago, I did. Knew she'd find her way to ye someday."

Gav's breath stopped a moment as he gripped the simple gold hilt, its design unadorned yet elegant. He lifted the sword high, feeling its balance, its weight, its purpose. It felt like an extension of his own arm, as though it had been waiting for him all this time.

"I'll get that for ye," Wiglaf said, stepping forward to attach the scabbard to Gav's belt. His large hands moved with surprising gentleness as he secured the blade at the boy's side.

"He be needing anything more, Wiggy?"

"None else," Wiglaf replied, his tone firm. "The academy be providing what he needs from here."

Gav turned to Morholt, his heart swelling with gratitude. "Thank you, Mr. Morholt, sir!" he said, his voice earnest. He stepped forward, extending his hand for a shake, but then hesitated, remembering the dwarf's earlier embrace. Instead, he bowed deeply, his knees bending in an awkward but sincere stoop.

Morholt chuckled, a deep rumble in his chest. "None o' that now, lad," he said, waving a hand dismissively. "Just see that ye take care of her, aye? Galatine's a fine blade, and she deserves a fine hand to wield her."

"I will," Gav promised, his voice steady. "I'll make you proud."

"Aye, I reckon ye will," Morholt said. "Now off with ye."

Wiglaf and Morholt exchanged a knowing chuckle as Gav bounded out of the forge, his steps light and his face alight with excitement. The boy's energy was infectious, and for a moment, the two old friends stood in the doorway, watching him with a mix of amusement and quiet pride.

"Wiggy. Look after him, would ye? He's got a long road ahead."

"Aye," Wiglaf replied, his tone steady and sure. He clapped a hand on Morholt's shoulder, the gesture heavy with unspoken understanding. Then, with a final nod, he turned and followed Gav, his long strides easily catching up to the boy's eager pace.

As they walked, Gav felt as though the world itself had shifted. The sunlight seemed brighter, the air sweeter, and even the distant sound of the waves carried a kind of music he hadn't noticed before. It was as if the encounter in the forge had awakened something in him—a sense of wonder, of possibility, that he hadn't allowed himself to feel before. The anxieties of leaving home, the queasiness from the sea voyage, all of it melted away, replaced by a bubbling excitement that he could hardly contain.

"Wiglaf!" Gav called out, his voice nearly a shout as he turned to face the man. "Did you see that fairy in there? And the sword Morholt made me?! So cool!" His words tumbled out in a rush, his eyes wide with giddiness.

Wiglaf chuckled, his deep voice rumbling like distant thunder. "Strange creatures, fairies. Powerful, aye. I'm sure old Morholt enjoys the company, even if he won't admit it. And that sword—aye, that's a fine piece he's forged for ye. We'll test her later, see how she feels in yer grip. But for now, we must make for Gamalaot 'fore nightfall. Can't be keepin' the academy waitin', can we?"

Gav nodded, though his mind was still racing with everything that had happened. He glanced down at the sword at his side, his fingers brushing against the hilt. Galatine. The name felt right, as though it had always been a part of him. He couldn't wait to learn how to wield it, to see what adventures lay ahead for them.

The pair walked on, leaving the bustling streets of Carlisle behind as they reached the edge of the town and stepped into the wide, open plains. The land stretched out before them like an endless sea of green, the grass swaying and rippling in the breeze as though alive. Gav felt a surge of exhilaration as he took it all in—the vastness, the freedom, the sheer beauty of it. It was as if Avalon was welcoming him, urging him forward.

"Look there," Wiglaf said, pointing to something far off.. "See that gray speck on the horizon? That be Gamalaot."

Gav squinted, shielding his eyes from the sun as he followed Wiglaf's gaze. Far off, barely visible against the rolling green, was a small, gray smudge. "That's so far away!" he exclaimed, his voice tinged with disbelief. "We'll never make it before sundown."

Wiglaf chuckled, a deep, rumbling sound that echoed across the plains.

He then reached over his shoulder and, with a practiced motion, drew a massive blade from the scabbard strapped to his back. Colossal would have been an understatement; the sword was impossibly huge, its blade nearly the height of Wiglaf himself. Gav stared, wide-eyed, wondering how he hadn't noticed it before. The sheer size of it defied logic, yet there it was, gleaming in the dwindling sunlight.

Before Gav could fully process what he was seeing, Wiglaf raised the sword high above his head and drove it into the earth.

"Breca!" he shouted, his voice carrying across the plains with an echo.

The blade erupted in a soft, green light, its glow spreading outward like ripples on a pond. Then, from what seemed like nothing but air, a massive form began to materialize. Gav's breath grew shorter and more frantic as a gigantic brown grizzly bear emerged, its size rivaling that of an elephant. The ground trembled beneath its weight as it let out a low, rumbling growl.

"Wah!" Gav cried, stumbling backward in terror. "Bear!"

"Easy, girl!" Wiglaf called out, his voice warm and affectionate. He stepped forward, placing both hands on the bear's massive head and scratching behind her ears. "I've missed ye, too!" he bellowed, leaning in to plant a kiss on the bear's broad forehead. "Ye been a good lass, Breca? A good lass?"

Gav stood frozen, his heart pounding as he watched the enormous bear nuzzle into Wiglaf's touch, her growls softening into a contented purring.

"Uhh, Wiglaf?" Gav called out, his voice trembling.

"Gav! Come here, boy! Say yer hellos to Breca!" Wiglaf beckoned, his tone cheerful and encouraging.

Gav hesitated, his feet rooted to the spot. But curiosity slowly overcame his fear, and he took a cautious step forward. Breca turned her massive head toward him, her dark eyes studying him with a calm, almost gentle expression. Gav reached out a trembling hand, and to his astonishment, the bear nuzzled her head into his palm.

"Hi, Breca," Gav said softly, a smile spreading across his face as he scratched gently behind her ears. "You like that?"

Breca let out a low, contented growl, her massive body swaying slightly as she leaned into his touch.

"Ha! She likes ye!" Wiglaf said with delight, his laughter booming across the plains. "A good thing, too. Makes this all the easier."

Without a moment's notice, Wiglaf hoisted Gav up and plopped him onto the saddle strapped to Breca's broad back. Gav let out a startled yelp, his hands flailing for something to hold onto.

"Wiglaf! Wiglaf!"

"Ye're alright!" Wiglaf said with a hearty laugh, swinging himself up in front of Gav with the ease of a man who had done this a thousand times before. "Onward to Gamalaot, girl!" he called, giving Breca a gentle pat on the side.

The titanic bear rose onto her hind legs, letting out a thunderous roar that shook the very ground beneath them. Then, with a powerful surge, she dropped back onto all fours and charged forward, her massive paws pounding the earth like drums. Gav clung to the saddle for dear life, his knuckles white as Breca hurtled across the plains with the speed and grace of a creature born to run. The wind whipped past his face, and the world blurred into a streak of green and gold.

In no time at all, the distant gray speck on the horizon began to grow larger and more defined. Soon, the outline of Gamalaot came into view, and Gav held his breath. The kingdom was immense, its towering stone walls stretching for miles in either direction, as though they had been carved from the earth itself. Beyond the walls, rising high on a hill, was a massive castle that loomed over the entire kingdom, its spires piercing the sky like the fingers of a giant.

"Whoa," Gav said automatically, his voice barely above a whisper.

"Just wait till ye see it up close," Wiglaf said with a grin.

True to Wiglaf's word, they arrived at the front gate of Gamalaot in what felt like mere seconds. Wiglaf dismounted first, then lifted Gav down from Breca's back, setting him gently on the ground.

"Run along, lass! Be good now!" Wiglaf gave Breca one last affectionate pat, and with a low rumble, the bear turned and bounded away into the open field. But after just a few yards, she vanished into thin air, as though she had stepped through an invisible door.

"Where'd she go?!"

"She's alright!" Wiglaf said, his voice steady and reassuring. "She's just between planes, that's all. Likely by some creek, huntin' or swimmin'."

"Between planes?" Gav asked, his brow furrowing in confusion.

Wiglaf scratched the back of his head, looking momentarily sheepish. "Oof, I keep forgettin' ye be new to all this, boy. Familiars are planeswalkers, ye see. And, well, they—uh—walk between the planes, I reckon."

Gav stared at Wiglaf, his expression a perfect mix of bewilderment and disbelief. "What does that even mean?"

"I suppose I've just made this all the more confusin' fer ye. Ye'll learn it all proper when classes start. I'm certainly not explainin' it well now."

Wiglaf clapped a hand on Gav's shoulder, steering him toward the towering gates of Gamalaot. "Come on, lad. Let's get ye inside."

They passed through the towering gates of Gamalaot and stepped into a bustling marketplace that, while similar to Carlisle, had an air of grandeur and formality that set it apart. The streets were lined with stalls and shops, but the crowd was thinner, more composed. Armored knights patrolled the area, their polished armor gleaming in the sunlight, while elegantly dressed nobles and dignitaries strolled about, their robes and gowns flowing elegantly in the breeze. The atmosphere was alive with the hum of conversation and the occasional clink of coin, but it lacked the chaotic energy of Carlisle's market.

"There be much to see," Wiglaf said, his voice urgent as he quickened his stride. "But we've not the time to take it all in now. We must keep movin'. Come on!"

Gav followed closely, though his eyes darted everywhere, trying to take in as much as he could. They moved through the marketplace, past the theater district with its grand, ornate buildings, and then through rows of pubs and mead halls, their doors open to the warm early evening air. The scent of roasted meat and spiced ale wafted out, mingling with the sounds of laughter and song.

They walked for what felt like miles, the castle looming ever larger in the distance but somehow never seeming to get closer. Gav's legs began to ache, but he was too captivated by the sights around him to complain. The homes they passed were as varied as the people who lived in them—some small and shabby, others grandiose and immaculate. Some manors even had their own gated communities, complete with high walls and guarded entrances.

At one point, Gav's gaze lingered on a particularly large estate, its grounds adorned with beautifully trimmed hedges and surrounded by its own set of walls. Wiglaf noticed and glanced over, his expression darkening slightly.

"The Lambelle's," Wiglaf said, his voice tinged with a hint of disgust. "A very 'well-to-do' noble house. I reckon they have a lad yer age."

"They must be loaded," Gav said almost absentmindedly, his eyes still fixed on the estate. He caught a glimpse of confusion on Wiglaf's face and quickly clarified. "I mean, they seem to be wealthy."

"Aye," Wiglaf nodded, his expression clearing. "Wealthy and powerful, aye. A bit too hoity-toity for me taste, but each to their own, I suppose." He shrugged his shoulders. "But I like what ye said before. Loaded?"

Gav chuckled. "Yeah. If someone is loaded, it means they're rich."

Wiglaf's face lit up with a grin. "I'm goin' to use that! Just tell me if I ever says it wrong."

The pair laughed, the sound light and carefree between them. But as they walked, Gav's attention was drawn to another massive estate on the opposite side. And unlike the Lambelle's pristine grounds, this one was a shadow of its former self. The manor stood in disrepair, its stone walls scorched and blackened, as though they had endured a great fire. Piles of charred logs and splintered paneling lay in gray-black heaps, scattered across the grounds like the remnants of a forgotten battle. The air around the estate felt heavy, almost mournful, and Gav couldn't help but feel a pang of unease as they passed by.

He glanced at Wiglaf, expecting some explanation or comment, but the man remained silent, his jaw tight and his gaze fixed straight ahead. The awkwardness of the moment hung between them, thick and unspoken. Gav didn't dare ask, but the weight of Wiglaf's silence told him everything he needed to know.

As they neared the estate's gate, Gav caught sight of a weathered crest hanging askew above the entrance. Though faded and cracked, the emblem was unmistakable—a symbol he had seen before, though he couldn't quite place where. And then it hit him. It was the same symbol etched into Galatine, the same symbol lightly embroidered on his sash. It must be the Ragnell crest. This must be the Ragnell estate.

His heart sank as the realization washed over him. This crumbling, fire-scarred manor was once his family's home. The place where generations of Ragnells had lived, laughed, and built their legacy. Now, it stood as a grim reminder of all that had been lost.

Gav's steps slowed, his eyes lingering on the ruins. He wanted to ask Wiglaf what had happened, to demand answers, but the words never came. The look on Wiglaf's face—a look of sorrow and resolve—told him that now wasn't the time.

"Come on, lad," he said quietly, his voice carrying a note of urgency. "We've still got a ways to go."

The golden hour bathed the world in a warm, amber glow as Gav and Wiglaf finally reached the base of the castle's towering gate. The sun hung low in the sky, casting long shadows across the stone path that led up to the fortress. Gav tilted his head back, his eyes tracing the immense walls that rose before him. They were foreboding and powerful, taller and thicker than any of the walls he had seen this far. Behind those walls, a steep motte rose, crowned by a palisade that encircled the castle like a protective ring.

"Final leg, boy!" Wiglaf said, his voice brimming with fervor. He clapped a hand on Gav's shoulder, his grip firm and encouraging. "Though she be a steep one! Don't lose heart now!"

Gav swallowed hard, his eyes still fixed on the castle. It was a marvel of stone and strength, its Gothic windows and ornate battlements standing as a testament to the craftsmanship of its builders. The tallest tower of the keep seemed to stretch endlessly into the sky, its spire piercing the clouds as though reaching for heaven itself.

"She's a beauty, ain't she?" Wiglaf said, his voice softening as he followed Gav's gaze.

"It's the biggest building I've ever seen!" Gav replied, his eyes sparkled with wonder as he took in every detail.

Wiglaf studied Gav's reaction, feeling a broad smile spreading across his own bearded face. The boy's wonder was infectious, and for a moment, the old warrior felt a fatherly swell of pride.

"Welcome to Castle Gamalaot."

Chapter 6
The Induction

Wiglaf guided Gav into the castle courtyard. Over a hundred recruits, all in crisp white tunics, milled about in small clusters, speaking in low murmurs, exchanging words and glances anxiously. Official knights of the castle stood stalwart, sentinels as still as unmoving stone, their eyes scanning the crowd with a vigilance that seemed more born of habit than necessity.

"Wiglaf, what's going on here?"

"It's the induction, lad!"

Gav's brow furrowed deeply, his forehead folding into tight lines as he looked up. Wiglaf's explanation didn't seem to reach him; it didn't do a thing to ease the twisting nerves in his stomach. The butterflies had returned, fluttering restlessly, and his heart beat a little faster in his chest. All around him, the recruits chatted, unaware, or perhaps just as uncertain as he was, but to Gav it felt as if he were standing at the edge of a steep cliff, with nothing but the tension in the air to guide him forward.

They began to approach the crowd. And that's when Gav started to notice the glares thrown upon him. More whispers and scowls like before. The further he walked into the crowd, the more they dispersed from him.

"Boy," Wiglaf said. "I hate to do this to ye, but I've got to be off."

"No!" Gav shouted, which only drew in more stares. "Please don't leave!"

"The induction's startin' any moment now! Ye'll be alright, boy. I swear it," Wiglaf said, patting Gav's head.

Before Gav could plead any further, his large companion was off and disappeared behind a grand set of oak doors leading into the castle.

Gav felt alone in that sea of prying eyes. He tried to approach someone, anyone, hoping to find a friendly face amidst the crowd. But no matter the direction he moved in, kids would pull each other away and whisper to one another. He couldn't hear what they said exactly, but he could feel the sharp, hurtful sting all the same.

"Don't worry about it too much," came a soft voice from over his shoulder. "Though I realize that's easier said than done."

Gav turned to find a girl in a white tunic standing behind him, her thick, dark brown curls tumbling past her shoulders. She studied him with a finger resting on her chin.

"You're Gavain, right?" she said. "I can tell by your eyes. Gavain Laurent of House Ragnell."

"Just Gav," he muttered.

"I'm Eleanora." She extended her hand. "Pleased to meet you."

He shook it, hesitating before asking, "What's your… House name? Eleanora of House…?"

"Just Eleanora." A flicker of amusement crossed her face. "I don't have a house. And I'd really prefer if you called me Nora."

"Oh. Sure thing, Nora."

"Thank you!" Her smile was so bright it was almost contagious—like he'd done her some grand favor instead of just saying her name.

"So wait," Gav said, "you don't have a house? How does that—"

"I think you misunderstand," she cut in. "I'm not homeless, which is what I assume you thought. No, 'houses' are for the wealthy. Nobility. Which I am not. My parents are merchants."

"Oh." Gav barely got the word out before she barreled on.

"But I do have a surname—Edmund. It's just a name, no repute attached. You should know, nobles and commoners don't usually mix. Except here!" Her entire demeanor shifted, her eyes alight with excitement. "In the Gamalaot Castle Court! Where honor can be earned instead of inherited. The knighthood is one of the only ways to change your fate. It's all so romantic, isn't it?" She paused, tilting her head. "Am I boring you?"

"What?" Gav's cheeks burned. "No!"

"I saw your eyes wandering," she teased, though her tone stayed kind. "My family says I talk too much and too fast. Probably from growing up with four brothers—three of them are knights here. Still in training, though."

"That's cool!" Gav said, still fighting the heat in his face.

Nora's expression softened. "I am sorry. I know I ramble. And it was probably too bold to approach you, me being a commoner and you…"

"I don't have a house either," Gav blurted. "Not anymore. I didn't even know about any of this until recently. So I'm… really glad you're talking to me."

Nora tilted her head, curiosity sparking in her gaze. "It's true your house has fallen. But you still have a legacy, and a rather famous one at that, you know."

"More like infamous," Gav muttered, frustration edging his voice. "Seems like everyone who recognizes me hates my guts."

"Hmm." Nora's brow furrowed. "That's probably because…"

Before she could finish, a triumphant blast of trumpets shattered the air, echoing from the keep's balcony. The crowd around them stirred, a ripple of excitement spreading through the courtyard.

"The induction!" Nora shouted, her eyes lighting up with excitement. "Come on, we must hurry!" She grabbed Gav by the hand, her grip firm, and pulled him through the throng of people. They wove their way to a spot closest to the balcony, the music growing louder with each step.

"What's happening?"

Nora turned to him, her expression one of amusement and disbelief. "You really don't know much of anything, do you?" she said, her voice carrying over the noise. "Oh, and have you ever been told you talk funny?"

Gav opened his mouth to respond, but the words didn't follow. The music swelled, drowning out any chance of reply, and he found himself staring up at the balcony, where figures in gleaming armor began to appear. The crowd roared, their voices rising in a deafening wave, and Gav could only stand there, his hand still in Nora's, his mind spinning with questions.

He cast his gaze upon the balcony, where a line of armored knights stood proud and powerful, their presence commanding the attention of all the children below. The fading light of the day hung in the air, the last breath of twilight, clinging to the horizon. Yet amidst them, among these regal figures of strength and honor, there was one who stood out, a face both familiar and striking in its own right.

"Wiglaf!" Gav bellowed, his voice echoing across the courtyard as he waved with abandon. "Wiglaf!"

The knight acknowledged him with a small, measured wave, but quickly gestured for him to hush, his eyes narrowing with a quiet admonishment.

A sharp jab to his ribs snapped Gav from his reverie. He turned to find Nora, her face alight with sudden realization. "You know The Bear?!" she hissed in awe, her voice barely a whisper.

"Huh?" Gav blinked, momentarily lost. "You mean Wiglaf? Yeah, he's my friend."

"Oh wow! So cool!"

The children huddled and shuffled into an unsightly formation, quieting their conversations and turning their attention to the castle balcony.

In the center of the knights stood a figure clad in golden armor, royal and radiant. Atop his brow sat a crown adorned with jewels that caught the last of the sun's weary light, glimmering like stars awakening for their nightly watch. The evening's fading warmth had already given way to the cool embrace of the moon, yet those gems—ruby, sapphire, citrine, emerald, and garnet—shone with an eternal vibrancy. Gav's eyes followed the stones, their order mirrored on the hilt of the king's sword, which now gleamed as he raised it high toward the sky. The gesture stilled the very air, silencing everyone and everything.

And then another figure appeared. This man, gaunt and draped in a cloak of vivid blue, stepped from the shadows beneath the archway. His robe shimmered as if it carried the very patterns of the stars themselves, and though his face was mostly obscured by a great white beard, his voice rang out with the weight of an ancient power, like the heavens themselves had deigned to speak through him.

"Attention!" the old man's voice thundered. "Before we proceed, King Uther Pendragon would like to bestow upon you all a blessing."

The king lowered his sword, and with a solemn, deliberate motion, he turned it toward the children below. The growing moonlight caught the blade, casting a soft glow that seemed to carry the weight of a supreme responsibility.

"May the Threefold Light shield you," the king said, voice steady, as if invoking the power of some sacred rite. "Gamalaot's gates before you, Merlin's wisdom within you, and the spirits of hill and stream beside you." His eyes swept over the children dressed in their humble white tunics. "May your path be straight as Taliesin's word, your heart steadfast like the knights of Camlann, and your fate brighter than the glass fort's fire. *Ni bo diawl yn dy ol, na brad yn dy galon. Gwyn fydy goroesi.*" The old king raised his sword once more toward the heavens before sheathing it with the quiet finality of a prayer. "Good luck to you all, brave would-be heroes. By the morning's break, may you be knights of the round."

The crowd bowed in reverence, a wave of white-clad figures bending like stalks in the wind. Yet Gav stood frozen, straight-backed and oblivious, still caught between Nora's words and the spectacle unfolding before them.

"Gav." Nora's whisper was razor-sharp. She jabbed her elbow into his ribs. "Bow."

"Ah—right." He lurched forward, his waist bending in a stiff, graceless dip.

Above them, the king paused. His gaze swept across the sea of lowered heads, lingering for a heartbeat too long—eyes dark, unreadable. Then he turned away, his cloak rippling behind him like spilled ink.

"Rise." The old wizard's voice was gentle but carried the weight of stone. "No need for such severity." He raised his wand—gnarled, weathered, as if it had been pulled from the roots of an ancient tree—and with a single flick, sent a streak of light arcing into the heavens. It burst like a star, showering the children in a cascade of shimmering dust. Their laughter and cheers rose like a tide, filling the night with a kind of wild, uncontainable magic.

"Who's that?" Gav asked, his voice barely audible over the clamor.

"The Archbishop," Nora replied, her hands clapping in rhythm with the others, her eyes alight with admiration. "The greatest wizard in all of Avalon."

Gav stared at the old man, his face etched with lines that seemed to tell stories of their own. There was something in his presence, something that settled over Gav. The knot of anxiety in his stomach loosened, not entirely gone, but softened, transformed into a flicker of anticipation. And as the Archbishop sent another bolt of magic spiraling into the sky, Gav felt it too—a spark of wonder, bright and alive, cutting through the darkness.

"And now," the Archbishop declared, his voice booming like a drum, his smile wide and full of a kind of joy that ignited the very air around him, "it is time for the induction!" From the folds of his robe, he drew a long scroll of parchment, its edges curling like dried-up leaves. He adjusted his spectacles, their lenses catching the glow of the torches, and peered down at the list with careful scrutiny.

The crowd of children fell silent, their breaths held tight, their eyes fixed on him, for he held the very threads of their futures in his hands. The night seemed to pause, the stars themselves leaning in to listen.

"Tristian von Blumenthal," the Archbishop called, his voice ringing clear.

A boy with hair like spun gold stepped forward, his steps hesitant, his shoulders tense. He glanced back at the others, his face a mask of nerves, before the great oak doors swallowed him whole. The silence deepened, heavy and expectant. Gav's eyes darted to where Wiglaf and the knights had stood, only to find their places empty. *Where had they gone?*

Moments later, this boy, Tristian, reappeared, standing now on the lower balcony beside the Archbishop. The old wizard raised his wand, its tip glowing faintly, and tapped it gently against the boy's chest. The white tunic Tristian wore began to shimmer, then blaze with a light so fierce it seemed to pull the very darkness apart. With a sweeping motion, the Archbishop aimed his wand skyward, and from its tip burst a bolt of crimson fire. It twisted and roared, taking shape as a lion of pure, ethereal light—its mane a plume of flames, its eyes burning with pride. It let out a roar that shook the earth, a sound so mighty it seemed to echo in the bones of every soul present.

"The Order of the Crimson Manes!" the Archbishop proclaimed, his voice swelling with pride. Tristian's tunic had transformed, now a deep, rich red, adorned with the crest of a lion that seemed almost alive in the flickering torchlight.

The crowd erupted, their cheers rising like a storm, their voices mingling with the fading roar of the spectral lion as it dissolved into a shower of stardust, drifting gently back to earth.

"Lucky!" Nora exclaimed, her eyes shining with both envy and hope. She turned to Gav, her voice low but fierce. "I want to be a Crimson Mane too. All my brothers are in the order. It's all I've ever wanted."

"Ewain de Boron!" the Archbishop's voice rang out, slicing through the murmurs of the crowd. This time, the silence was less absolute, the air thick with whispers and shifting feet. This boy, too, disappeared into the castle, the big doors shutting him in. When Ewain emerged from the keep, he stood tall beside the Archbishop, his face a mix of pride and apprehension. The wand tapped his chest, and again the night was split by a bolt of light—this one a vivid green. It twisted and roared into the shape of a bear, its massive form rippling with power, its growl low and menacing as it bared its teeth to the stars.

"The Order of the Verdant Claws!" the Archbishop declared, and Ewain's tunic bloomed into a deep, forest green, the crest of a bear now emblazoned upon it. The crowd cheered, though not as wildly as before, their voices mingling with the fading snarls of the spectral bear.

The ritual continued, each name called, each child stepping forward to vanish behind the oak doors, only to reemerge to be transformed.

"Perceval de Boron!" the Archbishop shouted, and again the crimson lion roared across the sky. "The Order of the Crimson Manes!" Gav watched as the crowd began to settle into the rhythm of it, the awe giving way to a kind of restless anticipation.

But then, something unexpected. He called out another name. "Lanval de Galles... The Order of the Azure Stripes!" The boy's tunic shifted to a deep, midnight blue, and the sky above erupted with the wild, cackling form of a hyena, its laughter echoing like a challenge to the stars. The crowd gasped, their murmurs rising to a buzz of excitement. This was new. This was different.

"Lucan Lucien Lambelle... The Order of the Azure Stripes!" Gav's eyes narrowed as he watched the raven-haired boy step forward, his expression smug, his walk deliberate, as if he already knew he was above the rest. Gav remembered the name from his walk with Wiglaf, and though he had never spoken to Lucan, he could feel the boy's disdain radiating like heat from a forge. Lucan's tunic turned blue, and the hyena reappeared, its laughter harsh and mocking, before it too dissolved into the night.

"Eleanora Edmund!" the Archbishop called, and Nora turned to Gav with a grin.

"Wish me luck!" she said, her voice bright with excitement as she skipped toward the keep. She was gone only a moment before reappearing, her face alight with triumph.

" The Order of the Crimson Manes!" The lion roared once more, and Gav clapped fiercely, his heart swelling with pride for his new friend.

"Irina de Maris… The Order of the Gilded Wings!" The girl's tunic shimmered into a rich, golden hue, and the sky was filled with the majestic form of an owl, its wings outstretched, its cry piercing the night like a call to battle.

And then, at last, the Archbishop's voice called out his name, "Gavain Laurent Ragnell."

The courtyard fell silent—a silence so heavy, it was hard for Gav to even move his feet. Every eye turned to him, their stares accusing, their judgment apparent. He felt their gazes like weights upon his shoulders as he stepped forward, his footsteps echoing in the stillness. The oak doors loomed before him, their hinges groaning as they swung shut behind him, sealing him in darkness. The world outside ceased to exist, and Gav was alone, waiting for whatever came next.

The corridor stretched before Gav, its walls lined with massive iron sconces, their flames flickering and casting long, dancing shadows. The air was thick with the scent of old stone and burning wood. Gav walked the uneven path, his footsteps echoing softly, until the hallway opened into a vast chamber. At its center stood a large round table, and seated there was Wiglaf, his familiar face a small comfort in the strangeness of it all.

"Wiglaf!" Gav called out, his voice bouncing off the stone walls as he hurried toward the table. But he stopped short, his breath catching in his throat, when he saw the others. The knights from the balcony were there too, their faces stern, their eyes piercing as they stared at him, their gazes seeming to pass straight through him.

"You go by Gav, is that correct?" a stern voice asked. Gav turned to see a man with sharp features, his graying blonde hair neatly combed, his red and white armor gleaming in the firelight. A black lion emblem adorned his tunic, its eyes fierce and regal.

"Yes, sir," Gav replied, his voice steady despite the knot tightening in his chest.

"Very good!" another voice chimed in, bright and full of energy. Gav's eyes shifted to a woman with dark, serpentine eyes and jet-black hair that spilled over her shoulders. Her tunic was blue, the hyena emblem stitched into the fabric seeming to leer at him. "Gav, let's say you receive a gift! But you don't know what's in it. You're curious, so what do you do?"

Gav blinked, caught off guard by the question. He glanced at Wiglaf, who sat silently, his green tunic bearing the proud emblem of a bear.

"I suppose I would open it?" Gav ventured, his voice tinged with uncertainty.

"Straight away? Or would you wait?" the woman pressed, her eyes narrowing slightly.

"You already asked your question," snapped another woman, this one dressed in yellow armor, the black outline of an owl emblazoned on her chest. Her voice was sharp, penetrating.

"Let the boy answer, Guinevere," the woman in blue retorted, her tone light but firm. She turned back to Gav, her expression softening. "Go on!"

"Well, yes, I suppose I would open it right away," Gav said, his voice gaining a little more confidence.

"Please approach the table, Gav," the man in red said, his tone commanding but not unkind. "Do you see the board before you?"

Gav stepped closer and looked down. A weathered chessboard lay on the table, its wooden pieces carved with intricate detail. The game appeared to be in progress, though some pieces were missing, as if it had been abandoned mid-play.

"Chess?" Gav asked, his brow furrowing.

"You know it?" the man in red inquired.

"Yeah, I've played before."

"Would you please make a move on the board? You're white."

Gav studied the game carefully. The black king was cornered, surrounded by white pieces. It was a winning position, but the path to victory wasn't immediately clear. He hovered his hand over the rook, then the knight, then the bishop, tracing their possible moves in his mind. Checking with the knight seemed strong, but was it the best option? He glanced up at the man in red, searching for a hint, but the knight's face was unreadable.

"Sir?" Gav said, his hand resting on his chin.

"Yes?"

"When you play, do you allow promotion?"

"Yes, I do," the man replied, a faint smile tugging at the corners of his mouth.

With that, Gav moved a white pawn to the eighth rank. "I promote to queen," he declared, his voice firm.

The man in red leaned toward the woman in yellow, exchanging a glance. He then looked to the woman in blue and finally to Wiglaf, who gave a subtle nod.

"Gav," Wiglaf said, his voice low and steady. "Ye can head upstairs now."

To his left, Gav saw a steep spiral staircase leading to a second-floor corridor. He hesitated, glancing at Wiglaf, hoping for some sign—a nod, a smile, anything—but the knight remained stoic. Gav would have to do this alone.

He ascended the stairs, each step echoing in the narrow passage. The flames in the sconces flickered and crackled, their light casting eerie shadows that seemed to follow him as he climbed. The air grew colder, the silence heavier, as he reached the top and walked down the dark hallway. At the end stood a door, its wood old and worn. Gav pushed it open and stepped through.

The Archbishop stood before him, his astral robes glowing faintly in the dim light. His smile was warm, his eyes kind. "Come," he said, gesturing for Gav to approach.

He stepped forward, his heart pounding, and looked out over the balcony. Below, the crowd of white-clad children stood in silence, their faces upturned, their eyes fixed on him.

Gav felt the tip of a wand pressed to his chest as warmth pooled within him. And then, the order was issued. "The Order of the Crimson Manes!" the Archbishop shouted, his voice ringing out like a bell. He raised his wand, and a bolt of red lightning shot into the sky, splitting the night with its brilliance. A spectral lion roared, its form twisting and dancing among the stars, its cry echoing across the courtyard.

Gav looked down at his chest and watched as the white fabric of his tunic shifted, staining itself a deep, vibrant crimson. The lion emblem appeared, its golden threads gleaming in the torchlight.

"Go on, Gav," the Archbishop said, his voice gentle but firm.

Gav turned and saw Nora waiting for him at the bottom of a small staircase, her face alight with excitement. She waved her hands wildly, her grin wide and infectious.

"Gav! You're a Crimson Mane! Just like me!"

A wave of warmth washed over him as Nora flung her arms around him, pulling him into a tight hug. For the first time since Morholt's forge, Gav felt like he belonged. Besides him and Wiglaf, he hadn't encountered many friendly faces. Nora's kindness was a relief to him, a blessing.

The Archbishop's voice cut through the din of the celebration, calling out the remaining children's names until none were left.

"Now that all the children have been properly inducted," he began, his eyes sweeping over the sea of young faces, their expressions a mix of awe and anticipation. He paused, letting the moment stretch, before his lips curled into a mischievous grin. "It is now time to make merry. Let's eat and dance. After all, this is a celebration!"

The words had barely left his mouth when the air erupted with the sound of bugles, their notes ringing out clear and bright. Drums joined in, their deep, rhythmic beats shaking the ground, followed by the lively trill of pipes and the sweet, soaring strains of fiddles. The Archbishop raised his wand one last time, sending a final bolt of magic streaking into the sky. The stars above seemed to ignite, their light dazzling and sharp, as if the heavens themselves were joining in the revelry.

Then, with a thunderous crash, the massive oak doors at the far end of the courtyard swung open, their hinges groaning under the force. Wiglaf stood in the doorway, his broad frame filling the space, his green tunic and bear emblem catching the firelight. "Who's hungry?!" he bellowed, his voice booming like a war horn. "Mead hall's open! There be food at the stalls too!"

The children exploded into cheers, their excitement palpable as they surged toward the doors, their laughter and shouts filling the night air.

"That's the bear!" one boy exclaimed, pointing at Wiglaf.

"He's huge!" another added.

"I hope they have hogget! I love hogget!" A third voice chimed in, barely audible over the clamor.

Gav hung back, watching as the other children found pairs and groups to walk with, waiting for Nora to take the lead; that is, until he noticed a boy watching him.

Perceval de Boron.

He recognized him from the induction ceremony. The crimson tunic, the lion crest. A fellow Crimson Mane. Gav glanced down at his own red fabric, suddenly self-conscious.

"You're a... Crimson Mane," Gav began, voice faltering. "Just like us."

Perceval's gaze swept over him. Recognition flashed—then vanished behind a wall of ice. His lips pressed into a blade-thin line.

"I'm Gav." He extended his hand, pulse jumping. A risk, but he was tired of cold shoulders.

"You're Perceval, right?" Nora cut in, her tone airy. "I think we've met."

"Percy," the boy sniped.

"Oh, right! My brother dated your sister. Mercie, was it?" Nora barreled on, words tumbling like dice. "And you're Percy. Oh, that's funny!"

Percy's head tilted, a fractional movement that conveyed utter bafflement and disdain. His eyes flicked back to Gav.

And there it was. That look. The one Gav had come to know too well in Avalon. Cold. Dismissive. A door slamming shut.

Percy turned without another word, not to Gav's face anyway. The boy's voice carried back, sharp as a dagger between Gav's ribs:

"You shouldn't be here."

The words lodged in Gav's chest, a barbed thing twisting deeper with every breath. His fists clenched.

Then Nora's hand settled on his shoulder. Warm. Steady.

"Let's get some milk, Gav." Her smile was a lifeline. "I find a nice pint makes most things better."

The night unfolded with laughter, music, and the warm glow of torchlight. Gav and Nora wandered through the courtyard, their steps light and unhurried, as they explored the food stalls laden with rich, aromatic dishes. They sampled roasted meats, sweet pastries, and spiced drinks, their laughter mingling with the lively tunes of the musicians. The air was sweet with the scent of honeyed mead and sizzling hogget, and the courtyard buzzed with the energy of celebration.

They danced, too, though their movements were small and awkward, more shuffling than anything else. But it didn't matter. The music swelled around them, a lively fusion of drums, pipes, and fiddles, and the knights—their faces flushed with drink and merriment—joined in, spinning and stomping with the children. The Archbishop's magic still lingered in the air, the gemstone sky above shimmering with a brilliance that seemed almost alive. It was a night of joy, of belonging, or so it seemed.

Even in the midst of it all, Gav couldn't shake the feeling of being watched. Unwanted glares followed him, sharp and piercing, rending asunder the warmth of the celebration. He caught the sideways glances, the whispered words, the subtle shifts in posture as he passed by. In a sea of shining faces and sparkling stars, Gav's deep emerald eyes seemed to glow brighter than all the rest—a beacon that drew disgust and disdain. And yet, as he stood there under the magic-lit sky, the warmth of Nora's new friendship at his side, he couldn't help but question it all. *Did he really belong here?*

Chapter 7
The Order of the Crimson Manes

"This way!" called out the older boy, a Red Mane knight in training, his voice piercing through the cool air. He was older than the rest of the recruits by only a small margin. He seemed to be fifteen years and a handful of months, just enough to shed the last traces of childhood baby fat. Now he stood, firm and solid, in that awkward space between youth and manhood, where the sharp edges of the world would soon test his years of knightly training. But for now, he simply led the younger recruits.

The line of weary cadets followed in his wake, their steps slow and heavy. The sky above them, once a dazzling canvas of magical diamond lights, had begun to fade, the shimmering constellations dimming as night settled in. The air grew thick with the weight of exhaustion.

"Keep pace," the older boy barked again, his tone a little sharper now. "I remember my induction. Hope you lot enjoyed yourselves."

"Nora!" Gav muttered in a low whisper, his voice barely more than a breath.

The girl, struggling to keep her balance, startled upright, her eyes barely open after nodding off mid-march. Her body had crashed into Gav's back with a thud, the sudden weight pushing him forward.

"Sorry!" she blurted out, the same apology escaping her lips for the third time that night.

The recruits trudged onward, each of them longing only for the solace of their beds, their limbs heavy with fatigue. The night had worn on, and dawn was still an hour away, yet it seemed an eternity.

"Halt!" The command rang out, severe and final.

They stopped in front of a long stone building, its form barely visible in the dim light, but the large door frame glowed faintly under the torch's flickering flame, casting long shadows across the ground.

"This is the Crimson Mane barracks. Boys take the basement bunks; girls, the ground-level bunks in the back." He led the children in as they fumbled over themselves in the dark. "I'd get straight to bed, rookies. Morning will be here before you know it."

This was far truer than anyone had realized. For it felt like only moments after finding their way to their beds did dawn break over Gamalaot as trumpets sounded with the morning cocks.

Gav's eyelids sprang open to the roaring noise outside. The room was well-lit from the sunlight pouring in from the window wells. And in this daylight, he was finally able to get a look about the room; he looked at his bed, which was small and standard for a cot, and a small wooden night table that appeared to be solely his own. Across the room was a wardrobe, which he assumed must be shared. Gav continued to scan the room, getting to know his new home for the foreseeable future. His eyes moved across the space until landing on the cot nearest his. Sitting on it was the boy from last night, Percy.

"Morning," Gav said with a slight wave.

Percy stared a moment before speaking. "Morning," he said obligatorily.

They dressed themselves in silence before joining the rest of the kids upstairs.

When Gav reached the top, he saw many of the familiar faces from last night. He watched on as boys and girls chatted with each other, trying to make friends like the first day of school. Small groups of threes and fours started to emerge within the crowd of red-cloaked children.

Gav found Nora across the room. She smiled and waved him over. It all felt so familiar, he thought. It was like his first day of middle school back home. And that's when it hit him. This would be his school this year, and all at once, a wave of nostalgia crashed over him. He missed his friends at Kingston Middle, especially Tommy. And while he didn't have too many close friends back home, everyone at least treated him like normal. Not like it was here, where each person would barely dare to look at him with anything other than loathing.

"Morning, Nora," Gav said.

"Percy!" She said, calling to him from over Gav's shoulder. "Percy!"

The boy trudged over unenthusiastically.

"Yes?"

"How was your night?" Nora asked.

Percy did not respond. But that didn't really matter because at that moment the barracks door swung open and the older boy who had led them only hours ago started shouting.

"Attention!" The command rang out. "Presenting Sir Arthur Pendragon, captain of the Order of the Crimson Manes."

As the man stepped into the barracks, his presence filled the room. "Arthur is fine," he said, his voice steady, with the weight of authority behind it. "Though, for those of you who prefer formality, Sir Arthur or simply 'sir' will do."

A sudden ripple passed through the ranks of recruits. Like a flock startled into flight, they broke from their huddled groups and quickly formed a single line. Straight backs. Squared shoulders. Each of them tried to stand tall, but there was a nervousness in the air, a tremor in the stillness.

For now, only the new cadets filled the room. Tomorrow, the older trainees would join them, and the line between youth and experience would blur. But today, it was just the fresh faces, stretching down the length of the barracks like a row of unfinished statues, still waiting to be shaped.

Sir Arthur moved down the line, his gaze sharp, inspecting each would-be knight with a look that could pierce through the armor they wore—or the lack thereof. Each recruit stood as though they could feel the full weight of his eyes, each of them silently aware that their mettle would soon be tested.

"Welcome," Arthur said, his voice firm and renitent, yet carrying an air of quiet respect. "New recruits, today is surely to be a special day, but I also anticipate a fair bit of nervousness."

Gav stood still, watching the man with an intensity that mirrored the captain's own. Arthur moved with a kind of purpose that seemed almost to resonate with the very walls of the barracks. His steps were measured, his gaze unwavering. If there had ever been any question about what a knight should be, Gav knew that Arthur embodied the pinnacle of it—of honor, of discipline, of chivalry.

"Starting today," Arthur continued, his voice steady, "everyone in this room bears the responsibility of our house." He paced slowly down the line of cadets, his eyes sweeping over each recruit, pausing just long enough to make them feel seen, heard, as though they were more than mere grunts. They were now a part of something larger. "You represent the Crimson Manes and the Academy at Castle Gamalaot. You must always strive to act in accordance with our knightly oath."

Arthur stopped, his gaze lifting to something distant, something none of the recruits could see—perhaps a vision of what lay ahead, a reminder of the weight of the mantle they had just taken on. Then, without warning, his eyes snapped to Gav's, locking with his own. There was no mistaking the intent behind that stare.

"We are a family." Arthur's voice softened but lost none of its steel. "We protect our own. You will not—under any circumstances—bring harm or dishonor to each other. Every cadet here has earned their place." He let the words settle like armor strapped to their chests. "By year's end, those unfit to wear the crimson will be gone. Am I understood?"

"Yes, sir!" The response cracked through the hall like a whip.

Silence followed—heavy, charged. The recruits stood motionless yet thrumming with newfound purpose. No room for doubt. No quarter for failure.

"Good. Today, we review your schedules."

Gav remained statue-still but tilted his chin just enough to catch Nora's eye. His lips barely moved: *Classes?*

She didn't answer, her own nerves locking her in place.

Arthur's words should have anchored him, but Gav's mind whirled with absurd images—knights hunched over grammar books, sparring with quills instead of swords. Would they line up for lunch pails next? Kick a soccer ball during recess? The mundane fantasy swallowed Arthur's voice whole, leaving Gav adrift until a pair of commanding boots halted before him. Stone-cold silence.

"Is that right, cadet?" Arthur's question cleaved through the haze.

Gav blinked. "Huh?" His face flamed scarlet as reality crashed back.

Arthur's gaze sharpened. "Repeat my last word, son."

"I—" Gav's throat closed. Nora's wide eyes screamed silent encouragement from his periphery.

"Miss Edmund." Arthur's tone carried warning. "Do not speak for him."

Nora stiffened, then lifted her chin. "With respect, sir—you just said we're family. He's overwhelmed." Her hands trembled, but her voice held. "Isn't that when family steps in?"

A beat. Then Arthur's laugh rang out—bright, startling, dissolving the tension like sunlight through storm clouds. "Well said." He turned to Gav, all business again. "Pay attention from now on. Understood?"

"Yes, sir." The words tasted like ash, but Gav nodded.

Arthur straightened, his next words a thunderclap: "All of you—take note of Miss Edmund's example!" The walls seemed to shake. "Fraternity and sorority are your creed. Accountability your foundation. Therefore..." A deliberate pause. "Twenty extra laps for the company today."

Groans died beneath Arthur's raised hand. No excuses. No weakness.

"Except Miss Edmund." A rare concession. "Your courage earns you choice, not obligation."

As the cadets about-faced, Percy shouldered past Gav and Nora, his whisper a venomous dart: "Thanks a lot."

"Ignore him," Nora breathed back.

"Morning warm-ups begin now. This is your training—structure it. Track it. Own it." Arthur's voice rolled over them like a tide. His gesture encompassed the sunlit fields. "I'll advise when asked, but the discipline must come from within. Clear?"

"Yes, sir!" The response came as sharp as blades being drawn. No one dared falter now. There was no room for complacency here. Each of them would have to find their own way, with only their discipline and their goals to guide them.

"Excellent!" Arthur's voice rang out with approval, his words crisp in the morning air. "Now, after morning training, you will head to your first class. As rookie cadets, your schedules are nearly identical, save for the timing. You all will take a survey of everything necessary for a knight to know: History, Chivalry, Combat, Magic, Strategy, and Husbandry. These are the cornerstones of your education here."

He paused, letting the weight of his words settle in. "Now, within these disciplines, you may choose to specialize in a particular area as you advance in your career here. I don't expect everyone to become an expert in all fields. Some of you may excel more in magic than in sword fighting. And perhaps, you'll find yourself more suited to magical study than to magical combat."

Arthur's gaze sharpened, his voice growing steadier, as though he were speaking to each recruit individually, letting them know that they would be seen for their strengths. "And to what you study, there is even more room to focus on your talents and interests. Divination, Apothecary, Incantation, Sorcery, Pyromancy, Cryomancy, and so on. The possibilities are vast."

He stepped forward, looking each cadet in the eye, as though drawing them into the gravity of the moment. "As you all grow and learn, we will help you determine what that specialty might be. Your path will not be the same as the next recruit's. It will be your own, shaped by your experiences and your choices. The road ahead is long, and the future is yours to shape."

Gav's mind ignited, all the possibilities lighting up within him like the sky had last night at the house induction ceremony. The world seemingly stretched endlessly before him, filled with options as boundless as the stars themselves. Each path sparkled with potential, each discipline rich with mystery and promise. And the best part—no one could tell him no. No more waiting for permission, no. This was his chance to explore, to immerse himself in everything without having to worry about his mother's watchful eye. His heart pounded with excitement, the thrill of freedom pushing aside the guilt that had clung to him as he'd left home. The future felt wide open.

"Ready?" Arthur's voice shattered the moment, sounding like a trumpet. "On my mark…"

The cadets looked up at him, their faces a mix of confusion and concern.

"You owe me twenty laps, cadets. Remember?" Arthur grinned, his eyes glinting with mischief. "Forward charge! Keep pace, cadets!"

The order was swift, the sudden energy in the air jolting every one of them into action. The sense of boundless possibility in Gav's chest remained, but now it was tempered by the immediate task at hand. There would be time for dreams later. For now, there were laps to run, and each step would carry him closer to the future he'd just imagined.

Nora took the lead, her strides long and determined, setting a pace that was quick but steady. Gav watched her for a moment, her figure cutting through the air with effortless confidence, before he pushed himself forward, falling into line behind her. With him came a reluctant wave of trainees, each one fighting their own battle with the burning sun, the heat slowly creeping in as the morning's crispness began to fade away.

"Keep it up, cadets!" Arthur's voice rang out from the sidelines. His encouragement was steady, but there was a hint of challenge in his tone, an implied reminder that this was just the beginning.

Gav's breath came in sharp bursts, his legs growing heavier with each lap. His mind struggled to keep track of the number of laps already run; the counting was lost somewhere between the beat of his heart and the rhythm of his footsteps. All he could focus on was the burning ache in his muscles, the steady rise and fall of his chest, and the constant need to move forward.

He clenched his teeth, willing his body to keep pace, to not falter, to push through the heaviness of fatigue that threatened to slow him down, and the sun beating down on him, but he didn't allow himself to think about it. There was only forward. Keep pace. Keep going.

"Ye got 'em runnin' already, eh?" said a gravel-hoarse voice.

Gav snapped his head around, following that familiar voice to that unmistakable frame.

"Wiglaf!"

Gav's legs burned, but even still, his determination pushed him to quicken his pace, the track beneath him blurring into a haze of dirt and sweat. He didn't know how much farther the end was, but that didn't matter. There was only one thing that drove him now, the need to finish, to reach the end as fast as he could. He had to get there. He had to see him.

Wiglaf was one of the few who didn't look past him or through him like everyone else. There was a connection there, something Gav hadn't found in anyone else, except maybe Nora. But that was it. Wiglaf and Nora—the only ones who offered a rare kind of understanding, a recognition that made him feel less miserable. It was that thought, that pull, that surged through him now, urging him forward with a force he couldn't resist.

His breath came in desperate, ragged pulls, his chest tightening with each inhale. But he couldn't slow down. His feet hit the ground faster, harder, the pounding rhythm matching the frantic beat of his heart. Every stride was driven by urgency, a single-minded rush to close the distance, to reach the moment where he could stop and finally see him again.

"At ease, cadets," Arthur said. "Catch your breath and then stand at attention over here."

Gav never broke his stride and made a beeline to Wiglaf, stopping only when hitting the man's mountainous frame.

"Aye, lad! Careful now. I'm not as spry as I once was."

Gav's heart thudded in his chest as he came to a halt, his breath ragged and his mind racing with a thousand things he wanted to say to Wiglaf. But now, standing there, he felt foolish. The words were lost somewhere deep within him, swallowed by the sight before him. His mouth hung open in a stupid expression as he stared at the squadron of cadets trailing behind his giant friend, all dressed in the green uniforms of their order.

As he took in the scene, he noticed the presence of two other groups now emerging onto the field, each with its own distinct uniform. His eyes darted to one group, and his stomach gave a slight lurch when he recognized the two women at the front. They were the knights who interviewed him at the induction ceremony. Their cadets followed closely behind them, dressed in bright gold and blue respectively, their movements sharp and disciplined, just like their leaders.

"At attention!" Arthur said firmly.

The children painted the field in the vibrant hues of their houses, each tunic a burst of color that caught the sunlight and shimmered like precious stones. Rubies glinted in the form of the cadets dressed in crimson, emeralds flashed with the green of Wiglaf's squadron, and lapis lazuli sparkled beneath the bright azure sky, while yellow citrine gleamed wisely through the golden uniforms. It was a spectacle of light and color, a living tapestry that spoke of the pride and potential of each house. The field, once a simple stretch of earth, had transformed into a canvas where every cadet's future seemed to shine as brightly as the jewels their uniforms represented.

"Good morning, cadets," Arthur said. "By now, you have been introduced to your house captain." He nodded to the Crimson Manes on the western lawn. "But your lone house does not make up the entirety of Castle Gamalaot. Each of us represents a pillar of our great kingdom on which the castle could not stand without. While friendly competition is perfectly acceptable, and perhaps encouraged, you must respect and honor your fellow knights."

"Aye! Just wait fer the Winter Festival," Wiglaf said with a hearty pound of his chest. "That be the best time to let all yer frustrations out."

"Winter Festival?" Gav whispered to Nora beside him. She said nothing. It was unclear if this was a decidedly purposeful act of ignoring him or if she was simply mesmerized by the commanding auras of the four captains.

"Let's not get ahead of ourselves, Sir Wiglaf."

"Quit yer formalities with the young ones! We ain't fancy folk!"

Arthur nearly fell forward from the hearty pat Wiglaf laid upon his back.

"Arthur," said the woman in gold and silver armor. "Why don't we move on to introductions?"

"Agreed," he said. "My name is Sir Arthur Pendragon; Order of the Crimson Manes." Arthur looked to Wiglaf with a rather awkward pause.

"Me?" he said with an obtuseness that visibly bothered the other captains. "Just Wiglaf, aye. Wiglaf of the Verdant Claws." The behemoth of a man then pounded upon his chest and shouted a battle cry passed down by his ancestors. "HAAAAA RAAAA!"

The cadets in green pounded on their chests in response and cried back with smaller shouts of their own.

"HURRR AHHHH!"

The woman in the gold and silver armor moved her jaw and massaged her temple before speaking. She wore an irritation that intimidated the crowd of cadets far more than anyone else they'd met so far.

"I am Lady Guinevere. Captain of the Gilded Wings and Gamalaot's current acting strategist."

"Brutes, the lot of you!" said the woman in blue. She smiled with thin, sallow skin that pulled her mouth into a slit just barely wider than her eyes. "I want you all to call me Miss Morrigan. I am captain of the Azure Stripes and head physician at the academy."

Gav found himself unsure about his house. A heavy disappointment lingered in his chest, a quiet ache that he wasn't under Wiglaf's command, and it felt as if that same sense of letdown had settled over the entire field, seen in the faces of the other cadets. To his credit, Arthur seemed a man of strength and repute, however distant, as if his mind wandered far from where his body stood. But the true weight of fear seemed to hover around Lady Guinevere and Miss Morrigan, each stirring something deep and unsettling in the hearts of the cadets, though for reasons as different as night and day. Nervous fear, in the end, had taken root in them all.

"Cadets," Arthur's voice rang out, steady and firm. "Today, we'll be guiding you through the castle. And because you'll soon find yourselves in classes alongside knights from other orders, we've decided to conduct the tours together. Use this time to make acquaintance with those beyond your own order."

"The castle's bigger than any of ye can rightly imagine!" Wiglaf boomed, his voice a warm chuckle in the cool air. "We'll be breakin' this great army into smaller bands."

The captains spread out across the field, their voices calling out the names of the cadets who would follow them. As each name was spoken, the cadets moved, like pieces on a chessboard. In truth, the whole affair reminded Gav of recess back home, when children would line up and take turns picking teams for kickball.

"Gav," called Wiglaf, his voice warmer, more familiar than the others. "Come on over now!"

A surge of joy washed over Gav at the sound of his name, spoken not by a commander, but by a friend. He quickened his step toward the group. But before he could settle, another voice, cool and smooth like oil, slithered across the field.

"Nora Edmund," said Miss Morrigan.

Their eyes met, Gav's and Nora's, and for just a heartbeat, the world seemed to slow. Then, as quickly as the moment had come, Nora had walked across the field to her group, away from him, the distance between them like an ocean.

Gav's heart sank. He had hoped to stay close to Nora. She was his only friend, and to have her familiar presence beside him as they navigated the castle grounds would have been nice. But as her name was called, she gave him a small, reassuring smile before walking away to join her group. Gav watched her go, feeling a pang of loneliness, but he quickly straightened his shoulders and turned his attention back to Wiglaf.

As he did, Gav felt the weight of the stares pressing down on him as he sought refuge in the shadow of the towering knight. The other cadets in their group exchanged glances, their expressions of thinly veiled disdain. Among them, Lucan Lambelle stood out, standing taller than the rest. His icy glare was fixed on Gav, his lips curled into a faint sneer that spoke volumes without a single word. The blue tunic he wore, marked with the emblem of the Azure Stripes, seemed to amplify his arrogance, and Gav couldn't help but feel smaller under his gaze.

"Let's be movin'!" Wiglaf's voice cut through the tension, his tone firm. He turned on his heel and began striding toward the south entrance of the castle, his broad shoulders and confident gait leaving no room for hesitation. Gav fell into step behind him, doing his best to ignore the whispers and sidelong glances from the other cadets. He focused on the sound of Wiglaf's boots crunching against the gravel path, using it as an anchor to steady his nerves.

The south entrance loomed ahead, its massive wooden doors carved with intricate designs of knights, beasts, and battles long past. Wiglaf pushed them open with ease, revealing a grand hallway that stretched into the heart of the castle. The air inside was cool, lightly blowing on the tapestries that lined the walls, their vibrant colors depicting scenes of heroism and legend, while suits of armor stood like silent sentinels, their polished surfaces reflecting the flickering torchlight flames.

"You're Gavain, ain't ya?" came a voice from behind.

Gav turned to find himself face-to-face with a large boy, broad in both fat and muscle. His hair was yellow and thick like straw, and his tunic a bold green.

"The Ragnell boy," came another voice, identical in pitch and tone, from the other side.

Twins.

Gav blinked, taken aback for a moment. "Yeah," he replied. "Just call me Gav."

"I'm Bor," said one of the boys, his grin wide and easy.

"And I'm Tor," the other followed, his voice carrying the same easygoing warmth.

"We're brothers," they said together, as if it were something they said a thousand times a day.

Gav opened his mouth, wanting to say something—anything—to keep the conversation flowing. They could be friends, something he was in short supply of. His words, though, stayed anchored somewhere inside himself, like stones in a stream. The silence stretched, but it didn't matter. Not with Wiglaf up ahead, his voice ringing through the air, breaking the quiet with stories of Gamalaot and legends of ancient heroes.

As they rounded the corner, Gav spotted Percy just a few paces ahead, stealing quick glances back at him, as if unsure of whether or not to acknowledge him.

"Hey." Gav's voice cut through the castle hall chatter.

Percy turned, eyebrow arched. "Yes?"

"Just wanted to say... sorry about the laps this morning." The apology hung between them like a poorly tied knot.

Percy's face did something complicated—a flicker of surprise, then something that might have been the ghost of understanding before his usual mask slid back into place. Gav considered mirroring his cold silence, but Nora's words echoed in his memory. *He's not so bad once you get past the prickles.* If she could find common ground with this walking icicle, maybe he should at least try.

Behind them, Bor and Tor bickered about syrup-drenched pancakes versus honey-glazed sausages, their easy camaraderie a stark contrast to the brittle quiet between Gav and Percy. The twins hadn't once glanced his way or tossed him an opening in their debate. Back home, friendships had been as simple as sharing a lunch bench. Here, every interaction felt like navigating a maze blindfolded.

"Anyway." Gav scuffed his boot against the cold, stone floor. "Just... yeah. Sorry."

For half a heartbeat, Percy's eyes thawed—just enough to suggest he recognized the olive branch, even if he wasn't ready to take it. The silence stretched, neither hostile nor welcoming, but perhaps, just maybe, a fraction less heavy than before.

"Hey! De Moron." The voice dripped like poison. Lucan shouldered through the crowd, his lip curled. "Should've known I'd find you cozying up to the Ragnell freak."

Percy's jaw tightened. "That's not my name." His voice stayed level, but a vein pulsed in his temple.

Gav stepped forward, eyes locked with Percy's in silent understanding. "I'm not his friend."

For half a breath, something passed between them—an unspoken thanks in the face of Lucan's venom.

"You're not?" Lucan's laugh was winter-cold. He circled them like a wolf sizing wounded prey. "For all his money, De Moron here couldn't buy a friend if he tried. And you..." He leaned in, breath hot against Gav's ear. "You're a walking curse. A damn blight on this kingdom. Guess trash sticks together."

Gav's fists clenched—knuckles white, muscles coiled. One punch. That's all it would take. But before he could move, there was a tug at his tunic. Percy's fingers twisted in the fabric, his eyes screaming *don't.*

Lucan loomed over them, all corded muscle and cruel smiles. "Where have you been all these years anyway? Showing up here out of the blue." He jerked his chin toward Wiglaf. "Don't tell me the oaf's been training you in secret?"

"What's your problem?" Gav's voice cracked like a whip.

"My problem?" Lucan's hands flashed—frost spiderwebbing across his fingertips before flames swallowed it whole. The air reeked of burnt ozone. "I've trained since I could walk. Cryomancy? Mastered. Pyromancy?" Another flare of fire erupted from his fingers. "Child's play."

Lucan stepped back, rolling his shoulders. "I'm only here as a formality. After this year, I'll be an active duty knight. The youngest since Lancelot. Mark me."

The shove sent Gav stumbling. Lucan vanished into the crowd, leaving frostbitten footprints in his wake.

Percy exhaled through his nose. "He's not wrong. About his skill." For the first time, he held Gav's gaze—not quite respect, but something closer to acknowledgment. "Picking fights with him is suicide."

"He already hates me," Gav muttered. "Same as everyone."

Percy opened his mouth—hesitated—then offered the closest thing to kindness he'd ever given: "He hates me too. Take some fencing lessons before you get yourself killed."

A startled laugh escaped them both. Percy smothered his quickly, as if caught doing something indecent.

"Aye!" Wiglaf cried out, his voice cutting through the awkwardness of the moment. "Over here, ye lads and lasses." With a grunt, he swung open yet another set of massive wooden doors and ushered them into a deeper part of the castle. "Stick close now," he warned, his tone rough but carrying an edge of earnestness. "Don't want none of ye wanderin' off. I once spent three whole days lost in these here cellar's passages 'fore the Archbishop stumbled upon me."

The cadets stood motionless for a moment, necks craned like saplings straining toward sunlight. Gamalaot Castle didn't merely surround them—it swallowed them whole. Each room bigger and more intimidating than the last.

They'd passed the archive first, its shelves stretching into shadowed heights, leather-bound tomes whispering secrets from their spines. Then the throne room, its vaulted ceiling lost in gloom, the weight of a thousand years pressing down upon their shoulders. Even the commissary, meant for breaking bread, felt like a cathedral—its stone ribs arching over tables that seemed to shrink beneath them.

Gav's breath hitched as he tilted his head back. Even Wiglaf, that mountain of a man, looked like a child's toy against these walls. The very air tasted old, thick with the ghosts of footsteps and murmured oaths. He could almost feel the castle's gaze upon his skin, ancient and patient as it watched these new ants scuttle through its veins.

His fingers twitched at his sides as they wound through the labyrinth. Every detail became a lifeline: the dent in the third suit of armor's breastplate, the way torchlight caught the jagged edge of a cracked sconce, the precise number of steps between the alchemy lab and the east stairwell. He mapped the turns like a scribe drafting a manuscript...*left at the falcon crest, right where the tapestries frayed.*

Night found Gav rigid on his bunk, eyelids burning. The others' breaths deepened into sleep while his mind raced along those remembered corridors. He flexed his hands beneath the scratchy blanket, murmuring directions to himself. Somewhere in the dark, a moth battered against a windowpane, drawn to the dim light from his lantern. Excitement and dread twisted together in Gav's gullet—a living thing with thorns. Tomorrow, the stones would judge him. Tomorrow, the real trial begins.

Chapter 8
The First Lessons in Combat and Sorcery

The morning broke with the shrill call of bugles and the cawing of roosters, their voices slicing through the sleepy morning as sunlight crept into the cramped basement barracks. Gav was already wide awake, his body buzzing with restless energy. Sleep had been a fleeting visitor, chased away by the mounting anticipation that had consumed him all night. His mind had raced through the day ahead, rehearsing his schedule, imagining the classrooms, the instructors, the challenges. Combat Training 101 and Elementary Magic filled the morning, while the afternoon promised Apothecary Science and Etiquette. Though the latter didn't spark the same excitement as the morning's offerings, the thrill of a fresh start was enough to carry him through. Gav had always loved first days back home; the clean slate, the new rhythms, the promise of starting from scratch.

He dressed quickly, lacing up his boots and securing his sword sheath across his back. As he glanced around the barracks, he noticed how similar he looked to the other cadets, their uniforms and gear mirroring his own. There was a strange comfort in that, a sense of belonging. Smiling softly to himself, he made his way up the stairs.

"Morning!" Nora's voice rang out through the chatter.

"Morning, Nora," Gav replied, offering a small smile. Her attention shifted to Percy, who was pulling on his boot strings with his usual air of detachment.

"Oh, Percy," she said, her tone teasing. "Are you less of a grouch today?"

Gav noticed a group of cadets nearby, their laughter bubbling up in stifled bursts as they exchanged knowing glances. Percy's expression darkened, though there was a flicker of amusement in his eyes. "I'm not a grouch," he said, his voice tinged with mock indignation.

"I'm not so easily convinced. Gav, what do you think? You believe him?"

Gav hesitated, caught off guard. His interaction with Percy the day before had been surprisingly civil, but Percy still carried himself with a guarded air that made him hard to read. "I believe him," Gav said finally, his voice soft and unsure.

"Yeah, I suppose you're right." Nora laughed, a bright, infectious sound. "So then you wouldn't be opposed to getting breakfast with us after our morning workout. Right, Percy?"

Percy shrugged, his expression neutral. "Sure," he said, before slinging his bag over his shoulder and heading outside.

"Great!" Nora exclaimed, her enthusiasm so intense that Gav flinched as a bit of spit landed near his ear. "Sorry about that!" she added with a sheepish grin. "Say, Gav, would you mind being my spotter today? I think I want to do strength conditioning."

"Sure thing," Gav replied, his shyness melting away in the face of her infectious energy. As they made their way to the training grounds, Gav felt a flicker of excitement. The day was just beginning, and already it felt full of possibility.

Gav and Nora stepped out into the crisp morning air, the dew still clinging to the grass as they made their way across the field. Gav couldn't help but notice the sideways glances and hushed whispers that followed him like a shadow. The girls exchanged knowing looks, their voices low and conspiratorial, while the boys' stares were harder, sharper, their expressions laced with a hostility that made Gav's skin prickle. He kept his head down, trying to ignore the weight of their judgment, but it was impossible to miss.

"Nora," Gav said quietly, his voice tinged with unease. "I appreciate you being friendly, but maybe you shouldn't…"

"Don't be thick," Nora interrupted, her tone as casual as if they were discussing the weather. "If you don't want to be friends with me because I'm strange, that's fine. But if you're only saying this because you're trying to be noble or chivalrous or whatever, well, that's really dumb. I can make my own decisions, and I'd like to be friends. Do you want to be friends with me or not?"

Gav blinked, caught off guard by her bluntness. Then, slowly, a smile spread across his face.

"I do," he said, his voice warm with gratitude. "Thanks."

"Excellent! Now, be a good friend and help me grab these kettlebells."

Gav followed her to the rack of weights, his hands wrapping around the cold, heavy metal of the kettlebells. They were far heavier than he'd expected, and he struggled to lift them, his arms trembling slightly under the strain. When he handed them off to Nora, he couldn't help but feel a pang of embarrassment as she hoisted them with ease, her strength evident in the way she carried herself. It was clear that Gav had a lot of catching up to do if he wanted to keep pace with his classmates.

The morning workout had left Gav drained, his muscles aching, and his breath still coming in short, heavy bursts. But the exhaustion only made the thought of breakfast more appealing, a reward for the effort he'd poured into the training. As he and Nora made their way into the castle through the southern entrance—the same one Wiglaf had shown him yesterday—Gav took pride in remembering the layout. The commissary was just beyond the second set of doors, and when they stepped inside, the sight that greeted them was nothing short of breathtaking.

Yesterday, the room had been empty, a vast, echoing space. But today, it was alive with activity and color. Dozens of long tables and benches filled the hall, each one laden with platters of food and pitchers of drink. The air was thick with the scent of freshly baked bread, sizzling meat, and sweet pastries. Cadets and knights alike moved through the room, their voices blending into a low, steady hum of conversation and laughter.

Gav's eyes widened as he took it all in. The room seemed even larger than he remembered, its grandeur magnified by the sheer number of people filling it. Hundreds of cadets bustled about, balancing plates and tankards, while fully uniformed knights sat among them, their presence commanding respect. At other tables, high-ranking officers gathered, their laughter and camaraderie loud and contagious.

"Nora! Over here!" said a voice, breaking through the noise.

Nora's face lit up at the sound, and she grabbed Gav's hand, pulling him toward the source of the call.

"Happy first day!" the boy who had called out to Nora said, his grin wide and welcoming.

"Did Arthur give you the whole 'we're family' speech?" another boy chimed in, his tone teasing but good-natured.

Nora's eyes sparkled as she replied, "I thought it was quite inspiring!"

"Arthur's good at that," said a third boy at the table, his voice carrying a note of admiration.

Nora turned to Gav, her laughter bubbling up as she gestured to the group. "Oh! Gav, these are my brothers!"

It all made sense. He should have seen it sooner; the resemblance was unmistakable. All three boys shared Nora's long, angular nose and the same bright, lively expressions.

"Hello!" Gav said, his voice tinged with awkwardness. He half expected them to be as cold and distant as so many others had been, but their smiles seemed genuine.

"You're Gavain, right?" asked the tallest of the three brothers, his tone curious but not unkind.

"I am," Gav replied, bracing himself for the usual reaction—the pause, the judgment, the silent reassessment. But it didn't come.

"He goes by Gav," Nora interjected, her voice firm. "Gav, this is Galeas. He's the oldest of these three."

"Call me Gale," the boy said, extending his hand toward Gav. Gav took it, shaking it firmly, and felt a flicker of relief at the warmth in Gale's grip.

"Nice to meet you," Gav said, his smile growing more confident.

"I'm Ed," said the boy next to Gale, offering his hand as well. "I'm a year younger than him. But I'm two years older than baby Nora here."

"And I'm Leif," said the last brother, his grin easy and relaxed. "I'm in my second year."

"It's great to meet all of you," Gav said, his initial awkwardness melting away. "You have a big family, Nora."

"This isn't even all of us," Ed said, cutting in before Nora could respond.

"First off, he wasn't talking to you," Nora shot back, her tone sharp but playful. "And secondly, Ed's right! We have another brother!"

"Here she goes," Leif said, rolling his eyes with mock exasperation. "Gwynn is her favorite."

"Yeah, we can't compete with him," Gale added, his tone light but tinged with amusement.

"You're seriously obsessed with him, sis," Ed said, shaking his head. "It's not healthy."

"You're all just jealous!" Nora shouted, her voice rising in protest. She turned to Gav, her eyes shining with pride. "He's famous!"

"Oh, really?" Gav said, his curiosity piqued. "Where is he?"

"On a mission, I think," Gale said, shrugging.

"What kind of mission?" Gav asked.

"We don't know!" Nora said, her voice brimming with excitement. "He gets sent on top-secret assignments all the time. He's that good!"

Gav couldn't help but smile at Nora's enthusiasm. It was clear that her admiration for Gwynn ran deep, and all her brothers' teasing only fueled her pride. As they settled into the conversation, Gav felt a sense of ease he hadn't expected. For the first time since arriving, he felt like he was among friends—or at least, people who might become friends.

"I mean, it is pretty cool," Leif admitted, his tone softening as he nodded in agreement. "Being sent out on the toughest missions and all."

"She's bad enough!" Ed interjected, gesturing toward Nora with a playful smirk. "The last thing Gwynn needs is another super fan. The dolt has a big enough head as it is!"

"I can't wait for you to meet him, Gav!" she said, her excitement bubbling over. "He's been gone a long time now. Oh! There's Percy. Percy! Over here!"

Percy approached the table, his usual air of quiet detachment intact, and took a seat beside Nora.

"Morning," he said plainly, his voice flat and even.

Nora's brothers greeted him warmly—all except Leif, who shifted uncomfortably in his seat, his eyes darting around the room as if searching for an escape. "How've you been, Percy?" Leif asked, his tone awkward and forced.

"I am well," Percy replied, his expression unreadable.

"That's good. That's good," Leif muttered, his gaze still wandering. "And, uh, how's your family?"

"Specifically, your sister," Ed added with a mischievous grin, elbowing Leif in the ribs.

Percy's eyes flicked toward another table, where a group of girls sat in animated conversation. "Mercie?" he said, nodding in their direction. "She seems fine."

"Now that she's not weighed down," Ed said, bursting into laughter as Gale joined in, nearly spilling his drink. The two brothers were clearly enjoying themselves, their teasing relentless.

"I thought you said you broke up with her?" Nora asked Leif, her tone innocent.

At this, Gale and Ed erupted into even louder laughter, their amusement drawing the attention of nearby tables. Leif's face turned a deep shade of pink, his embarrassment palpable as he sank lower in his seat. "It's not…it's not like that," he stammered, though his protests were drowned out by his brothers' laughter.

In their mirth, Gale knocked over a pitcher of milk, spilling across the table and drawing even more eyes their way, including those of Mercie de Boron. She glanced over, her expression a combination of curiosity and mild annoyance, before turning back to her friends with a dismissive shake of her head.

Gav couldn't help but chuckle at the sight of it, though a quiet sympathy tugged at him for Leif. His brothers' teasing was clearly harmless, all in good humor, but it was plain to see that Leif wasn't entirely at ease with it.

"Excuse me," Leif muttered, his face still flushed as he hurriedly stood and left the commissary.

"Way to go!" Nora said, scolding her brothers with her hands on her hips, a biting glare thrown at them. But Gale and Ed were too caught up in their laughter to care, their amusement only subsiding when they finally ran out of breath.

Gav managed a small smile and a quiet chuckle, but the weight of the lingering stares around him was impossible to ignore. He sank lower into the bench, his shoulders hunched as if trying to make himself invisible. The laughter at the table had drawn even more attention, and Gav could feel the eyes of the room on him, their judgment stinging.

"Don't pay them any mind," Gale said, swallowing a mouthful of sausage..

"I just don't understand why everyone hates me so much."

"You scare them," Gale said bluntly, as if it were the most obvious thing in the world.

Before Gav could respond, Percy abruptly stood and left the table, his departure as quiet and unceremonious as his arrival. Nora watched him go, then turned to Gav with a reassuring smile. "Give him some time," she said. "I'm working on him. The fact that he sat with us bodes well."

Gav sighed, his hands gripping the edge of the table as he leaned forward. "Can you guys please tell me what everyone's problem is?"

Ed leaned in closer, his voice dropping to a whisper. "They think you're evil."

"Evil?" Gav repeated, his voice rising in disbelief. "How can they think that? I haven't done anything!"

"It's obviously not true," Nora said quickly, her tone firm. "People are idiots."

"But why do they even think that? I didn't do anything!"

Gale sighed, his expression softening with something that looked like pity. "You really have no idea, do you?" he said quietly. "Look, we don't have all the details, Gav. I'd ask Arthur or Wiglaf, or maybe even the Archbishop. They know the truth. We only know rumors."

Gav's chest tightened at the mention of rumors. He'd always known there was something people weren't telling him, some reason for the way they looked at him, the way they whispered behind his back. But hearing it laid out so plainly—that they thought he was evil—was like a punch to the gut.

"Rumors about what?"

Nora reached out, placing a hand on his arm. "We don't know the whole story," she said gently. "But whatever it is, it's not your fault. You're not what they say you are."

Nora, Gale, and Ed could see the turmoil brewing in Gav's expression, the way his shoulders slumped and his hands clenched into fists under the table. Before he could voice another question, Ed cut in, his tone softer now, more earnest.

"I know it doesn't help much," Ed said, "but try to ignore them. People love to talk, especially when they don't know what they're talking about."

Gav's eyes flicked up, his frustration mingling with confusion. "Why don't you guys hate me?"

"Because we're not pearl-clutching morons," Nora said bluntly, her usual sharpness bisecting the tension. But when Gav didn't smile, she sighed and leaned in closer. "No, really. We don't hate you because we don't believe the nonsense everyone else is spouting."

"But why does everyone else think I'm evil?" Gav pressed, his voice rising slightly. "I just don't understand any of this."

Ed exchanged a glance with Gale before speaking, his tone cautious. "Look, Gav," he said, lowering his voice. "No one here really knows the specifics, but there's some kind of legend or prophecy about you or your family. The boy with the emerald eyes. He's supposed to bring the end of the world, or something along those lines."

Gav felt the words like a blow, his stomach twisting as the pieces began to fall into place. Wiglaf's cryptic comments about his eyes, the burned building they'd passed—*had he done that? Was it his fault?* His mind spiraled, a whirlwind of doubt and fear threatening to swallow him whole.

"But Gav," Nora said, her voice holding him. "You need to know that there are people who don't believe any of it."

"It's true," Ed added, nodding. "Our whole family thinks it's a load of dung."

"Nora reached out, placing a hand on Gav's shoulder. Her touch was firm, grounding. "I can't tell you what to feel," she said gently. "And I know this is a lot to think about. But people are just scared and trying to figure you out. I think the more you focus on being the best you can be, people will come around. Look at Percy!"

Gav's expression didn't change, his eyes still clouded with worry. Nora's attempt to reassure him fell flat, and she exchanged a concerned glance with her brothers.

"Talk to Arthur," Gale said finally, his tone steady. "He'll sort you out. He knows more about Gamalaot than anyone else here."

"Well, besides the Archbishop. The man is ancient," said Ed to himself more than anyone else.

Gav nodded slowly, though the weight of their words still pressed heavily on him. "Thanks, you guys. I really appreciate it."

"That's what friends are for!" Nora said, her usual cheerfulness returning as she slapped him on the back. "Now, I think we're in the same Combat Training class. We should get going soon."

Gav managed a small smile, though his mind was still racing. As they gathered their things and headed toward the training grounds, he couldn't shake these rumors. There was obviously more to this, but without the whole truth, his mind was left to fill in the blank spaces. For now, he did his best to cling to Nora's words and the small flicker of hope they offered. That he wasn't alone—not entirely.

The morning air was crisp and invigorating as Gav and Nora made their way to the training field, the sun casting a golden glow over the freshly trimmed grass. The field was alive with activity, cadets milling about, their voices a low hum of excitement and nervous energy. Gav's eyes scanned the crowd, noting the mix of uniforms—Azure Stripes, Verdant Claws, and Gilded Wings. Many of them already held wooden training swords, their grips practiced and confident, while others inspected the straw-and-wool dummies with varying degrees of skepticism.

Gav overheard snippets of conversation as they walked, the complaints of some cadets cutting through the morning calm.

"These things are ancient!" one boy in blue exclaimed, holding up a wooden sword with a chipped edge.

His friends laughed, their voices carrying across the field. Gav's gaze lingered on the group, and his stomach tightened when he spotted Lucan among them. Their eyes met, and for a moment, the air between them seemed to freeze. Lucan's expression was cold, his lips curling into a faint smirk before he turned back to his friends, dismissing Gav with a flick of his gaze.

Before the tension could escalate further, a hush fell over the field as Sir Arthur Pendragon arrived. His presence commanding, his stride confident and purposeful as he made his way to the center of the gathering. The cadets quickly fell into line, their chatter replaced by an eager silence.

"Good morning," Arthur began. "Today marks the beginning of your combat training. This is where you'll learn not just how to fight, but how to think, how to adapt, and how to work together. The tools you see before you may seem simple, even crude, but they are the foundation upon which your skills will be built."

Gav glanced down at the wooden sword in his hand, its weight unfamiliar but not unwelcome. He tightened his grip, determination flickering in his chest. This was his chance to prove himself, to show that he was more than the rumors.

Arthur's gaze swept over the group, his eyes perspicacious and assessing. "Combat is not just about strength or speed," he continued. "It's about discipline, focus, and respect—for your opponent, for your weapon, and for yourself. Today, you'll begin with the basics. Pair up and we'll practice strike forms. Remember, this is about control, not force."

As the cadets began to pair off, Gav felt a nudge from Nora. "You're with me," she said with a grin, raising her wooden sword. "Don't go easy on me just because I'm a girl."

"Wouldn't dream of it," Gav smiled, falling into position across from her.

Arthur's voice carried across the field, firm and authoritative, as he addressed the gathered cadets. "Looks like everyone has a training sword," he said, his eyes scanning the group. "There are extras up here if you need them. Everyone, stand on the white line."

The cadets shuffled into position, their feet aligning with the painted white line that stretched across the field. Gav adjusted his stance, his wooden sword feeling awkward but purposeful in his hands. He glanced at Nora, who gave him an encouraging nod, her own sword held at the ready.

"Sword fighting is an art form all its own," Arthur continued, his tone steady and instructive. "It shares much with dancing, if you can believe it. Now, I want everyone to stand with their feet square with your shoulders and to hold the blade up in front of you like this."

Arthur demonstrated the stance, his movements precise and deliberate. The cadets mirrored him, their bodies shifting into position as they raised their swords. Gav focused intently, his feet shoulder-width apart, his grip tightening on the hilt of his wooden blade.

"Very good! Now I'm going to demonstrate a combination by walking you through some basic positions."

He took a step forward, his body flowing into the first position as he brought the blade up in a diagonally vertical slice. "This is the first position!" he announced, his voice clear and commanding.

Next, Arthur slid his weighted foot out, his body lowering closer to the ground as he brought the blade down, gripping the hilt closer to his hip. The movement was smooth and controlled, his posture steady. "This is the second position."

In one fluid motion, Arthur lunged forward, his blade slicing horizontally through the air with a sharp whooshing sound. The cadets watched in awe, their eyes wide as they absorbed the demonstration. "And that's the third position," Arthur said, resetting his stance to the ready state. "This is a basic combination we call 'The Windsweep.' Watch again carefully."

He repeated the sequence, this time at double the speed. The cadets gasped as Arthur's movements became a blur of precision and power, the wooden sword slicing through the air with practiced ease. Gav felt a surge of admiration and determination. He wanted to move like that, to wield a sword with such grace and confidence.

"Do not worry about speed," Arthur said, his voice breaking through the cadets' murmurs. "You must first master the positions. Form is the most important part of armed combat. Poor form can cost you your life."

Gav nodded, his focus sharpening as he repeated the stance in his mind. He glanced at Nora, who was already practicing the first position. Around them, the other cadets began to mimic Arthur's demonstration, their wooden swords slicing through the air in uneven arcs.

Gav's attention was momentarily drawn to Lucan, who was moving through the positions with an ease that bordered on arrogance. Beside him stood two other Azure Stripe cadets—a girl Nora identified as Lilah von Trier and a boy whose name she wasn't entirely sure of.

"I think his name is Hubert," Nora said, her tone dismissive.

The two cadets hung on Lucan's every move, their admiration evident as they watched him execute the Windsweep combination with pinpoint precision. Lucan's face was a picture of triumph, his smug grin flashing at anyone who dared to look his way.

"C'mon, Gav," Nora called to him, bringing him back. "Give it a go!"

"Right," Gav said, nodding. He widened his stance, his worn wooden sword feeling more familiar in his hands now. He took a deep breath, closing his eyes for a moment to steady himself. And then, almost instinctively, his body moved. Despite Arthur's warning about speed, Gav's motions were fluid and unrestrained, as if his body had a mind of its own. He flowed through the positions seamlessly, the wooden sword slicing through the air with a sharp whoosh.

"Whoa!" Nora gasped, her eyes wide with surprise. "That was so fast!"

Gav nearly stumbled in shock, his own disbelief catching up with him. He had done it. He had performed the Windsweep effortlessly, as if he'd been practicing it for years. But could he do it again? Determined to find out, he reset his stance and tried again. This time, his movements were even smoother, even faster, the combination executed with a precision that left no room for doubt.

"You're incredible!" Nora cheered, her voice ringing out across the field.

Gav couldn't help but grin, the smile spreading across his face as he felt a surge of pride. He was drawing attention now, the eyes of the other cadets turning toward him. While some still regarded him with suspicion or disdain, he noticed a few of those hard stares softening, replaced by looks of curiosity and even respect.

"Gav," Arthur's voice called, acerbic and parting the murmurs of the cadets. The instructor approached, his expression unreadable but his tone firm. "Show me your Windsweep."

Gav nodded, his heart pounding as he prepared to demonstrate the combination once more. He took a deep breath, his body moving almost instinctively as he flowed through the positions. The wooden sword cut through the air with precision, each movement precise and deliberate. When he finished, Arthur's eyes gleamed with approval.

"Absolutely brilliant," Arthur said, clapping a hand on Gav's shoulder. "Keep it up, cadet." He turned to Nora, his tone shifting to one of encouragement. "Miss Edmund, show me your Windsweep combination."

As Arthur guided Nora through the transition between the second and third positions, Gav continued to practice, his confidence growing with each repetition. It felt good—no, it felt amazing—to finally feel successful, to prove to himself and everyone else that he could belong here. And the seething, jealous glares from Lilah, Hubert, and Lucan only fueled his determination further.

For the first time since arriving at the academy, Gav felt a real sense of belonging. There had been moments, but they were always undercut by the knowing stares and whispers. No, right now he wasn't just the boy with the emerald eyes, the subject of whispers and rumors. He was Gav, the cadet who could execute the Windsweep with power and speed and grace, and on his first try no less. And as he moved through the combination once more, he knew this was only the beginning.

The exhilaration from Combat Training carried Gav through the rest of the morning, the lingering unease from his earlier conversation with Nora's brothers fading into the background. The rush of mastering the Windsweep combination had left him buzzing with energy, and as he climbed the castle's winding staircase toward Elementary Magic, that excitement only grew. It fluttered in his stomach like a swarm of butterflies, a combination of anticipation and nervousness that made his steps feel lighter.

Nora walked beside him, her usual cheerfulness undimmed, but their group had grown by one. Percy had joined them on the way, his presence a quiet but noticeable addition. He didn't seem angry or uncomfortable, but Gav couldn't shake the memory of Percy's abrupt departure at breakfast. Despite Nora's reassurances, he couldn't help but feel that Percy still disliked him, maybe even resented him for being here.

The path to the magic classroom was a long one, taking them high into the castle's eastern rampart. The journey itself was an adventure, the trio passing through a covered parapet walk that offered a breathtaking view of the castle town of Gamalaot below. Gav paused for a moment, his eyes sweeping over the sprawling kingdom. From this height, the world seemed both vast and small, the bustling streets and towering buildings reduced to a patchwork of rooftops and winding roads.

When they finally reached the corner tower where Elementary Magic was held, Gav's excitement only intensified. The room was unlike anything he'd ever seen in real life. Small cauldrons lined a shelf at the back. Glass jars filled with pickled animal parts sat on another shelf, their contents floating eerily in murky liquid. The tables were adorned with skulls and pentangles that glowed with a faint, otherworldly light. The air was thick with the scent of herbs and something metallic, while whispered conversations filled the space.

Other students were already inside, their eyes wide with wonder as they explored the room. Gav felt a surge of curiosity, his eyes drawn to everything all at once.

Nora didn't hesitate. She grabbed both Gav and Percy by the arms and pulled them toward a table at the front of the room.

"Good morning," Miss Morrigan greeted the class, her voice slithering through the air like a serpent's hiss. She began by taking attendance, her sharp eyes scanning the roster with a meticulous attention to detail. When she reached Gav's name, she paused, her lips curling into a faint, unreadable smile. "Ragnell?"

"Present," Gav said softly, his voice barely above a whisper. He glanced over his shoulder, his stomach sinking as he noticed Lucan, Lilah, and Hubert seated a few rows back. They were whispering to each other, their eyes darting toward him.. *Of course, they were in this class too.* It felt like just his luck.

He turned back to face his teacher. Miss Morrigan was an enigma; her words kind, her smile frequent, but there was something unsettling about the way she spoke. Her voice carried a weight that pressed down on the room, her tone both soothing and unnerving. It was as if her very manner of speaking was a spell, weaving its way into the minds of her students. Her reputation as a wizard on par with the Archbishop only added to her mystique. Having a wizard so powerful and esteemed as their commander, the Azure Stripe cadets in the room sat a little taller, their pride evident.

"You are here to learn the basics of magic," she began, her voice soft and delicate, yet laced with an eerie cadence that held the cadets' attention captive. "I hate to start with the boring bits, but I think it helps to conceptualize this early on. Magic is a science. It requires precision and accuracy to execute to fidelity. I don't expect any of you to master all dimensions of magic. Quite the opposite, in fact. This class will survey many of the popular aspects: sorcery spells, incantations, and curses. And we will also learn the art of summoning, potion brewing, and enchantment."

Her words were measured, her tone almost hypnotic, but as she continued, her voice began to shift. It grew darker, more ominous, as if she were drawing them into a shadowy world they couldn't yet comprehend. "But cadets... Magic is an ocean. The deeper you go, the more horrific and terrifying it becomes. Darker and darker until all you can see is nothing at all, but you know there's an endless abyss in that blackness, and one misstep can send you sinking down some irrecoverable chasm. You can easily drown without the proper care."

The room fell silent, the weight of her words settling over the cadets like a heavy fog. Gav exchanged a worried glance with Nora, her usual cheerfulness replaced by a look of unease. Percy, however, leaned forward in his seat, his eyes alight with fascination. He seemed enthralled, hanging on Miss Morrigan's every word.

And then, as quickly as the darkness had descended, Miss Morrigan's demeanor shifted. Her face brightened, her smile returning as she clapped her hands together. "And that is why I will be your guide...your buoy in that ocean!" she declared, her voice suddenly chipper and bright, as if the previous moment had never happened.

Gav glanced at Nora again, his concern mirrored in her expression. Percy, however, looked ready to dive headfirst into whatever challenges Miss Morrigan had in store.

"Let's start with notes. Where does magic ultimately come from?"

"Dragons," chorused every cadet in the room, everyone except Gav. He was busy fumbling with his notebook, the unfamiliar quill slipping in his grip as he tried to dip it into the inkwell without making a mess. Even if he hadn't been distracted, he wouldn't have known the answer. The ease with which everyone responded embarrassed him; it was as if she'd asked, *What color is the sky?* Or *how many fingers do you have on your right hand?* This moment was a stark reminder that he was a stranger in this strange land of Avalon, an outsider trying to catch up.

"Very good," Miss Morrigan said, her smile widening. "And who can list all of the magical attributes?"

Percy's hand shot up immediately, his eagerness evident.

"Can you say your full name when you answer? It'll help me learn quicker," Miss Morrigan instructed, her tone light but firm.

"Perceval de Boron. Magic is broken into the following: Pyromancy, Cryomancy, Geomancy, Miracles, and Hexes."

"Oh my," Miss Morrigan said, clasping her hands together in delight. "How deliciously technical!"

Gav scribbled furiously in his notebook, the quill scratching against the paper as he tried to keep up. He hadn't quite mastered the art of dipping the quill into the inkwell, and his notes were already marred by sloppy pools of black ink.

"While young Perceval is absolutely correct," Miss Morrigan continued, "we should simplify for first-time mages." She cast a fleeting glance in Gav's direction, which only seemed to fuel the snickering from Lucan and the others seated at the back of the room. "Pyromancy is the technical term for fire magic, cryomancy is ice magic, geomancy is earth magic, miracles are light-based magic, and hexes are dark magic—sometimes called black magic. And we will practice all of these this year."

"Even black magic?" Gav muttered aloud to himself, his brow furrowing. If video games back home had taught him anything, dark magic was usually the weapon of villains.

"Please remember to state your name before speaking," Miss Morrigan said, her smile never wavering.

"What? Oh, I didn't mean…" Gav's face flushed red as he stammered.

"It's okay. I'm only teasing," Miss Morrigan said, her smile stretching even wider. "Dark magic has been misunderstood for centuries. You wouldn't be the first to presume that evil witches and warlocks practice the dark art of black magic. But as a black mage myself, I take offense to this!"

Gav didn't audibly gasp, but his eyes widened, and he exchanged a quick glance with Nora, who looked equally surprised. Around the room, other students reacted with similar expressions of shock. It wasn't entirely surprising to hear that Miss Morrigan was a black mage—her appearance and demeanor certainly fit—but there was an obvious stigma attached to the practice, evident in the reactions of the students around him.

"Statistically," Miss Morrigan said, raising a finger as if to emphasize her point, "based on the incarceration records within all of Avalon from the last twenty years—and mind you, this includes dozens of other kingdoms on the continent—more than sixty percent of criminal mages were pyromancers by disposition."

Gav quickly jotted down the figures in his notebook, his quill scratching vigorously. He caught a playful grin from Nora out of the corner of his eye, but he figured she must already know much more than he did. Still, he thought it was better to be safe than sorry. After all, it might be on a test.

"All this is to say, magic itself is not born of evil. There are those who, with dark hearts, wield it for harm, just as there are knights of honor who harness it in the name of justice and virtue."

From the back of the room, an arm shot up, followed by a voice brimming with certainty. "Lucan Lucien Lambelle," the boy declared.

"Yes?"

"Just to clarify, you're saying there is no such thing as evil spells? Or evil magics?"

"Essentially, yes," Morrigan replied, her tone flat. "But I'm not here to stir a debate on magical ethics. That's a matter for Sir Galahad to tackle, not me."

"With all due respect, Captain Morrigan, aren't you overlooking malefic sorcery?"

The ever-present smile that had been a fixture on Miss Morrigan's face vanished as if it had never been there at all. In its place, her eyes widened, hardening into a glare that carried a weight of sharp irritation.

The room stilled in an instant. An oppressive silence hung about them, thick and suffocating, as if the very walls themselves held their breath. After a long, heavy pause, she spoke, her voice low and taut.

"I was obviously excluding malefic sorcery when I spoke earlier," she said darkly.

"Miss Morrigan?" Gav asked, his curiosity getting the better of him as he looked up from his notebook. "What exactly is malefic sorcery?"

Both Percy and Nora shot him a glance that immediately made him regret the question. But as his gaze returned to Miss Morrigan, he braced himself for a sharp reprimand, or perhaps a harsh lecture. Instead, to his surprise, she let out a long sigh, her shoulders sagging in a rare moment of sympathy.

"Of course, you wouldn't know innately," she said, her voice softening. "Malefic sorcery—or what most simply call maleficence—is the sixth magical attribute." She shot a venomous look toward Lucan at the back of the room, one that spoke volumes of a simmering fury the boy would feel the weight of later. "And unlike the other five attributes, maleficence is, by its very nature, evil."

She straightened, her gaze turning sharp once more as the energy in the room shifted.

"We will not be covering it in this class because it's irrelevant to our studies and outside our purview. However," she continued, her tone shifting with a quiet authority, "since it has been raised, I will answer any questions you have now. But after that, we're done with it. Understood?"

The class nodded as one, a stiff, mechanical motion, as if pulled by the same string. No one stirred, no one spoke. It was as though the weight of the unspoken words had pinned them all in place. Just as Miss Morrigan drew a breath to break the spell, to push them forward, Percy's hand rose.

"Yes, Perceval?"

"What denotes maleficence?" he asked, his words careful. "I understand it's rare, but how would one even recognize it? What does it look like?"

Miss Morrigan paused, her lips pressing into a thin line. "That is an excellent question," she said, though her tone carried a hint of resignation, as though she wished he hadn't asked. "All malefic spells," she began, her voice low and deliberate, "manifest in a deep maroon color. Not the bright red of life, but the dark, almost black red of something dead and rotted." She hesitated then, her gaze drifting upward to the ceiling, as if searching for the right words among the cracks and shadows. "And..." she continued, her voice dropping lower still, "the air will smell sickly sweet, rank and rotten, all at once. Maleficence bears the sweet smell of death."

The class never quite shook the weight of that moment. The lesson had taken a turn none of them had anticipated, least of all Miss Morrigan, whose usual composure had faltered, if only for a heartbeat. For the rest of the hour, the room felt smaller, the walls closer, the light dimmer. And Gav, sitting stiffly in his seat, could feel Lucan's gaze like a brand on the back of his neck.

He didn't understand why, not entirely, but there was no mistaking the intent behind those eyes. The question Lucan had asked wasn't just a question. It was a message, a warning, something meant to cut deep and leave a mark. Gav clenched his jaw, refusing to turn, refusing to give Lucan the satisfaction of seeing the unease that coiled in his gut. But if Lucan's aim had been to unsettle him, to plant a seed of fear, then he had succeeded. And though Gav would never admit it, not even to himself, the truth lingered, cold and undeniable, in the pit of his stomach.

Chapter 9
Tending the Garden

Gav's first week was drawing to a close, the days folding into one another, and he had begun to settle into a rhythm, a cadence that felt almost natural, as though the edges of this new life were starting to soften and blend into something resembling familiarity. Each morning, he found himself in the commissary, sharing breakfast with Percy, Nora, and her brothers: Gale, Ed, and Leif. Percy still carried himself with a certain wariness, a guardedness that Gav couldn't quite penetrate, but there was something steadying about his presence all the same.

"It's the last Friday!" Ed burst out, his words muffled by a mouthful of hogget. He pounded his fists against Gale's shoulder, his excitement spilling over like an overfilled cup. "It's the last Friday!"

"The last Friday?" Gav echoed, raising an eyebrow as he glanced around the table.

"The last Friday!" Ed cheered again, thrusting a hand toward Gav for a high five. Flecks of hogget flew from his lips, landing on Gav's tunic, but Ed was too caught up in his own exuberance to notice.

"On the last Friday of each month," Gale explained, his voice tinged with amusement as he watched his brother bounce in his seat, "we get our mission assignments for the month."

"Mission assignments?" Gav asked, his curiosity piqued.

"Arthur will explain it," Gale said with a confident nod. "It's part of your basic training."

"One time we took on a bugbear!" Ed interjected, slamming his hands on the table for emphasis.

"Wicked cool," Nora murmured, her eyes glazing over with a dreamy sort of awe.

Gav stroked his chin with contemplation. He tried to picture a bugbear, some grotesque hybrid of a bear and an insect, perhaps? The image eluded him, vague and formless. It wasn't until later, in the hushed solitude of the library, that he would flip through the pages of a bestiary and find a crude rendering of the creature. It bore a striking resemblance to a werewolf, he thought.

"I can't imagine they'd send first years to fight a bugbear," Percy said, his tone cool and measured.

"We dispatched bandits my first year," Leif chimed in from the far end of the bench.

"Wait, really?" Percy and Nora exclaimed in unison, though their tones couldn't have been more different. Nora's eyes sparkled with excitement, while Percy's widened with concern.

"There's no way that's true," Gale said firmly, his voice carrying the weight of authority. As the oldest of the group, his word settled the matter, and Percy visibly relaxed, his shoulders dropping as the tension left his body.

"I'm serious!" Leif protested, though his words were met with skeptical glances.

Gav and Nora, however, were captivated by the fantasy of it, real or not, their imaginations running wild. *What would their task be?* Nora's eyes gleamed with the promise of adventure, something high-octane and thrilling. Gav, on the other hand, had no frame of reference, no expectations. For him, almost anything would do, so long as it didn't involve an eight-legged bear with claws and antennas.

"I can't wait," Nora exclaimed.

She didn't have to wait long, but that didn't stop her from riding that wave of excitement through breakfast and into their morning combat training. Her energy was infectious, and it seeped into Gav, fueling his imagination as he tried to picture himself in the thick of it, sword in hand, shield raised, facing down some villain or monster. It was a far cry from where he'd been just a month ago, a regular kid on summer break, counting down the days until school started and hoping his mom would let him try out for basketball or volleyball. Now, here he was, swept into a world of knights and dragons, of missions and magic. It was surreal, almost impossible to wrap his head around.

Yet, whenever he looked around at the others, at Nora, Percy, Gale, Ed, and Leif, he saw how naturally they spoke of this world, how easily it fit into their lives. It wasn't some fantastical dream to them; it was their reality. And slowly, almost imperceptibly, it was becoming his reality too. The image in his mind, of himself as a young knight in some grand fairytale, began to feel tangible. It was as possible as the idea of being a soccer player or a wrestler. It was a strange and wondrous shift, one that left him both exhilarated and uneasy, like standing on the edge of a great, uncharted sea.

"Attention, cadets," Arthur's voice rang out across the training field, cutting through the crisp morning air. The students stood in neat rows, their eyes fixed on him, their anticipation palpable. "I'm sure some of you have already heard from your peers about the importance of today."

A low murmur rippled through the group, a buzz of excitement and curiosity. Gav felt it too, that electric hum in the air, the kind that made his stomach tighten and his pulse quicken.

"Today, you will receive your assignments. As knights of Gamalaot, part of your chivalric duty is to assist and aid those in need. You've been cleared of all other responsibilities for the day, and you will commit all of your energy to your mission."

The cadets hung on his every word, their imaginations electric. Gav's mind raced with possibilities. *Would it be a bugbear, like Ed had mentioned at breakfast? Or a band of bandits terrorizing a nearby village? Maybe a lost unicorn in the woods, or some other fantastical creature he couldn't even begin to picture.* The anticipation was almost too much to bear.

But when the assignments were handed out, the reality was far from the grand adventures they had envisioned.

"Garden hobs," Nora groaned, her voice dripping with disappointment. She knelt in the dirt, wrestling a large turnip from the ground. The turnip had a little face, its tiny eyes squeezed shut as it wailed like an infant. "It's not fair!" she protested, her frustration boiling over. "The second years get to rout a powrie camp, and we're stuck here picking up garden hobs!"

With a huff, Nora tossed the crying turnip creature into the wheelbarrow, where it joined its wailing companions. Gav stood nearby, shovel in hand, watching the scene with both amusement and resignation. It wasn't the heroic mission he'd imagined, no bugbears, no bandits, no lost unicorns, but it was something. And as he glanced at Nora, her face flushed with indignation, he couldn't help but smile. Even in the mundane, there was a kind of magic, though he doubted Nora would see it that way.

Gav bent down and plucked another turnip from the ground. He sighed with relief when he saw it was just a regular turnip, its surface smooth and unmarked by any tiny, crying face. He tossed it into the basket beside the wheelbarrow, where it landed with a soft thud among the other normal vegetables.

"I suppose you've never seen a hob before," Percy said, appearing at his side. In his hands, he held a garden hob shaped like an ear of corn, its tiny face scrunched up as it wailed pitifully.

"What are they, exactly?" Gav asked, wincing at the sight of the crying creature.

"They're imps," Nora answered, grunting as she heaved another hob from the ground. This one resembled a potato, its lumpy form squirming in her grip.

"They're technically demons," Percy corrected, his tone matter-of-fact. "But calling them imps isn't wrong. They just come in different varieties. Some hobs can be really nasty."

Gav nodded along, trying to appear unfazed by the casual mention of demons. Inside, though, his mind reeled. Demons. Real, actual demons. It was one thing to hear about them in stories or lessons, but another entirely to see one wriggling and crying in Percy's hands. He glanced back at the wheelbarrow, where the hobs continued to sob, their tiny voices blending into a dissonant chorus. It was strange, unsettling, and yet somehow ordinary to the others. Gav took a deep breath, steadying himself. If this was part of being a knight of Gamalaot, he'd have to get used to it—demons, hobs, and all.

"Ugh, but garden hobs are just so lame!" Nora whined, her voice carrying across the garden as she yanked another squirming hob from the soil.

"You're doing a marvelous job, dearies!" called a warm, cheerful voice. A plump woman emerged from a small hovel near the crop beds, her hands clutching a basket filled with golden, fried breaded balls. "Would you dears care for some gastelets?" she offered, holding the basket out with a kind smile.

"No thanks," Gav and Percy said in unison, their voices overlapping. They glanced at each other, surprised by the accidental duet, before quickly looking away.

"Yes, please!" Nora exclaimed, already reaching into the basket and grabbing three of the fried treats. "I'm taking their shares, too. Is that alright, Mrs. Judith?"

"Oh, take as many as you want, sweetheart," Mrs. Judith said, her laughter light and musical. "I'm just glad you're getting rid of these disgusting pests before they ruin all the usable veggies left in my little garden. Oh, and be sure to check the squash. I think I heard some when I walked over here."

The three cadets smiled at her as she bustled away, her presence leaving a lingering warmth in the air. Though the work was tedious and far from glamorous, helping someone as kind as Mrs. Judith made it easier to swallow their complaints. This was part of their training, after all. To be a knight of Gamalaot wasn't just about wielding swords or facing down monsters; it was about character, about serving those in need, no matter how small or mundane the task might seem.

Gav sighed, glancing at the squash patch Mrs. Judith had mentioned. "Well," he said, hefting his shovel, "let's get to it. The sooner we finish, the sooner we can get out of here."

Nora groaned but didn't argue, popping another gastelet into her mouth as she trudged toward the squash. Percy followed, his expression as stoic as ever, though Gav thought he caught the faintest hint of a smile tugging at the corners of his mouth.

"So these little... things... these are demons?" Gav asked, holding up a wailing hob with a squash for a head. Its tiny face contorted in distress as it squirmed in his grip.

"Yes," Percy replied, his tone carrying that familiar air of confidence, as though he were lecturing from an invisible podium. "They usually possess household items—things like dusters or candles. They're not inherently malicious; they just want a job. A hob that possesses a duster will dust your house. A candle hob will light your home." He paused to pluck another hob from the ground, this one with the face of a beet, its expression equally pitiful. "But in this case," he continued, "they've taken hold of organic matter. And because they're rooted, the main concern is that they now have a means of rapid reproduction."

"I see," Gav said, though his voice was distant, his mind still grappling with the idea of a vegetable being a demon.

"It's a big deal," Percy insisted, his passion flaring. "If left unchecked, they could completely upend the food chain. Imagine a world where potatoes don't exist because they all became potato hobs."

"I wouldn't care for such a world," Nora interjected, her tone grave. "A world without potatoes…that would be miserable." She shuddered at the thought, as though the very idea were a personal affront.

"Can they possess people?" Gav asked, his brow furrowing as he considered the implications.

"Oh, absolutely," Percy said without hesitation. "Hobs can be a serious threat."

"Should we be wearing protective gear?"

"No," Percy said. "A hob only attaches to an object once. Unless forcibly removed, these little guys are stuck."

Nora stared into the screaming face of the garden hob she had just plucked from the ground. Its tiny eyes were wide with what could only be described as terror. For a moment, she hesitated, her expression softening. Then she sighed, her resolve hardening once more.

"Sorry, little guy. I like potatoes way too much."

"So what will they do with them?" Gav asked, rising to his feet and brushing the dirt from his hands. He glanced at the wheelbarrow, now nearly overflowing with wailing hobs.

"They'll probably be deseeded and rehomed," Percy explained, his tone softening as he looked down at the beet hob in his hands. "Garden hobs like these can make for good pets, under the right circumstances. They just need a purpose, something to do." He smiled faintly before gently placing the hob into the wheelbarrow with the others.

The cadets worked slowly, methodically, their movements steady despite the monotony of the task. The sun climbed high overhead, then began its slow descent, casting long shadows across Mrs. Judith's garden. By the time the last hob had been plucked from the soil, the sky was painted in hues of orange and pink, the horizon swallowing the sun whole.

An older cadet, the one who had technically been in command of the mission, appeared as they finished. He gave the rookies a curt nod before leading them back toward the castle, the wheelbarrow of hobs creaking as it rolled behind them. The air was cool now, the day's warmth fading with the light, and the cadets walked in silence, their exhaustion making it impossible to form words.

By the time they reached the castle, the smell of dinner wafted through the halls, pulling them toward the commissary like a siren's call. They were famished, their stomachs growling in unison as they shuffled inside.

Gav settled onto the bench, flanked by the usual crowd. Percy and Nora sat on one side, while Nora's brothers, Gale, Ed, and Leif took the other. But the seating arrangement didn't last long. Almost as soon as they sat down, Nora's brothers were pulled away by classmates from their respective years. Their seats were left empty for only a moment before two burly boys with identical green uniforms and nearly identical faces slid into the vacant spots.

"Hiya, Gav!" they said in unison, their voices booming with enthusiasm.

"Oh, hi," Gav replied, scrambling to recall their names. "Bor and Tor, right?"

"Spot on!" they chimed together, grinning broadly.

"Except I'm Bor," said the boy on the right, pointing to himself.

"And I'm Tor," said the boy on the left, mirroring his brother's gesture.

"Oh, right," Gav said, his tone reserved but polite. He gestured to the others at the table. "This is my friend Nora, and this is my…" He hesitated, glancing at Percy, unsure how to label their relationship.

"I'm Percy," he interjected smoothly, his tone calm and matter-of-fact, as if deliberately sparing them all from further awkwardness.

"Nice to meet yous both!" Bor and Tor said together, their voices overlapping in perfect harmony.

Nora leaned over and gave Gav a playful punch on the shoulder. "Look at you!" she teased, her eyes sparkling with mischief. "Making friends all on your own!"

"Oh, shut it," Gav shot back, though his irritation was softened by a laugh.

"Captain Wiglaf told us to sit with cadets from one of the other orders," Bor explained, his tone cheerful.

"And then we remembered yous from our tour," Tor added, nodding toward Percy and Gav. "Thought it'd be a good chance to get to know yous better."

The twins piled their plates high with mounds of hogget filets, their appetites seemingly insatiable. Gav, Percy, and Nora watched in mild disgust as Bor and Tor shoveled food into their mouths with an almost mechanical efficiency. The boys were massive, easily twice the size of the others at the table, and though their manners were rough around the edges, their easygoing nature made them pleasant company.

"So," Bor began, his words muffled by a mouthful of hogget, "how's yous liking the Crimson Manes?"

"Yeah," Tor chimed in, his own mouth full. A small piece of food fell from his lips and landed back on his plate, unnoticed. "You liking it good?"

"Uh, yeah," Gav replied, trying to keep his tone neutral despite the spectacle before him.

"You know what the worst is?" Bor asked, leaning in as if sharing a secret.

"Etiquette!" the twins exclaimed together. Flecks of meat and bread sprayed across the table as they spoke, a clear sign that the etiquette lessons hadn't quite taken root.

"Too bad yous aren't Claws," Bor continued. "Captain Wiglaf is awesome."

"What's 'The Bear' like?" Nora asked, her eyes lighting up with curiosity. "Is he as strong as they say?"

"Stronger," Tor said without hesitation.

"Oh yeah," Bor added, nodding vigorously. "First day of morning workout, he lifted up our beds and shook us awake."

"He lifted your beds?" Percy asked, his usually stoic expression cracking into one of surprise.

"And shook 'em like pepper shakers," Tor confirmed, his tone matter-of-fact.

"We wake up on our own now," Bor said with a grin.

"So cool," Nora murmured, her voice dreamy as she leaned back in her seat.

"I'm surprised you're not a Claw," Gav said to Nora, his tone thoughtful. "You seem to really look up to Wiglaf."

"It doesn't work that way," Percy interjected, his voice carrying that familiar air of superiority. "They place a knight exactly where they're meant to be at the induction. That's why they conduct the interview. Nora is a Crimson Mane because she's supposed to be."

"I'm happy as a Mane," she said, her tone firm but not defensive. "I just admire Wiglaf's raw strength. I mean, he became a famous knight despite having no noble lineage. He's a bona fide rags-to-riches story!"

Gav studied her for a moment, pieces of the puzzle falling into place. Nora had mentioned before that her family didn't have any social status, and now he understood why she looked up to Wiglaf so much. It wasn't just about his strength; it was about what he represented. A man who had risen from nothing, who had carved out his place in the world through sheer will and determination. And then there was her oldest brother, Gwynn, whom she idolized for similar reasons.

At this, Gav couldn't help but smile at her, a soft, genuine expression that caught her off guard. Nora tilted her head, her brow furrowing slightly in confusion, but she smiled back all the same.

The commissary buzzed around them, the clatter of plates and the hum of conversation filling the air, but for Gav, the noise seemed to fade into the background.

"I'm stuffed," Bor announced, leaning back in his seat and patting his now distended belly with a satisfied grin.

"You said it," Tor echoed, mirroring his brother's posture and gesture.

The saucer of hogget that had once been piled high was now empty, save for a few scraps of fat and charred edges. But just as the twins declared their victory over the meal, a matronly woman appeared, carrying a fresh tray piled high. The meat steamed as she set it down, its rich aroma wafting through the air. The boys exchanged a glance, their eyes narrowing as if they'd just been issued a challenge.

"You finding your second wind?" Tor asked, a mischievous glint in his eye.

"Pile it on," Bor replied, already leaning forward, his fork at the ready.

Gav, Nora, and Percy watched them in awe and mild horror as the twins dove back in. The trio lingered for a while longer, enjoying the lively company, but eventually, the call of the barracks grew too strong to ignore. With full stomachs and tired limbs, they bid their new friends goodnight and made their way to the Crimson Mane barracks.

"Good night!" Nora called out, her voice echoing down the staircase that led to the boys' sleeping quarters. She stood at the top, her silhouette framed by the soft glow of the hallway lanterns, her hand raised in a casual wave.

"Good night!" Gav and Percy shouted back in unison, their voices carrying up the stairs as they descended. The sound of their footsteps faded as they made their way to their bunks.

Gav removed his tunic and boots, placing them neatly at the foot of his cot. He stored his sword carefully underneath, part of the nightly routine he'd adopted since arriving at Gamalaot. As he reached to extinguish the oil lamp on his night table, Percy's voice cut through the quiet.

"Gav?"

"Yes?" Gav paused, his hand hovering over the lamp.

"I want to say something."

"Okay."

Percy hesitated, his eyes scanning the ceiling as if the words he sought were etched into the stone above.

"I want to apologize for how I've treated you."

"Oh," Gav replied, caught off guard. "That's okay."

"No," Percy said firmly. "It's not. I don't want to make excuses, but I have to tell you... my family... well, they..."

"I understand," Gav said. "It's the prophecy, right? Nora's brothers explained it to me."

Percy's jaw tightened, and for a moment, Gav thought he might say more. But when Percy spoke again, his voice quavered with an anger Gav had never heard from him before.

"We don't even know what the prophecy is. Has anyone told you that?" Percy's words were sharp, frustration seething beneath them. "No one's seen it. No one's heard it. They're just afraid of you because someone told them to be. How stupid is that? The details matter! They must!" He hesitated, then added quieter, "And they don't know you. You're a good person. It's obvious, and I've only just met you."

The room fell silent. Gav sat on the edge of his cot, hands resting on his knees, absorbing the words. He hadn't expected anyone to so openly challenge the prophecy aloud, let alone question the fear that clung to him like a second skin.

"Thank you," Gav said at last, voice low but sure. "That...means a lot."

Percy's face softened in a way Gav hadn't expected. For a breath, the silence between them felt heavier, fuller—like the air before a storm breaks. Then Percy huffed a half-laugh, shrugging.

"And you can introduce me as your friend from now on. That is, if you want to."

Gav extended a clenched fist. Percy blinked, then his eyes brightened with understanding. Their knuckles brushed, a silent pact wrapped in a shared smile.

"I'm exhausted," Gav murmured, reaching to extinguish the lamp between them. "It's been a long day."

"Yeah." Percy's voice was warm in the dark. "Sleep well, Gav."

The light went out, and darkness fell upon them both like a soft blanket, whisking them off to the best sleep either boy had since beginning their training.

Chapter 10

A Meeting with the King

Another week in Gamalaot passed for Gav and his friends. He had quickly risen to the top of his combat training class, mastering several advanced combinations with surprising ease. The Windsweep, the Knight-Kneeler, and the Helm-Splitter had become second nature to him, his movements fluid and precise. He felt a growing confidence in his abilities and genuinely looked forward to each session, eager to push himself further.

Elementary Magic, however, was a different story. The class had begun to ramp up in complexity, and Gav found himself struggling to keep up. Where combat training felt intuitive, magic required a level of focus and understanding that didn't come as naturally to him. He was determined though, and refused to let himself fall behind.

"Good morning, cadets!" Miss Morrigan's voice rang out, sing-songy and bright, though it carried that undertone, the one that made the hairs on the back of Gav's neck stand on end. Coming from her, even the most cheerful greetings felt disarming and eerie. "You may have noticed this table here. The one I've moved to the front of the room."

She gestured to a small, peculiar table standing at the front of the classroom, its surface etched with an intricate pentangle. The design seemed to shimmer faintly, as if breathing, alive.

"This is an old enchanting table I've personally modified. I'm still working on the name. The Archbishop suggested 'the sigil sorter,' but I think that sounds too hokey for her, and I don't care much for rhymes."

The cadets exchanged glances, some amused, others wary. Gav leaned forward in his seat, his curiosity piqued despite his lingering unease. Miss Morrigan's lessons always walked a fine line between fascinating and unsettling, and this one seemed no different.

"Today," she said, her voice dropping to a conspiratorial whisper, "we'll be using this table to explore the fundamentals of sigil identification. Pay close attention, cadets. This is where the real fun begins."

Gav felt a mix of excitement and apprehension as he watched Miss Morrigan begin her demonstration. The table radiated with energy, the pentangle glowing faintly as she traced her fingers along its surface.

The cadets in the room eyed the strange device with cautious curiosity. Miss Morrigan's presence always seemed to cast a peculiar shadow over the classroom, and her Azure Stripe students, while impeccably well-mannered, carried themselves with the kind of quiet deference that suggested more than just respect. It was as if they were treading carefully around a force they didn't fully understand, or perhaps didn't dare to.

"The purpose of this device is to identify your magical affinities. Can someone here explain to us what magical affinity is exactly?"

The room fell silent. Percy's hand shot up immediately, but Miss Morrigan's gaze swept past him. "Anyone besides young Perceval," she said, her tone losing a fraction of its calm.

Gav glanced around the room, his eyes meeting those of his fellow cadets. They exchanged silent looks, a wordless debate about who would be brave enough to speak up. The tension in the air was palpable, broken only by the faint creak of chairs and the rustle of parchment. Finally, a hand rose, belonging to a thin boy with round spectacles, the boy who always seemed to hover around Lucan.

"Yes, Hubert."

"I believe magical affinity refers to a person's magical inclination," Hubert said, his voice steady but soft.

"Oh, splendid!" Miss Morrigan exclaimed, clasping her hands together with delight. "You make your captain proud! That is correct. Every person has a certain disposition that makes them more adept at performing particular types of magic. For instance, hex magic comes easier for me because I have a 'derk' sigil. But I can still perform any magic I care to learn outside of hexes! It just takes more energy."

The classroom erupted into the sound of scratching quills as the cadets furiously scribbled down her words. Gav's own quill moved quickly across the parchment paper, though his mind was racing ahead. *Magical affinities, sigils, the idea that some types of magic might come more naturally to him than others*—it was a lot to take in. He glanced at Percy, who was already nodding along as if this were all second nature to him, and then at Nora, who was doodling little stars in the margins of her notes.

"I want you to think of magical energy the way you would physical energy. Let's call it stamina. Picture yourself running a mile, but not just any mile—one where you're fully geared up in heavy armor. That's a lot harder than running the same distance with nothing but your boots, right? Well, magic that aligns with your affinity is like that lighter load. It takes less energy for you to wield, as though you've stripped off all that heavy gear when casting those spells. In essence, your sigil basically tells you what kind of magic will be easiest to master."

The scratching of quills grew louder and more frantic as the cadets tried to keep up with Miss Morrigan's lecture. Gav's own hand moved quickly, his notes a messy scrawl as he struggled to capture every word. The analogy of magical energy being like physical stamina made sense to him, though the idea of having a specific affinity still felt abstract. He was so focused on writing that he didn't notice the sudden silence that fell over the room until the sound of quills slamming onto desks startled him. He looked up to find Miss Morrigan staring directly at him, her sharp eyes waiting expectantly.

"Now...Who would like to volunteer to go first? Everyone must go at some point."

Before Gav could even consider raising his hand, Lucan stood from his seat with an air of confidence that bordered on arrogance. He strode to the front of the room, his posture straight and his expression smug, as if he'd been waiting for this moment all along.

"Excellent," Miss Morrigan said, her thin smile returning. "Lucan, place your hand in the center of the table where all the lines of the pentangle intersect."

Lucan followed Miss Morrigan's instructions, placing his hand firmly within the center of the pentangle. Almost immediately, his body stiffened as the table latched onto him with an invisible force. The cadets watched, wide-eyed, as Lucan tried to shift his hand, but it remained firmly stuck, as if fused to the surface. A faint hum filled the room, growing louder as the pentangle began to glow with an eerie light.

"No fussing," Miss Morrigan said with a light laugh, though her tone carried a warning. "You'll only make her angry."

Gav saw Lucan's eyes widen slightly, a flicker of fear breaking through his usual mask of confidence. The sight was enough to make Gav crack a smile, and he wasn't alone. The rest of the class stifled giggles as Lucan's composure wavered, his bravado slipping for the first time.

"What do you mean, angry?" Lucan asked, his voice tight as he tried to maintain his cool.

Miss Morrigan sighed, her expression tinged with mild exasperation. "I told you all at the beginning of class that I modified her," she said, as if this were the most obvious thing in the world. "You don't need to be frightened. She really takes her job seriously. I think she's going to make a fine arcane table." She reached out and set her hand gently on the table's edge, stroking it almost affectionately, as if it were a living animal.

The room continued to buzz with snickering, the cadets exchanging uneasy glances as they giddily watched on. Gav's smile widened as he witnessed Lucan struggle against the table's grip.

"Professor Morrigan," Percy said, raising his hand with his usual air of calm curiosity. "Is that table… possessed?"

"Yes!" Miss Morrigan replied, her voice brimming with pride. "King Uther was kind enough to let me keep some of the hobs you cadets plucked in town! I'll tell you, she didn't like giving up her turnip, but she took to the table quite nicely in the end!"

The class's laughter grew louder, as did Lucan's expression, shifting from fear to mild horror. He began subtly tugging at his hand, trying to free it from the table's grip, which only fueled the laughter in the room.

"Remarkable," Percy said automatically, his tone thoughtful.

"Settle down," Miss Morrigan said, her voice sharp but not unkind. "Lucan, be still."

Lucan froze, his body stiffening as he obeyed, though the concern didn't leave his face. The table shuddered slightly, and a stream of magical light shot forth, bending and twisting itself into a shape that hovered above the pentangle.

"Ah," Miss Morrigan said, her eyes narrowing as she studied the glowing symbol. "'Bhel'—the flame sigil."

The table shook again, more violently this time, and Miss Morrigan's eyebrows lifted in surprise. Another stream of light burst forth, replacing the first and forming a new, intricate shape.

"'Vorst,'" she said, her voice tinged with a genuine admiration. "The frost sigil. Exceptional! Two affinities! You'll make a fine knight, Lucan."

The table released Lucan's hand, and he stepped back, his earlier fear replaced by a look of smug satisfaction. He stood tall, his chest puffing out as he basked in the class's awe. Gav could feel the room's admiration for Lucan, but he could also sense the swelling of Lucan's ego, like a balloon about to burst.

"Two affinities," Nora whispered, her voice conveying hints of both envy and disbelief. "That's… rare, isn't it?"

"Incredibly," Percy murmured, his tone neutral, though his eyes lingered on Lucan with a hint of skepticism.

Miss Morrigan clapped her hands together, drawing the class's attention back to her. "Well done, Lucan. Now, who's next?"

"Can I go next?" Nora said, her hand shooting up with eager enthusiasm.

"Of course, dear. Step forward."

Nora bounded up to the table, her energy infectious as she placed her hand on the pentangle with swift deftness. Almost immediately, she felt the table's pull, tugging her down slightly as it began to rumble and shake. A stream of magical light burst forth, twisting and bending into a familiar shape.

"'Bhel' again," Miss Morrigan said, her tone approving. "Another flame sigil."

Nora grinned, pulling her hand away and returning to her seat with a spring in her step. "Flame sigil," she said under her breath, as if testing how it sounded. "Wicked."

One by one, the cadets took their turns at the table, each one stepping forward with both curiosity and apprehension. Gav paid particular attention to those he knew better, watching as their sigils were revealed.

Hubert went up next, placing his hand on the table, and after a moment, the light formed into a new shape.

"'Derk,'" Miss Morrigan announced. "A fellow black mage! How delightful."

Hubert adjusted his glasses, a small, proud smile tugging at his lips as he returned to his seat.

Lilah followed, her steps graceful and measured. The table's light shifted again, forming a different symbol.

"'Leht,'" Miss Morrigan said. "The light sigil. A fine affinity for a healer."

Lilah nodded, her expression serene as she stepped back, her sigil glowing faintly in her mind.

Finally, it was Percy's turn. He approached the table with his usual calm demeanor, his hand steady as he placed it on the pentangle. The table shuddered, the light forming into a shape that seemed heavier, more solid than the others.

"'Rocc,'" Miss Morrigan said. "The earth sigil. Quite extraordinary, young Perceval."

Percy's lips curved into a small, satisfied smile as he removed his hand. "Thank you, Professor."

Gav watched as Percy returned to his seat, his nerves tightening with each passing moment. He was last, and the weight of everyone's eyes on him only made it worse. *What if he didn't have any magical ability whatsoever? What if he was the only one in the class without a sigil? Or worst of all, what if he had a malefic sigil—something dark and dangerous that would confirm him as a threat?*

Lucan leaned forward in his seat, his gaze shrewd and calculating, as if he were waiting for Gav to fail. The rest of the class seemed just as curious, their whispers filling the room with a low hum of anticipation. They all wanted to know, perhaps even more desperately than Gav himself.

"Come now," Miss Morrigan said, her voice breaking the tension. "No need to be frightened."

Gav took a deep breath and stepped forward, his legs feeling like they might give out at any moment. He placed his hand on the table, and the instant his palm touched the cool surface, he felt a powerful pull, as if the table were trying to draw something out of him. It tingled and prickled his skin before suctioning him in. He staggered slightly, catching himself before he could fall.

The room fell silent as the table began to hum, the lines of the pentangle glowing with a soft, swirling light. Gav's heart pounded as he watched the light twist and form into a shape—a symbol that pulsed with a gentle, airy glow.

"'Aer,'" Miss Morrigan announced, her tone matter-of-fact. "A wind sigil—that would make you a green mage. Though I suppose you're more interested in swordsmanship, so a green knight, then!"

Gav let out a breath he didn't realize he'd been holding, a hot wash of relief crashing over him. *A wind sigil. Not malefic, not nothing—just wind. He could work with that.* He pulled his hand away from the table and returned to his seat, his legs still a little shaky but his mind clearer now.

As he sat down, he caught Percy's eye. He offered him an approving nod. Nora, on the other hand, was grinning from ear to ear, excited to put their sigils to the test.

"Now that we know our natural affinities," Miss Morrigan said, clapping her hands to regain the class's attention, "your homework is to master the most basic spell of your given affinity. Check the index of your book—*Pantagruel's Practical Spellcraft*. You will have a demonstration exam next Friday. Class dismissed!"

The room erupted into chatter as the cadets gathered their things. Gav flipped open his spellbook, his fingers tracing the index as he searched for the section on wind magic. *A basic spell. He could do that. Right?* Only time would tell.

So each morning, Nora, Gav, and Percy made their way to the castle's grand archive, a place of towering shelves and dusty tomes, where the air smelled of parchment and the faint, lingering scent of magic. There they pored over their notes and the well-worn pages of *Pantagruel's Practical Spellcraft*, their brows furrowed in concentration.

"Which spell is the easiest?" Gav asked one afternoon, leaning in close to Nora and her open textbook. His eyes scanned the page, but the words seemed to swim before him, elusive and foreign. *Abjuration. Conjuration. Divination. Evocation. Transmutation.* They were heavy words, weighted with meaning he couldn't quite grasp. It seemed like every spell he read over was too hard.

Nora, too, seemed lost, her face a mirror of his own confusion.

"Here," Percy said, reaching over and flipping through Gav's book with ease. His fingers moved quickly, sure and steady. "You'll want this page. Read the section on 'Gust.' That's the one you should practice."

"Thanks," Gav said.

Nora, silent and thoughtful, handed her own book to Percy without a word. He took it, his eyes scanning the pages before he folded down a corner and handed it back.

"There," he said. "You'll want to look at 'fireball.' That's your spell."

"Thanks, Percy," she said, her tone carrying a note of playful exaggeration.

"What about you?" Gav asked, glancing over at Percy. "Which one are you workin' on?"

"Entangle," Percy replied, his eyes fixed on the page. " *'Create a dense network of vines, capable of slowing down and immobilizing targets.'* Sounds straightforward enough."

"Ooh!" Nora exclaimed. "Here's mine: *'Throw a mote of fire at target.'* Now that sounds cool!"

Gav turned back to his own book, his finger tracing the lines of text as he read aloud. " *'Summon a strong wind that clears clouds and mist, pushes target back, forcing them off balance, and/or increase the caster's movement speed.'* Percy, this doesn't sound all that easy."

"It is," Percy said absently, keeping his gaze fixed upon the book.

The three of them sat there in the quiet of the archive, studying as they bent their heads over their books.

Day after day, they practiced, their lives falling into a rhythm as steady as the turning of the earth. Between classes and meals, even in the quiet hours of the night, they huddled together beneath the faint glow of the flickering torchlight, their heads bent over their books, studying the proper stances and incantations. The days blurred together, and before they knew it, a week had slipped by, the day of the exam upon them.

On the morning of the test, the air was thick with anticipation. But before they could prove themselves to Miss Morrigan, Gav and Nora found themselves in Combat Training, sparring with wooden swords under the watchful eye of Arthur, who paced the field like a shadow, his gaze discerning. The clack of wood against wood echoed across the training grounds as partners practiced their combinations.

"Ouch," Nora muttered, tumbling onto her backside as Gav's training sword found its mark. She winced, rubbing her shoulder. "You got me again."

"You all right?" Gav asked, extending a hand to pull her to her feet.

"Yeah, I'm good," she said, brushing herself off and squaring her shoulders. "Let's go again."

But before they could resume, a uniformed knight approached Arthur at a brisk pace, his expression grave. He stopped a few paces away, his eyes sweeping over the cadets before he leaned in and spoke in low, urgent tones.

"Sir, you're needed. Now."

Arthur's gaze flicked to the cadets, still engrossed in their practice, and then back to the knight. A subtle nod passed between them. Without a word, Arthur turned and followed the knight, his departure so quiet and swift that few even noticed he was gone.

But Lucan noticed. And as soon as Arthur was out of sight, he strode up to Gav with a face like a storm cloud, his presence commanding the attention of everyone on the field. The clatter of wooden swords fell silent as the cadets turned to watch, their breaths held, their eyes wide with curiosity and unease.

"Ragnell," Lucan said, his voice bitter and cutting as he raised his wooden sword high above his head. The blade caught the pale light filtering through the overcast sky, and his eyes burned with a fierce intensity. "We're partners now."

Gav glanced at Nora, who stood at the edge of the field, her arms crossed and her expression one of mild indifference. Around them, a circle of cadets had begun to form, their faces alight with curiosity and excitement.

"Fine," Gav said, his voice steady despite the unease coiling in his gut. He gripped the hilt of his training sword tighter, the rough wood biting into his palm.

The two boys marched to opposite ends of the field, their boots crunching against the dirt as the crowd of classmates closed in around them, chanting and cheering. The sound rose and fell like the tide, a rhythmic pulse that reverberated in Gav's chest.

"Go!" Lucan shouted.

They lunged at each other, their wooden swords swinging in wide, aggressive arcs. The clash of wood against wood rang out, loud and percussive, as they traded blows. Their movements were fluid, almost like a dance, each step and strike calculated and precise. But Gav was quicker, his reflexes sharper. He ducked low, his body coiled like a spring, and landed a solid blow to Lucan's side.

"Again!" Lucan barked, his voice trembling with barely contained fury. He didn't wait for a response, already striding back to his starting position.

Gav hesitated, glancing at the faces around him, but the crowd was electric, their eyes gleaming with excitement. Reluctantly, he followed suit, his feet dragging slightly as he returned to his mark.

The second round began, and this time Lucan's swings were harder, more forceful, but less controlled. His strikes came wild and unrelenting, each one carrying the weight of his frustration. Gav dodged and parried, his movements deliberate and measured. Then, in a flash, he slid back, his sword arcing downward in a cross-chop that struck Lucan squarely on the shoulder.

"Again!" Lucan roared, his face flushed with anger. He didn't even pause to acknowledge the hit, his eyes blazing as he turned back to his starting position.

"Lucan," Gav said, his voice tinged with exhaustion and a hint of pleading. "Let's just—"

"Again!" Lucan snapped, cutting him off. His fists were clenched, his chest heaving as he glared at Gav across the field.

Gav sighed, his shoulders slumping slightly, but he nodded. Once more, they took their positions. The third round began, and the sound of their swords colliding filled the air, a relentless staccato that seemed to echo the tension between them. The cadets on the perimeter whispered and pointed, their voices a low hum beneath the clash of wood.

Lucan's strikes grew more erratic, his frustration boiling over with every swing. Gav, though weary, held his ground, his movements still precise, still controlled. But as the fight dragged on, it was clear that this was no longer just a sparring match.

Just as Gav raised his wooden sword, poised to deliver what would have been the final strike, a sudden, searing plume of flames erupted from Lucan's body. The fire roared to life, licking hungrily at the air, its heat washing over Gav in a suffocating wave.

"Whoa!" Gav shouted, stumbling backward, his eyes wide with shock. "What the heck?!"

"What's the matter, Ragnell?" Lucan sneered, his voice dripping with malice as he laughed. "Can't get close?"

Gav's feet moved instinctively, carrying him backward as he tried to put distance between himself and the inferno surrounding Lucan. But after only a few steps, his boot slipped on something slick, and he crashed to the ground. He looked down, his breath rough and ragged. The grass beneath him had frozen solid, patches of ice glinting in the pale light, their surfaces jagged and treacherous.

He scrambled to his feet, his eyes darting back to Lucan, who stood at the center of the chaos, flames and frost swirling around him in a bizarre, terrifying dance. The air crackled with energy, the heat of the fire and the bite of the cold warring against each other.

"Come on, Gav!" Lucan bellowed. His eyes burned with a manic intensity as he spread his arms wide, daring Gav to strike. "Hit me! Hit me!"

"You're insane," Gav muttered, his voice low but steady as he rose to his feet. His heart pounded in his chest, but he forced himself to stand tall, his grip tightening on the hilt of his wooden sword.

"You a coward? Is that it?" Lucan taunted, his voice rising to a fever pitch. "I should finish you right here! Everyone would be happy to see you gone!"

The words struck Gav painfully, but he didn't flinch. Instead, he felt something inside him harden, a resolve that burned brighter than the flames surrounding Lucan. His fingers clenched around the wooden sword with a grip so tight, he thought he heard the faintest crack of the wood straining under the pressure.

"Alright, Lucan," Gav said, his voice calm but firm, a small, resolute smile tugging at the corners of his lips. "You asked for it."

Gav whispered an incantation under his breath, like a man speaking to the earth itself. Beneath his feet, a faint green pentangle shimmered into existence, its edges glowing with an otherworldly light. A fierce wind began to rise, swirling around him, gathering strength until it howled like a wild thing unleashed. The force of it was so great that nearby cadets were swept off their feet, tumbling backward like fallen leaves.

Lucan's laughter cut through the chaos, shrieking and unhinged, a sound that seemed to feed the flames that danced around him. The fire grew brighter, hotter, hungrier, as though it fed on his madness. It wrapped him in a cloak of burning fury, a living inferno that dared anyone to come close.

But Gav did not hesitate. He planted his foot firmly, then launched himself forward, faster than any man had a right to move. His sword was poised, steady in his grip, a promise of what was to come. He was a streak of motion, a force of will, hurtling toward the blazing figure in front of him. The flames roared, an inferno waiting to consume him, but Gav did not falter. He would not falter. This was his moment, his chance to prove—not just to Lucan, but to himself—that he belonged here. That he was meant to be a knight. That he had earned his place.

The cadets on the field shielded their eyes, squinting against the blinding wind and the searing light of the flames. They strained to see, to witness the clash, but fear held them back. Fear of what might come after. They waited for the explosion, the deafening crash, the moment when the two forces would collide and one would emerge victorious. But that moment never came. The sound of impact never rang out. Instead, the boys lay still, facedown on the ground, pinned by some unseen force, a spell as unyielding as the earth beneath them. The field fell silent, save for the faint crackle of dying flames and the low, mournful sigh of the wind.

"Ragnell! Lambelle!" Arthur's voice thundered across the field, severe and deadly as the blade of his sword. His weapon, his golden sword, stood driven into the earth, its hilt trembling faintly, glowing with the same eerie light that held Gav and Lucan pinned to the ground. "Class is dismissed," he barked, his tone carrying a weight that could have sent a grizzly bear slinking into the shadows.

The cadets needed no further urging. They scattered like roaches, their footsteps quick and nervous, leaving Gav and Lucan alone on the field with Arthur. The man's presence was a tempest, his anger palpable, a force that seemed to bend the very air around him. He strode forward, his boots crunching against the earth, and seized each boy by the arm, hauling them to their feet with a strength that brooked no resistance. The light that had bound them flickered and dissolved, fading into the atmosphere like smoke on the wind.

"I'm sorry," Gav muttered, his voice small, almost swallowed by the heavy silence that followed. Arthur did not respond. His face was a mask, unreadable, his jaw set like stone. He offered no acknowledgment, no sign that he had even heard.

Lucan, watching carefully, held his tongue, his own defiance tempered by the way Arthur had dismissed Gav's apology.

Without a word, Arthur turned and began to march toward the castle, his grip firm on the boys' arms as he led them across the field. They moved in silence, the only sound the rhythmic crunch of boots on gravel and the distant echo of their footsteps as they entered the castle's towering gates. Up they went, flight after flight of stairs, the air growing cooler, the walls closing in around them as they ventured deeper into the heart of the palatial fortress.

Finally, they arrived at the king's personal chambers. Arthur released his grip, his hands falling to his sides after rapping sharply on the heavy wooden door. The sound echoed down the hall, a sharp, furious knock that demanded attention.

"Your majesty," Arthur said, his voice low but carrying, a tone that blended respect with an undercurrent of urgency.

"Enter!" came the reply, a booming, jovial voice that filled the space beyond the door. It was a voice that carried the weight of authority, yet rang with a warmth that felt almost out of place in the cold, stone corridors of the castle.

Gav's heart pounded in his chest, a rapid, unsteady rhythm that sounded in his ears. He hadn't seen much of the king since the induction ceremony. In fact, he hadn't ever really interacted with him at all. And now, standing before him, he felt the weight of his own apprehension pressing down like a stone. He had never been in trouble like this before—never even been sent to the principal's office, let alone summoned to face the king of Gamalaot. His mind raced with thoughts of what might come next, the consequences looming large in his imagination.

But when the door swung open, the scene before him was nothing like what he had expected. King Uther was not standing sternly by the window, gazing out over his kingdom with the gravity of a ruler. No, the old king was seated comfortably, his feet propped up on the desk, a delicate teacup cradled in his hands. His laughter filled the room, warm and rich, as he shared a moment with an even older man. It was the Archbishop, Gav realized, recognizing the old man's figure too from the induction ceremony. The two men seemed at ease, their camaraderie a stark contrast to the tension Gav felt coiled in his chest.

"Arthur," the king said, his grin widening as he turned to address the knight. "What seems to be the trouble?"

"My lord," he began, bowing slightly, "these two cadets have violated academy rules and displayed a complete disregard for the chivalric code that binds the knights of Gamalaot. I found them using magical attacks during an unsupervised sparring match. Had I not intervened, I fear the consequences could have been dire. Mortal wounds, perhaps even worse."

The king's expression shifted, his smile fading into a more thoughtful look. He exchanged a glance with the Archbishop, who sipped his tea with an air of quiet amusement. "I see," the king said after a moment. "Arthur, please go find Morrigan and bring her to my office."

"Yes, milord," Arthur replied, bowing once more before turning on his heel and striding out of the room, his footsteps echoing down the hall.

Once the door had closed behind him, the king leaned back in his chair, his demeanor softening. "You'll have to forgive my son," he said, his tone almost apologetic. "He takes his role very seriously—as he should. But I think he sometimes forgets that he was once a cadet himself."

"A mischievous one at that," the Archbishop added, his voice tinged with laughter as he raised his teacup to his lips. The old man's eyes sparkled with amusement, as though recalling some long-forgotten memory.

The king turned his gaze to Gav, his eyes lingering on the emerald shine that swirled within the boy's irises. There was a curiosity there, a quiet intensity that made Gav feel both seen and exposed. Then the king's attention shifted to Lucan, his expression thoughtful as he assessed both boys.

"I was excited to learn that both of you would be attending the academy this year," the king said at last, his voice warm and encouraging. "I think you each have the makings of fine knights."

Just then, a knock sounded at the door.

"Enter," said the king, his voice carrying the same easy authority as before.

The door swung open, and Arthur stepped inside, followed closely by Morrigan. Her presence was like a sudden shift in the air, her sharp eyes immediately scanning the room until they landed on Gav.

"Gav!" she cried, her voice offering both relief and concern. "Are you alright?"

"Yeah," Gav replied, his voice steady despite the knot of anxiety in his chest. "I'm fine."

Morrigan's lips curved into her usual enigmatic smile, but it was fleeting. When her gaze shifted to Lucan, her entire demeanor changed. Her expression hardened, her eyes narrowing with a sharpness that could cut steel.

"I expect better of you," she said, her voice low and cold, each word dripping with a quiet fury that sent a shiver down Gav's spine. It was a tone that inspired true terror.

Arthur, still kneeling, bowed his head respectfully. "Your majesty," he began, his voice tight with regret, "please forgive the impudence of my cadet."

"And mine as well," Morrigan added, her tone softer now as she too took a knee, her head bowed in deference to the king.

"Rise," the king said, his voice calm but firm. He waited until both Arthur and Morrigan had stood before turning his attention back to Gav and Lucan. His expression was serious now, the warmth in his eyes tempered by a gravity that made the room feel heavier.

"Lucan Lucien Lambelle and Gavain Laurent Ragnell," the king began, his voice carrying the weight of his station, "you must understand the severity of your actions. The use of deadly force is strictly prohibited when training or sparring. And the use of lethal magic must always be supervised so long as you are still classified as trainees." He paused, letting his words sink in, his gaze shifting between the two boys. "With that being said, I do not wish to exact too extreme a punishment for a first-time offense."

The king glanced over his shoulder, locking eyes with the Archbishop, who had been quietly observing the proceedings. The older man nodded, understanding the unspoken cue, and rose to his feet with a grace that belied his age. He stepped forward, his robes whispering against the stone floor, until he stood before the boys.

"Please present your hands," the king said.

Gav hesitated for a moment, his heart pounding, before extending his hands, palms up. Lucan followed suit, though his expression remained guarded, his jaw clenched tight.

The Archbishop's hands were cool and dry as he took Gav's hand first, cradling it gently within his own. For a moment, there was only silence, a stillness that seemed to stretch endlessly. Then, with a suddenness that made Gav flinch, a flash of light erupted from the Archbishop's fingers, stark and bright, stinging his palm like the bite of a spider. Gav hissed through his teeth, pulling his hand back instinctively, clutching it to his chest as he stared down at the mark now etched into his skin.

There, glowing faintly on his palm, was the image of a clock. Its hands moved slowly, almost imperceptibly, ticking away the seconds with a quiet, relentless precision. Gav blinked at it, his breath stilled, before glancing over at Lucan. The other boy's hand bore the same mark, but his reaction was far more visceral. Lucan's face had gone pale, his lips pressed into a thin line, his eyes wide with something that looked like panic. He held his hand close to his chest, his fingers trembling ever so slightly, as though the weight of the spell was too much to bear.

"You will be placed under probation for seventy-two hours," the Archbishop said, his voice calm and measured, "during which time you will be unable to perform any magic."

Gav nodded, accepting the punishment with a quiet resignation. It was fair, he thought, and temporary. He could endure it. But when he looked at Lucan again, he saw something that gave him pause. The other boy's usual composure was cracking, his mask slipping to reveal a raw, unguarded fear. It was as if the idea of being stripped of his magic—even for a short time—was unthinkable, unbearable. Gav could see it in the way Lucan's jaw tightened, the way his eyes darted to the mark on his palm and then away, as though he couldn't stand to look at it for too long.

For a moment, Gav almost felt sorry for him. Almost. But then he remembered the flames, the laughter, the way Lucan had reveled in the chaos. Whatever fear Lucan felt now, Gav couldn't bring himself to pity him entirely. Still, there was something unsettling about seeing him like this—vulnerable, shaken, as though the ground had been pulled out from under him.

The king's voice broke the silence, pulling Gav's attention back to the present. "Use this time to reflect," he said, his tone firm but not unkind. "Consider the weight of your actions and the responsibilities that come with the power you wield. At the end of your probation, you will present a letter of apology to your captain. This is not just a punishment, it is an opportunity to learn."

Gav nodded again, his gaze dropping to the floor. He could feel the weight of the king's words, the truth in them settling heavily on his shoulders. But when he glanced at Lucan one last time, he saw that the other boy wasn't listening. His eyes were fixed on the mark on his palm, his expression unreadable, his mind clearly elsewhere. Whatever lesson the king hoped to impart, Gav wasn't sure Lucan was ready to hear it.

"In addition," said the king, his gaze sweeping over Gav and Lucan, "you both will be responsible for cleaning the stables this weekend, polishing all the gear in the armory, and washing the dishes in the commissary kitchen."

The boys stood stiffly, their heads bowed, the weight of the king's words settling over them. They could feel the simmering anger radiating from Arthur and Morrigan behind them, a reminder that their punishment could have been far worse. Yet neither boy dared to speak, to protest, or even to breathe too loudly. They both knew better than to test the patience of those around them.

The king waited a moment, his eyes narrowing slightly as he studied the boys. When no one spoke, he turned his attention to Arthur, his expression expectant. "Anything else?" he asked, his voice calm but edged with authority.

"Nothing further, milord," Arthur said, his tone clipped.

The king sighed, a faint flicker of disappointment crossing his features as he glanced back at the Archbishop. "Well," he said, his voice lighter now, though still tinged with regret, "I suppose tea time is over, and we should all get back to work." He waved a hand dismissively, his gaze returning to Gav and Lucan. "Dismissed."

Arthur and Morrigan bowed one final time to the king, their movements precise and respectful, before turning to guide Gav and Lucan out of the chamber. The walk through the castle was silent, the only sounds the soft scuff of boots on stone and the distant murmur of voices echoing through the halls.

When they finally stepped out onto the training field, the sunlight felt almost too bright, too sharp, after the dim interior of the castle. Morrigan paused, her sharp eyes flicking to Gav and Lucan. "I'll see you in class," she said, her voice cool and clipped. "Best not be late." Without another word, she turned and strode away, her cloak billowing slightly in the breeze.

The boys stood there for a moment, the space between them charged with tension. Lucan broke the silence first, letting out a derisive scoff before turning on his heel and storming off. Gav watched him go, his own thoughts churning, before his gaze dropped to the mark on his palm. The glowing clockface stared back at him, its hands creeping forward with agonizing slowness. He flexed his fingers, as if testing whether the mark might fade or shift, but it remained stubbornly in place.

Gav's thoughts churned, anxiety pressing down on him with a quiet force. The exam was only an hour away, and he could not shake the dread that coiled in his gut. Without magic, how could he hope to pass? The question clawed at him, a burr lodged deep in his mind. And then it came to him. It was part of the punishment, wasn't it? Not just the calluses on his hands from the labor, not just the mark burned into his skin, but the gnawing uncertainty, the bitter taste of helplessness. The king's words echoed in his ears, sharp and deliberate: *This is your chance to learn.* Gav drew in a long, steadying breath, his shoulders squaring as though bracing against a heavy wind. He would endure. He had no choice but to endure. And perhaps, if the fates were kind, he might emerge from this trial tempered, stronger than before. But for now, there was only the waiting, the slow, ticking of time marked by the clock etched into his hand.

Chapter 11
Familiar Day

The weekend descended upon Gav, and the aftermath of his clash with Lucan left him shackled to the dim, musty storage room. The air was thick with the scent of old metal and damp stone, and the two of them worked in a silence so heavy it seemed to press against the walls. Gav's hands moved methodically over the suits of armor, polishing the tarnished steel until it gleamed faintly in the weak light. Across the room, Lucan hunched over a pile of axes, the rhythmic scrape of his sharpening stone the only sound between them.

"At least we finished the stables," Gav said, his voice trying to cut through the quiet. It was the first time either of them had spoken in over an hour, and the words felt clumsy, out of place. Lucan didn't answer, not really. Just a grunt, low and dismissive, as he kept his eyes fixed on his work. Another hour slipped by, marked only by the steady progress of their tasks. Gav's pile dwindled faster, and soon he stood, brushing the dust from his hands, his side of the room cleared.

He glanced at Lucan, who still had a small mountain of blades and armor before him. "Would you like some help?"

"No."

Gav shrugged, undeterred. "I'm all done. I'll just grab some from your pile. We'll get out of here faster."

"Whatever," Lucan muttered, his voice dripping with disdain.

Gav's patience, thin as it was, began to fray. He reached for a couple of swords and a breastplate, his movements quick and forceful. "You can hate me all you want," he said, his voice steady but edged with frustration. "But it's your fault we're here in the first place."

Lucan's head snapped up, his composure cracking like brittle ice. "You shouldn't be here!" he burst out, his voice louder than he likely intended, raw and unguarded.

"Well, I am," Gav shot back, his tone flippant. He had tried to make the best of their punishment, to shoulder it with some semblance of grace, but Lucan's simmering resentment had worn him thin. Today, of all days, he found he had no patience left for it. He carried the swords and breastplate back to his side of the room, the silence between them now charged, electric.

"This was supposed to be my time!" Lucan's voice cracked like a whip as he surged to his feet, his face flushed with both anger and desperation. "I was going to be the youngest knight in Gamalaot court history! Everyone should be looking at me, but instead, all anyone can talk about is you. You and your damn curse. You're nothing special without it. So you can swing a sword around. Big deal. You're nothing! Nothing!"

He began pacing, his boots striking the stone floor with sharp, uneven steps. His words spilled out in a torrent, half directed at Gav, half at the walls, as though he were arguing with some invisible force that had wronged him. "It wasn't supposed to be like this," he muttered, his voice trembling. "It wasn't supposed to be like this…"

Gav watched him, his own frustration tempered by something softer, something that felt uncomfortably like pity. "Lucan," he said, his tone earnest, "you're still the best knight in our class. And you can still be the youngest knight to…"

"It wasn't supposed to be like this!" Lucan interrupted, his voice breaking as he dropped back onto the stool, his hands gripping the edge of the workbench. He bent over the pile of equipment, his movements slow and defeated, his words now a low, disjointed stream of self-reproach and bitterness.

Gav opened his mouth to speak, but no words came. He felt a strange ache in his chest, not for Lucan himself—the boy had been nothing but cruel to him—but for the weight he carried, the invisible burden of expectations that seemed to press him into the ground. It was a pressure Gav could sense, even if he didn't fully understand it.

They worked in silence after that, the only sounds the scrape of metal and the occasional clatter of tools. The hours dragged on, the dark light in the storage room fading as evening approached. By the time they finished, the sun had dipped below the horizon, and the faint smell of dinner wafted through the halls.

When they reached the commissary, they parted ways without a word. Lucan stalked off, his shoulders hunched, while Gav lingered for a moment, watching him go. The air between them was heavy with unspoken things, but Gav knew better than to try to bridge the gap. Some wounds, he thought, were too deep to mend with words.

"Gav!" Nora's voice rang out, crisp and bright, cutting through the low hum of the commissary. She waved him over to their table, her smile wide and welcoming. And it wasn't just her. Percy, Bor, Tor, Gale, Ed, and Leif were all there, sitting tall, their faces lit with eager grins as they watched him approach.

He hurried over, his steps quickening, the weight of the weekend's punishment lifting immediately just at the sight of them.

"We've missed you!" Nora exclaimed, her voice carrying across the table.

"Yeah, yeah," Ed interjected, his tone sharp but his eyes gleaming with curiosity. "Enough of that. Tell us what happened! We've been dying to hear!"

Gav hadn't seen any of them in days, not since he'd been stuck on kitchen detail. He and Lucan had been tethered together like a pair of stray dogs, eating their meals in hurried silence between scrubbing plates and tankards. But tonight, their punishment was finally over, and they were free to rejoin the lively chaos of the commissary, to sit among friends and housemates once more.

"I'm pretty sure the entire academy knows," Gav said, scratching the back of his head, his cheeks warming with embarrassment.

"Not about the fight," Ed said, leaning forward, his elbows on the table. "About the king! And the Archbishop! I can't believe you guys didn't get expelled."

The table fell quiet, all eyes fixed on Gav, waiting, expectant. He hesitated for a moment, then took a seat, the weight of their curiosity pressing against him.

"Wait, really?" Gav said, his voice tinged with disbelief. "The king was really kind, and the Archbishop seemed nice too."

Ed snorted, leaning back in his chair with a smirk. "Lambelle do some smooth talking? Or wait—let me guess, his mother came marching in, throwing around how much money they spend on the academy. Ugh, they're the worst."

Nora tilted her head, her brow furrowing as she drew a breath. "You really think they're that bad? I don't know, Lucan doesn't seem evil. Just... stressed."

"It wasn't like that at all," Gav cut in, his voice firm.

Percy adjusted his glasses and leaned forward, his expression thoughtful. "That is peculiar," he said. "King Uther is not known for his mercy. Nor is the Archbishop. According to *The Avalon Historia*, Gamalaot is as great as it is today because of their ruthless pragmatism."

Gav shrugged, his tone flat. "They seemed very friendly and fair. Not much else to say, really."

Gale, sitting at the edge of the table, raised an eyebrow, a hint of jealousy creeping into his voice. "Seems like they like you. That bodes well for your future here, Gav."

"Let's just drop it!" Nora protested, her voice rising as she shot Gale a sharp look. "We're just glad you're alright and that you're free again."

"Well, just about," Gav said, holding up his hand. The clock was still there, ticking slowly, its glow faint but unmistakable.

Percy's eyes lit up, and he snatched Gav's arm, pulling it closer to examine the glowing insignia on his palm. "This is insane magic," he muttered, more to himself than to anyone else. His voice was low, almost reverent. "Silencing all magical ability is simply unheard of. I mean, to block the flow of spiritual energy… It's just all so fantastical—like something out of one of the ancient epics. *Onela and Eofor* or *The First Flame of Heoroweard*."

Gav blinked, confused. "What are you talking about?"

"I'm sorry," Percy said quickly, his tone earnest. "I forget you're still new to all this. The running theory is that magic comes from dragons."

"I remember that from class," Gav said, nodding slowly.

"Right," Percy continued, his enthusiasm undimmed. "There are countless ancient myths and stories about them. *Onela and Eofor, Hygd the Bold,* and *Merlin the White*—though, interestingly enough, despite Merlin's story being the most famous, large parts of it are lost to time. The original written account was damaged in a library fire centuries ago."

"You should teach a class, Percy," Nora said, her tone teasing but with a hint of disinterest as she picked at her food.

"How do you know all this stuff?"

Percy shrugged, a faint blush creeping across his cheeks. "My dad," he said, his voice tinged with both pride and embarrassment. "He's a historian."

"And makes loads of money," Ed said, his voice drifting off dreamily. "Sells massive tomes, he does."

"He's required reading in my Magical History class," Leif added, his tone matter-of-fact.

Percy sighed, a small, self-deprecating smile tugging at his lips. "It's dry, I know," he said, anticipating the inevitable conclusion. No one disagreed with him, but they didn't press the point either, letting the comment hang in the air like a faint, familiar joke.

"How long until you can cast magic again?" Nora asked, her voice gentle but curious.

"Midnight tonight," Gav replied, his eyes dropping to his hand. A small smile played on his lips as he watched the clock's slow, steady march.

The conversation shifted then, easing into the comfortable rhythms of normalcy. They talked about the classes they liked, the teachers they hated, the crushes that bloomed and faded like wildflowers in the academy's halls. Gav appreciated it, the simplicity, the familiarity. But his mind kept drifting back to his hand, to the faint glow of the clock etched into his skin.

Even after dinner ended, and the commissary emptied, and he lay in his cot, the day's exhaustion tugging at his limbs, he couldn't stop staring at it. The clock's hands moved with a quiet, relentless precision.

He had half-expected some grand, theatrical moment to mark the end of the spell; a burst of light, a shimmering glow, or perhaps an ethereal chime ringing out as the clock faded. But there was nothing. No fanfare, no spectacle. Gav had stayed awake, his eyes fixed on his hand, waiting for the moment the spell would lift. And then, quietly, without warning, the clock was simply gone. His palm was bare again, unmarked, as though it had never been there at all.

It was strange, almost disappointing in its simplicity. Gav had grown used to the idea that magic was something extraordinary, something that defied explanation. Yet here it was, slipping away as quietly as it had arrived, leaving no trace behind. He stared at his hand for a long moment, flexing his fingers, half-expecting the clock to reappear. But it didn't.

The more he thought about it, the more he realized how little he truly understood about this world. Some magic felt like it had been ripped from the pages of a storybook; grand, sweeping, and impossible. Other times, it felt almost scientific, rooted in rules and logic he couldn't quite grasp. It was a strange duality, one that left him both fascinated and unsettled.

A small smile tugged at his lips as he thought back to his birthday at Wonder World, the way the illusions and tricks had seemed so real, so magical. Maybe, he thought, Miss Morrigan was right, and magic and science weren't so different after all. Maybe they were two sides of the same coin, each explaining the world in its own way. And maybe, just maybe, the magic he had seen here in Avalon wasn't so far removed from the world he had left behind in Kingston.

The thought lingered as he finally lay back, his hand resting on his chest. The room was quiet, the only sound the soft rhythm of his breathing. He closed his eyes, letting the stillness settle over him, and drifted into sleep.

The next day, Gav's Elementary Magic lesson more than made up for the anticlimactic end to his punishment.

"Follow me, cadets," Miss Morrigan said, her voice carrying a sharp, almost musical lilt as she led the students out onto the green field. The sun hung high in the sky, casting a warm, golden light over the grass, and the air was filled with the faint hum of insects and the distant chatter of birds. "At ease! And take a seat," she commanded, her tone both firm and oddly playful.

The students obeyed, settling onto the grass in loose rows. Gav sat cross-legged, enjoying the feel of the sun on his face and the softness of the ground beneath him. It was a relief to be outside after days of being cooped up in the storage room, but the usual undercurrent of unease that seemed to follow Miss Morrigan like a shadow tempered his enjoyment. Her presence was always a little unsettling, her sharp eyes and sharper smile giving the impression that she always knew far more than she let on.

"Today is such a special day for you all," she announced, her voice brimming with a kind of gleeful anticipation. "It's Familiar Day! Oh, I'm just so excited for you!" She clasped her hands together, her grin widening as she surveyed the class.

The students around Gav perked up immediately, their faces lighting with excitement. All except Gav, who sat there, bewildered. He glanced at Nora, who was practically bouncing in place, her eyes shining with delight.

"Familiar Day?" Gav whispered to her, his voice low. "What's that?"

Nora turned to him, her grin infectious. "You'll see," she said, her tone teasing.

But before Gav could press further, Miss Morrigan's voice cut through the air acutely. "That's right, Gav," she said, her eyes locking onto his with an intensity that made him sit up straighter. "It's your familiar's birthday today!"

Gav blinked, his confusion deepening. "My... familiar's birthday?" he repeated. He had no idea what she was talking about, and the way the other students were grinning at him made him feel like he was the only one not in on the joke.

Morrigan extended her arm out, her fingers splayed, and called out into the air with a voice echoing with power. "Ofnir!" she cried.

As if summoned from the very fabric of the sky, a massive serpent materialized, its scales glinting like polished obsidian in the sunlight. The creature coiled itself around Morrigan's outstretched arm, then wound its way down to her waist, its movements fluid like a river. The snake's head rose from the curve of its body, its forked tongue flicking out as it let out a low, polite hiss in her direction.

"Everyone, meet Ofnir," Morrigan said, her voice brimming with pride. The snake turned its head toward the students, its golden eyes gleaming, and gave a slow, regal bow.

Gav's breath caught in his throat. His entire body felt weightless, his mind racing as he realized where this was going. He remembered Wiglaf summoning his bear, Breca, to carry them to Gamalaot's castle town. The memory of that moment, the sheer awe he'd felt, flooded back to him now. And as he watched Miss Morrigan with Ofnir, his excitement surged, matching that of the other students.

"I remember when you were born," Morrigan said softly to the snake, leaning in to press a kiss to its snout. The serpent hissed softly in response, its tongue flicking out again. Then she turned to the class, her expression shifting back to its usual sharp intensity. "Today, class, you're going to birth your familiars. But first..."

The collective groan that rose from the students was almost comical. They reached into their rucksacks, pulling out notebooks, quills, and inkpots with the resigned air of those who had been through this routine before.

"I'll keep the notes short, I promise," Morrigan said, her tone light, almost teasing. "I know it's hard to write quickly out here."

Despite her words, no one believed her. Miss Morrigan had a notorious habit of diving into the finer points and mechanics of magic with a speed and enthusiasm that left most students scrambling to keep up. She had a way of sharing crucial details just as the bell rang, leaving everyone frantically scribbling as they packed up their things.

Morrigan's voice carried across the field, her words weaving a spell of their own as she spoke. "Familiars are born from your soul," she began, her tone both commanding and tender. "So you must treat them with respect and kindness. To nurture your soul is to nurture your familiar. And in kind, your familiar will do all they can to support you." She paused, scratching gently beneath Ofnir's chin. The serpent let out a soft, contented hiss, its golden eyes half-closing in pleasure.

"To birth your familiar," she continued, "you will need to break off a small piece of your soul. Now, I know that sounds complicated, and that's because it is. Later on in your careers, cadets, you'll have the opportunity to learn more about how this spell works…if you're up to muster." Her gaze flicked to Percy as she said this, her lips curling into a sly smile. Percy straightened, his cheeks flushing slightly, but he didn't look away. "But most knights," Morrigan added, "just visit a qualified spiritualist for all familiar care. And lucky for you all, I happen to be a qualified spiritualist."

With a dramatic flourish, she clasped her hands together, and a powerful magical circle flared to life around her and the students. The air pulsated with energy, the ground beneath them glowing faintly with intricate runes and symbols.

"Now, class," Morrigan said, her voice dropping to a softer, almost hypnotic tone, "I want you to lay your hand across your heart. Close your eyes and feel the warmth emanating from your chest. Slowly move your hand around until you find what seems to be the hottest spot…and then quickly pluck it! Keep it tightly closed within your grip. Once you have it, you can gently release them from your grasp. Go on now!"

The students obeyed, their movements hesitant at first but growing more confident as they focused. Gav placed his hand over his heart, his fingers splayed against his chest. He closed his eyes, letting his breath steady as he searched for the warmth Miss Morrigan had described. At first, it was faint, a subtle heat that pulsed in time with his heartbeat. But as he concentrated, the sensation grew stronger, more distinct. It was a soft, quiet warmth, like the gentle kiss of sunlight on water, comforting and alive.

He moved his hand slowly, his fingers tracing the contours of his chest as he sought the source of the heat. It wasn't easy; the warmth seemed to shift and dance, elusive and fluid. But then, something deep within him stirred, an ancient, instinctive call that urged him to reach out, to seize it. His fingers closed around something, and to his surprise, he didn't find a stone or a coin, as he'd half-expected. Instead, his hand closed around something soft and malleable, a glowing orb that pulsed faintly in his grasp.

Gav's eyes fluttered open. He slowly opened his hand, his breath catching as he stared at the orb cradled in his hand. It shimmered with a faint, golden light, its surface shifting and swirling like liquid starlight. Around him, the other students were holding similar orbs, their faces alight with wonder and excitement.

Morrigan's voice broke the silence, her tone warm and approving. "Well done, cadets. You've taken the first step. Now, let's see what your souls have chosen to become."

Gav's heart raced as he stared down at his hands, the light within them flickering in time with his pulse. He could feel it: a connection, fragile but undeniable, between himself and the glowing sphere. Whatever it was, whatever it would become, it was a part of him.

"It's an egg?" Nora said, her voice tinged with wonder as she stared at the glowing oval cradled in her hands.

"They aren't exactly eggs, Miss Edmund," Miss Morrigan said, her tone gently corrective. "But I like how you're thinking! Let's run with it! Now, watch those eggs, cadets. Very soon, they will hatch, and you must call their name. Don't overthink it. When your eyes meet theirs, simply call out to them."

Gav, Nora, and Percy huddled together, their eggs held close to their chests. The air was electric with anticipation, the kind of excitement that made Gav feel like a child on Christmas morning, waiting to unwrap a long-awaited gift. He could see the same eagerness reflected in Nora's wide eyes and Percy's barely contained grin.

Percy's egg was the first to stir. It began to shake, gently at first, then more and more rapidly, its glow intensifying as it expanded in his hands. Gav and Nora watched, their own eggs clutched tightly, as Percy's trembled and pulsed, the light within it growing brighter and brighter.

And then, with a sudden burst of radiance, the light itself exploded, not violently, but in a breath of light that seemed to hang in the air for a moment before coalescing into a small, black pup with a tuft of white on its chest. The little creature landed at Percy's feet, its ears perked and its eyes sharp, though the severity of its expression was softened by the adorable tilt of its head as it looked up at him.

Percy knelt down, his face breaking into a wide grin as he brought his nose close to the pup's. "Orf," he said, his voice soft but sure.

The pup's tail wagged once, and then it leaned forward, giving Percy's nose a quick, affectionate lick, as if to confirm the bond between them. Percy laughed, a sound of pure joy, and scooped the pup into his arms, holding it close.

Gav and Nora exchanged glances, their excitement growing as they turned their attention back to their own eggs. The field held the clamor of the young cadets and their familiars, a commotion of light and sound bursting from the ground and filling the air.

"Percy!" Nora shouted, her voice brimming with delight. "A puppy! How cute!" She beamed, her eyes sparkling with joy. Both Gav and Percy could see she was itching to drop to the ground and shower the little pup with affection, but the glowing egg in her hands kept her rooted in place, her excitement bubbling over.

It wasn't long after that Nora's egg began to stir. Unlike Percy's, the shaking was subtler, the burst of light less dramatic. The glowing orb in her hands split in two, and from it emerged a small, delicate creature with scales and a tail.

"A salamander?" Nora tilted her head, studying the little lizard in her palms. "Wait, where are the legs?"

The creature had only two pronounced legs, thick and sturdy in proportion to its slender body. On its upper torso were two tiny nubs that might have been arms, though they were barely developed. It blinked up at her with bright, curious eyes, its tail flicking gently.

"Nora," Percy said, his tone suddenly serious and urgent. "That's not a salamander."

"No?" Nora replied, still staring at the little lizard. She stuck out her tongue playfully, and the creature mirrored the gesture, its tiny forked tongue flicking out in response. Nora giggled, her disappointment melting away.

"That's a wyvern," Percy exclaimed, his eyes wide with awe and concern.

"Is that right?" Nora said, her voice softening as she looked down at the little wyvern. "Are you a wyvern, Minerva?" she cooed.

At the sound of her name, the small wyvern jumped up and down in Nora's hands, its tiny nubs fluttering as if she had wings, excitedly. "But you're so small!" Nora laughed. "I'll call you Minnie! Short for Minerva, of course! You like that, Minnie?"

The wyvern let out a tiny, high-pitched chirp, its tail wagging furiously as it nuzzled against Nora's fingers.

"They start small," Percy said, his expression growing more serious. "She's going to get big. Really big. You think you can handle that, Nora?"

Nora didn't answer. She was too engrossed in her own little world, her nose brushing gently against Minnie's as the wyvern chirped and wriggled in her hands. Her smile was radiant, her earlier disappointment completely forgotten.

Gav watched the exchange, his own egg still cradled in his hands, its warmth growing more intense by the second. He couldn't help but smile at Nora's joy, even as Percy's warning lingered in the air.

Gav looked down at his glowing egg, watching as it shifted slightly in his hands, and he felt a jolt of excitement mixed with nervousness. *What would it be?* He'd never had a pet before, never been responsible for anything like this.

The egg cracked, a thin fracture splitting down the middle. But it didn't simply break in half. Instead, the tip of the oval burst open in a small plume of flame, and something shot out of it with a flash of fiery light. The shell disintegrated into shards of glowing light, scattering like sparks into the air. A blur of vibrant red darted around the space, moving so quickly it was almost impossible to follow. Then, with a graceful swoop, it landed on Gav's shoulder, its tiny claws gripping gently.

Percy and Nora crowded around, their eyes wide as they leaned in to get a closer look. Gav turned his head slowly, his nose nearly touching the little beak of his new familiar. The creature was small, its feathers a brilliant, fiery red that seemed to shimmer in the sunlight. Its black eyes twinkled with intelligence, and it tilted its head, studying Gav with a curious chirp.

"It's a bird!" Nora exclaimed, her voice filled with delight. "A little firebird!"

"A cardinal?" Gav said, squinting at the creature. It certainly looked like one, with its vibrant red plumage and small, sturdy frame. But there was something different about it, something he couldn't quite place.

"Remarkable," Percy said, his brow furrowed as he examined the pattern on the bird's wings. "I have no idea what kind of bird this is."

"Wait, really?" Nora and Gav said in unison, their voices tinged with disbelief.

"I don't know everything," Percy replied defensively, though his cheeks flushed slightly.

"Yes, you do!" Gav and Nora shot back, their words overlapping again. They glanced at each other and laughed, the tension breaking for a moment.

"It looks like a cardinal," Gav said, turning his attention back to the bird. He peered into its dark, shining eyes. "Is that what you are?"

The bird hopped in place on his shoulder, its head tilting as if to say, *who knows?* It let out a cheerful chirp, its tiny wings fluttering.

"And your name," Gav said, a smile tugging at his lips. "You're a girl."

The bird chirped again, louder this time, and hopped closer to Gav's cheek. He leaned in, half-expecting her to whisper something in his ear. Instead, he felt a sudden clarity, a name forming in his mind as if it had always been there.

"Lavinia," Gav said, the name rolling off his tongue with certainty.

The little bird let out a delighted trill, her wings flapping excitedly before she took off, zipping around the field in a blur of red. Gav tried to follow her with his eyes, but she was impossibly fast, her movements almost fluid, as if she were phasing in and out of reality. She darted between the other cadets, her fiery feathers leaving faint trails of light in her wake, before finally returning to Gav. She landed on top of his head, her tiny talons tangling in his hair as she pecked at his scalp with playful affection.

Gav laughed, reaching up to gently stroke her feathers. "Alright, Lavinia," he said, his voice warm.

"Cadets!" Miss Morrigan's voice rang out a penetrating command, pushing through the excited chatter of the students. "It looks like each of you has successfully birthed your familiars!"

Gav glanced around the field, taking in the sight of his classmates, each cradling or interacting with their new companions. There were creatures of all shapes and sizes—birds, mammals, even a few that defied easy categorization. For a moment, his gaze locked with Lucan's. The other boy sat a short distance away, his familiar, a small white lion cub with a golden mane, resting in his arms. Lucan's expression was cool, almost calculating, and the intensity of his stare sent a faint shiver down Gav's spine. He quickly looked away, focusing instead on Lavinia, who was now perched on his shoulder, her fiery feathers brushing against his cheek.

"But before you all go," Miss Morrigan continued, her tone shifting to one of mock sternness, "I have homework to assign."

The class groaned in unison, the sound a combination of exasperation and resignation.

"Oh, hush it," Miss Morrigan said, waving a hand dismissively. "Does anyone know one of the primary utilities a familiar provides for a knight?" She paused, her sharp eyes scanning the group before landing on Lucan. "Ah, yes, Lambelle."

Lucan didn't stand, but his voice carried the confidence of someone used to commanding attention. "They can send and deliver missives," he said, his tone crisp and assured. As he spoke, he absently stroked the lion cub's mane, the creature purring softly in response.

"Excellent! Yes, familiars are the most reliable and secure means of communication, especially for a knight in the field. As planeswalkers, they can travel much greater distances than we can, and they do it exponentially faster…but we will cover the mechanics of this in more detail later. Your homework is to send a letter using your familiar. Understood?"

"Yes, Miss Morrigan," the class replied in a pained, unison chorus.

"Excellent! Class dismissed!" she declared, clapping her hands together with a flourish.

Nora, Gav, and Percy retreated to the barracks, their familiars trailing behind them. They settled at the long bench in the common room, parchment spread out before them, quills scratching against the paper as they worked on their letters. The room was alive with the soft rustle of pages and the occasional murmur of conversation, but the trio worked in relative silence, each lost in their own thoughts.

"Who are you writing to, Gav?" Nora asked, her eyes still fixed on her own letter as she carefully formed each word.

"I was thinking about sending one back home," Gav replied, his voice soft. "To Mom."

"That's sweet!" Nora said, glancing up briefly with a smile before returning to her work.

"And you?" Gav asked, dipping his quill into the inkwell.

"My brother Gwynn!" Nora said, her tone brightening. "I want to tell him all about Minnie!"

"I think I'll write to Great Aunt Candace," Percy said, more to himself than to the others. He absently stroked Orf's head as the pup dozed in his lap, his quill moving steadily across the parchment.

The trio fell back into silence, the only sounds the scratch of quills, the occasional cough, or the tap of a shoe against the floor. Cadets drifted in and out of the common room, their conversations buzzing faintly, but Gav barely noticed. He was absorbed in his letter, his thoughts flowing onto the page as he tried to capture everything he wanted to say. The sun dipped in and out of the windows, casting long shadows across the room before finally sinking behind the tree line, leaving the barracks bathed in the warm glow of lantern light.

Gav wrote through it all, his focus unwavering. Hours slipped by, and the common room gradually emptied. He had a faint memory of Nora and Percy bidding him goodnight, their voices soft and tired, but he couldn't be sure if it had actually happened or if he'd imagined it. It didn't matter. What mattered was finishing the letter to his mom. He was almost done, the final words taking shape on the page as the night deepened around him.

But then, a cold wind swept through the room, carrying with it a shadowy shape that seemed to materialize out of the darkness. Gav instinctively threw his arms over his papers, shielding them from the sudden gust. Something light and feathery landed on his head, and he froze, his heart pounding. Slowly, he reached up and felt the weight of an envelope resting there. He plucked it off, his hands trembling as he stared at it.

Before he could open it, the envelope slipped from his fingers and fluttered to the table. Gav reached for it, but a sharp, pointed beak pecked at his hand, making him yelp and pull back.

"Ouch!"

He looked up, his eyes widening as he saw a large raven standing on the table, its glossy black feathers shimmering in the dim light. The bird's eyes were sharp and piercing, fixed on Gav with an intensity that made his skin prickle. The raven tilted its head, then used its beak to nudge the letter closer to Gav, as if urging him to open it.

Gav hesitated, catching his breath. Slowly, he picked up the envelope and broke the seal, unfolding the parchment inside. The handwriting was elegant but hurried, the ink dark and bold against the page. He read the words, his pulse quickening with each sentence.

I possess the truth kept concealed from you. The prophecy; the reason for their ire and hate—I know it all. Ask me your questions, but let them remain between us. Share this secret with none, or else I vanish. I leave you Titus—trust him with your writings. - MLR.

Gav's hands shook as he lowered the letter, his mind racing. He looked at the raven, its eyes still locked on his. "Titus?" he asked, his voice barely above a whisper.

The raven nodded once, a deliberate and almost human gesture.

Gav exhaled sharply, his thoughts swirling. He glanced back at the letter, the initials *MLR* burning into his mind. *Who was this person? And did they really know the prophecy?*

His quill was still in his hand, the ink drying on its tip. Without thinking, he pressed it to a fresh sheet of parchment, his hand moving almost of its own accord. The words spilled out, his questions forming faster than he could write them.

Chapter 12
Under the Winter's Shadow

Christmas' grip had tightened around the realm of Avalon, and Gamalaot found itself, on some December morning, covered in a thick sheet of white. The cadets trudged through feet of snow, bundled in the fur-lined winter variant of their house uniforms. They marched through the knee-deep drifts, continuing their daily workout regimens as usual.

The nearby lake was frozen solid; Nora and Gav looked longingly at the children playing on the ice, their laughter calling out to them antagonistically. The pair watched with a pining as they lunged around the field.

But a festive spirit hummed through the castle as Christmas break loomed overhead. The anticipation was incontrovertible, a tangible excitement that fluttered down from the sky interposed with the icy snowflakes.

Classes had been largely uneventful in the days leading up to the break. Many of the more privileged students had already left the academy, retreating to their second homes or family estates outside the country. But for those like Gav and his friends, Castle Gamalaot remained their world. Before they knew it, the final day of classes came and went, and the excitement of the approaching Christmas break overtook the air.

Dinner in the commissary that evening was a lively affair. The long tables were crowded with cadets, their voices rising and falling in a symphony of laughter and chatter. The scent of roasted meat and spiced cider filled the room, mingling with the warmth of the crackling hearths.

"I can't believe we're on Christmas break!" Ed exclaimed, his voice booming as he raised his tankard high. Mead sloshed over the rim, foamy droplets spilling onto the table as he grinned broadly.

"Wassail! Wassail! To Christmas!" Leif shouted, clashing his tankard against Ed's with a loud clank.

The two brothers sprang to their feet, throwing an arm around each other and kicking out their legs in a clumsy, exuberant dance.

"Wassail, everyone!" Ed shouted at everyone in the hall.

"Sing it with us!"

They teetered on the edge of the bench, nearly falling off, laughing as their voices rose in a raucous song:

Wassail! Wassail! All over the town,
Our cup it is white and the ale it is brown;
Our cup it is made of the good ashen tree;
And so is the malt of the best barley!

For it's your Wassail and it's our Wassail
And joy to be you and a jolly Wassail!

Gav sat stiffly at the table, his posture hunched as if trying to make himself smaller. He watched the brothers with a mixture of amusement and unease, his fingers tightening around his own cup of cider.

"Percy, are they...?" Gav began, his voice low as he leaned toward his friend.

"No," Gale interrupted, smirking as he stirred his bowl of porridge. "It's not real mead."

"They only serve real mead at the Captain's bench," Percy added, sipping his apple cider with a calm, almost scholarly air.

"How d'ya know we didn't sneak any?!" Ed retorted, collapsing back onto the bench with a thud, his cheeks flushed and his grin wide.

"See for yourself, Gav!" Leif said, sliding the frothing tankard across the table toward him.

Gav hesitated, his stomach tightening as he stared at the drink. The frothy surface shimmered in the firelight, and the faint scent of honey and spices wafted up to him. But the thought of drinking it made his insides twist.

"Oh," Gav said, forcing a small, polite smile. "No, thank you."

The brothers erupted into laughter, their voices blending with the general din of the commissary. Gav sat back, his shoulders relaxing slightly as he sipped his cider. The warmth of the drink spread through him, and for a moment, he allowed himself to enjoy the chaos. The holiday spirit was infectious, and everyone couldn't help but feel a constant burning of joy. Christmas break was here, and for a little while, at least, the weight of the world could wait.

"Ya all seem ta be in high spirits!" Wiglaf's booming voice cut through the chatter as he appeared behind Gav, his broad frame casting a shadow over the table. "Excited fer Christmas, no doubt!"

Ed and Leif froze, their faces turning even brighter red as they stiffened in their seats, suddenly trying to blend into the background.

"We were just talking about our holiday plans," Gav said, his tone casual but firm. He caught the subtle nod of gratitude from the Edmund brothers across the table.

"Our family is going to Carlisle!" Nora chimed in eagerly, her eyes sparkling with excitement. "Mom, Dad, and Gwynn split the cost for a room at the Griff-Inn!"

"Sounds like fun!" Wiglaf said, his smile widening. "How 'bout ye, Percy?"

"We're going outside The Veil," Percy replied, his voice calm and measured. "Mom and my sister want to visit Brussels for the holiday while Dad is away on his book tour."

"The Veil?" Gav muttered under his breath, his brow furrowing. He had been in Avalon for months now, but there were still moments when he felt like an outsider, stumbling over terms and concepts that everyone else seemed to take for granted. The twinge of embarrassment was familiar, but it didn't sting any less.

"The unprotected lands," Percy explained, noticing Gav's confusion. "The Veil is the magic spell that hides and protects the realm of Avalon from the rest of the world."

"Oh," Gav said, nodding slowly as the pieces clicked into place.

"Aye, lad," Wiglaf added, his tone warm and reassuring. "We passed through it when we sailed into Carlisle, ye remember?"

"So wait," Gav said, his curiosity piqued. "How big is Avalon exactly?"

Percy set his cider down and leaned forward, his scholarly demeanor taking over. "Roughly fifty percent larger than Asia," he said matter-of-factly.

Gav's eyes widened. "Oh wow! That's ginormous!"

"No more lessons!" Nora said from the end of the table. "We're on break! Anyway, how about you, Wiglaf? Any fun plans for Christmas?"

Wiglaf's usual boisterous demeanor faltered for a moment, his expression softening into something uncharacteristically flat. "I ain't goin' nowhere special," he said, his tone lacking its usual warmth. He paused, then turned to Gav. "I don't mean to be rude, but could I steal ye a moment, lad?"

"Huh? Oh, sure," Gav said. He took a breath and rose from the bench, following Wiglaf as the big man led him to the far end of the commissary. As they walked, Gav glanced out the windows they passed, watching the heavy white snowflakes dance in the cold darkness outside. The sight was beautiful, but it did little to ease the knot of worry forming in his chest.

"What's wrong?" Gav asked once they were out of earshot of the others.

"Nothin' too bad, laddie," Wiglaf said, his eyes fixed on the window, his reflection blurred by the frost creeping up the glass. He turned suddenly, his gaze meeting Gav's. "I just didn't want to embarrass ye in front of yer friends." He clapped a hand on Gav's shoulder, his grin returning, though it didn't quite reach his eyes. "Speakin' of, look at ye makin' all them friends! Good goin', lad!"

Gav smiled faintly, but the unease in his stomach only grew. "What do you mean, embarrass me? What's going on, Wiglaf?"

Wiglaf's expression sobered, and he let out a heavy sigh. "Well, I reckon ye were thinkin' ye could head home fer Christmas. See Miss Hrethel… or, uh, Ethel, I mean. Yer mom, boy!"

Gav's heart sank. "I mean," he said slowly, "I was hoping so, but I didn't exactly know who to ask about going home."

"Me, boy," Wiglaf said firmly, his hand still resting on Gav's shoulder. "Ye come to me, understand?"

"Yes, Wiglaf," Gav said, forcing a smile despite the sinking feeling in his chest.

"Aye, don't be doin' that, lad!" Wiglaf said, his voice heavy with regret. "I can't be tellin' ye the bad news after ye go an' smile at me with them sad eyes!"

"What bad news?"

Wiglaf's shoulders slumped, and he looked Gav straight in the eye. "Yar stuck here, boy," he said, his tone heavy with regret. "I spoke with King Uther and the Archbishop. They said the safest place fer ye is here at the castle."

He stared at Wiglaf, the words sinking in slowly. "Stuck here?" he repeated, his voice barely above a whisper.

"Aye, lad. I'm sorry. It's fer yer own safety. They don't want ye riskin' anythin' by leavin' the protection of the castle."

"But safe from what exactly?" Gav asked, his voice tinged with frustration and confusion. He stared at Wiglaf, searching for answers in the man's weathered face.

"But if ye like," Wiglaf began, his tone softer, almost shy, "I've got a cottage near the castle. King said it'd be alright if ye wanted to go there with me fer Christmas. Don't mean ta boast, but it's nicer than the barracks."

Gav blinked, caught off guard by the offer. "Spend Christmas together?"

"I know I be a lousy substitute fer yer mum, boy. But ye'd be doin' me a big favor with yer company. Don't have family 'round here no more."

A warmth spread through Gav's chest, pushing back the cold disappointment that had settled there. "I'd really like that, Wiglaf!" he said, his voice breaking slightly as he threw his arms around the behemoth of a man.

Wiglaf let out a hearty laugh, patting Gav on the back. "Ha! Well, good! I'll come by ta fetch ye in the mornin'!"

Gav stepped back, grinning up at him, but as Wiglaf turned to leave, a sudden thought struck him. "W-wait," Gav called out, but Wiglaf didn't turn around. *What did he mean I'll be safer here?*

Wiglaf paused for a moment, his broad shoulders stiffening, but he didn't answer. Instead, he gave a small wave and continued walking, his heavy footsteps echoing down the hall.

Gav stood there, his hands tucked into his pockets, staring after him. The question lingered in his mind, unanswered, and the weight of it settled heavily on his shoulders. He turned back to the window, watching the snow fall in thick, silent flakes. The glass fogged with his breath as he leaned closer, his mind drifting to thoughts of home.

He pictured his mom alone on Christmas, the house quiet without him there. He thought of Veteran's Park, the snow untouched, no forts or snowmen built by him and Tommy. The ache in his chest grew sharper, and before he could stop them, tears welled up in the corners of his eyes.

Gav swiped at his face with an open palm, his movements quick and furtive. He glanced around, making sure no one had seen, then ducked out into the cold, the icy air biting at his cheeks as he hurried back to the barracks. The snow crunched under his boots, and the night seemed to press in around him, heavy and silent.

As he walked, the tears came harder, and he let them fall, his breath hitching in the cold. For all the magic and wonder of Avalon, it couldn't fill the void he felt.

Gav moved quickly, his head down, his shoulders hunched. For once, he was grateful for the way people seemed to avoid him, their unwillingness to get too close giving him the space he needed to retreat mostly unnoticed. He reached the barracks and threw himself onto his cot, the thin mattress offering little comfort, but at least providing the solitude he craved. Alone with his thoughts, the dam finally broke, and he gave in to the overwhelming wave of nostalgia and homesickness. Tears streamed down his face, silent at first, then growing into quiet sobs that shook his chest.

And then, a tapping.

At first, Gav ignored it, convinced it was just the wind battering against the old, warped windowpanes. But the sound grew louder, more insistent, until it was impossible to ignore. A sharp, piercing caw followed, the sound of a bird in distress.

Lavinia appeared as if summoned, darting into the room in a streak of red light. She flew straight to the window, her tiny beak pecking furiously at the glass.

Gav craned his neck to see what had agitated her and spotted a familiar black beak pecking back from the other side.

"Titus?" Gav said, his voice hoarse from crying. He wiped his face with his sleeve and got up, crossing the room to open the window. "Lavinia, it's just Titus. Stand down."

The raven hopped inside, his glossy black feathers glinting in the dim light. From his talons dropped a small, folded note. Gav snatched it up, his heart racing as he glanced around the room, half-expecting someone to burst in and catch him. When no one did, he unfolded the note, his hands trembling as he read the words scrawled in elegant, hurried handwriting:

Are you not tired of their cryptics? What did Wiglaf mean by keeping you safe? Why did he ignore you? The next time you two meet, ask him about your brother. Don't let him evade you. You deserve to know the truth. - MLR

Gav stared at the note, his mind reeling. "My brother?" he whispered to himself. "I don't have a brother."

The voices of other cadets drifted in from outside, their laughter and chatter growing louder as they approached the barracks. Gav stiffened, his instincts kicking in. He quickly folded the note and tucked it into the box beneath his cot, where a dozen other mysterious messages from this MLR lay hidden. Just as he turned to open the window and let Titus out, the raven was gone, vanished as if he had never been there at all. All that remained was a single black feather, resting on the windowsill.

Gav picked up the feather, turning it over in his hands as his mind raced. The note's words echoed in his head, each one a puzzle piece that didn't seem to fit. *Ask him about your brother.* But Gav had no brother—or at least, he had never been told about one. The idea was absurd, and yet... There was a nagging doubt, a flicker of curiosity that refused to be extinguished.

He sat back on his cot, the feather still clutched in his hand, and stared at the ceiling. The voices outside grew louder, the cadets filing into the barracks, their laughter and chatter filling the room. Gav closed his eyes, trying to steady his breathing, but the questions lingered, swirling in his mind like the snow outside.

"Hey, Gav," Percy's voice called from the top of the stairs, breaking him from the trancelike state he was in. "You decent? Nora wants to come down."

"Yeah," Gav replied, quickly wiping his face with his sleeve and shoving the black feather under his pillow. He forced a smile, snorting snot and swallowing it before anyone could see him.

"Race ya!" Nora's voice rang out, followed by the sound of her bounding down the stairs. There was a pounding of footsteps, but before Gav could react, a fuzzy black snout poked through the doorway.

"No fair, Orf!" Nora's voice whined from behind. "You have more legs! And a lower center of gravity!"

"Good boy," Percy said, following at a more leisurely pace as he descended the stairs. He reached down to scratch Orf behind the ears, the pup wagging his tail contentedly.

"What are you guys doing here?"

"We wanted to check on you!" Nora said, her voice bright and cheerful as she stepped into the room.

"Even if it means breaking house protocol," Percy added, shooting a disapproving look at Nora.

"Oh, relax," Nora said, waving a hand dismissively. "There isn't anyone around! And Gav is more important than some stupid dorm rules." She turned to Gav, her expression softening. "You left in a bit of a hurry. Everything alright? What did Wiglaf say?"

"Oh," Gav said, his mind racing as he nervously kicked the box of letters further under his bed. "He was just telling me that I have to stay here for Christmas."

"Well, that's a bummer!" Nora exclaimed, her face falling.

"Did he say why?" Percy asked, his head tilting slightly as he studied Gav.

"Uhh, not really," Gav replied, avoiding Percy's gaze. "Probably too much of a hassle to take me home."

"I see," Percy said, his tone neutral but his eyes narrowing slightly.

"Guys!" Nora said, springing up onto the tips of her toes. "We should do something fun before break!"

"What did you have in mind?" Gav asked, grateful for the change in topic.

"I don't know! We could... build a snow fort outside!"

"It's a little late for that, don't you think?" Percy said.

"How about a snowball fight? Gav and me against you, Percy."

"Be serious," Percy said, crossing his arms. "I have to be up early to catch the morning ferry. And I'd rather not get sick right before the holiday."

"How about cards?" Gav suggested. "Or a board game. I think I saw a chess set in the commons..."

"Irish!" Nora said, her face lighting up with glee. "Let's play Irish! I'll go grab my set!"

Before anyone could protest, Nora had disappeared up the stairs, her footsteps echoing in the narrow stairwell.

"Irish?" Gav turned to Percy with an inquisitive look on his face.

"It's a lot like Backgammon," Percy explained, his tone matter-of-fact.

"Oh. Cool."

The two boys ascended the weathered steps, the silence between them somewhat awkward. There was a question hanging in the air, something neither of them felt bold enough to ask. Gav could feel Percy's eyes on him, the weight of his curiosity pressing against him, but he kept his gaze fixed on the stairs, his mind still fixated on the note he received and the questions it had raised.

Gav had been writing back and forth with this mysterious MLR for a month or two now, and he suspected Percy perhaps had picked up on his secrecy. Something was tense between them, but he didn't want to lose access. For now, though, he pushed those thoughts aside, focusing instead on the sound of Nora's laughter as she rummaged through her things upstairs. Whatever secrets lay hidden, whatever truths he still had to uncover, they could wait. Tonight, he would play games with his friends, and for a little while, he would let himself forget all of it.

Nora spilled the stones onto the table in the barracks common room, the clatter of pebbles breaking the quiet. Minnie and Lavinia immediately seized the opportunity for play. The two creatures began tossing a stone back and forth, Minnie using her snout and Lavinia her beak, their movements quick and playful. Orf lay curled at his master's feet, snoring softly, completely unfazed by the commotion.

The room was filled with a comfortable buzzing, punctuated by the occasional clink of stones and the distant sounds of cadets stomping snow and slush off their boots as they returned from the cold outside. Gav sat at the table, his eyes fixed on the game board.

"I'm sorry you can't go home," Nora said. "That really stinks."

Before Gav could respond, the door swung open, and Gale stepped inside, kicking his heels to dislodge the snow caked on his boots. "What really stinks?" he asked.

"It's probably Nora," Ed said, following close behind. He smirked as he unwound his scarf. "That girl barely washes when we're at home, and that's with Mom badgering her all the time."

"I washed!" Nora shot back, her cheeks flushing with indignation.

"Oh yeah? When?" Ed challenged, leaning against the table with a grin.

"This morning!" Nora declared, crossing her arms.

"Not a chance! "Leif, conduct the sniff test."

Leif, who had been quietly unwrapping his scarf, rolled his eyes. "Leave her alone, Ed," he said, his tone weary. "Last thing we need is Mom to be on us right as the holiday starts."

"You hear that?" Ed said, his voice dripping with mockery. "You're a tattletale, Eleanora!"

Nora stuck out her tongue at him, her expression a combination of defiance and amusement.

Just then, an abrupt hush fell over the barracks as a girl entered, a vision in gold and black. Her skin, pale and luminous, seemed to radiate in the dim light. She marched past them with an air of regal authority, her presence commanding the room. Gav couldn't help but blush as she leaned her face close to Percy's, her cascade of golden waves framing a face of timeless beauty.

"Are you packed?" she asked, her voice edged and impatient.

"Mercie," Percy said, wincing slightly. "Not exactly."

"And why not? We need to leave soon."

"I'll be ready by the morning," he replied flatly, his tone defensive.

"But we're leaving within the hour."

Percy's whole body stiffened, and he turned to his sister with a look of shock, disbelief washing over his face. "What are you talking about? We're leaving early tomorrow morning."

"No," she said, her voice scathing. "We need to be there by morning."

"No, that's wrong," Percy said, his voice rising as he stood to his feet. "In her note, Mother clearly said…"

"That we should be there by morning," Mercie interrupted, her tone dripping with condescension. "Did you forget how to read?"

"Mercie, you're wrong."

Percy's sister stood tall and stoic, her posture radiating authority. Despite being only a year older than him, she carried herself as if she were decades his senior. Her gaze, cold and dismissive, swept over Gav and Nora, lingering for a moment as if silently disgusted by their presence. She also made sure to keep her shoulder pointed toward Leif, who remained frozen in the doorway, clearly uncomfortable.

"Hold a moment," Percy said, his voice tight with frustration. He disappeared down the steps, his footsteps echoing in the stairwell.

Mercie remained still, her arms folded, her expression unforgiving. The room felt heavy with tension. Gav shifted uncomfortably, his eyes darting between Nora and the floor, unsure of where to look.

Percy returned moments later, clutching a letter in his hand. His voice grew louder as he climbed the stairs, his words spilling out in a rush.

"Mercie, it says right here that *'you and your sister must ensure that your preparations for the journey are completed well in advance, as the voyage is lengthy. It is imperative that we arrive in Carlisle promptly to catch the ferry, therefore kindly plan to...'"*

" *'Be present at the break of dawn,'*" Mercie said loudly, interrupting him and finishing the sentence in unison. Her voice was sharp, her tone laced with disdain. "If we leave in the morning, there is no chance of catching the ferry on time. I cannot believe you didn't think ahead. Honestly, Percy, you're too careless these days."

Percy stood frozen, staring at the letter as if it were a forgery, a lie. His face was a mask of confusion and disbelief. "I swear I thought it said..."

"You thought wrong," Mercie said, her words venomous. She turned her attention to Gav, her gaze piercing. "Perhaps you ought to keep better company. Companions that keep you sharp."

Percy's shoulders slumped, and he nodded reluctantly. "I'm sorry. I'll go get ready now."

"I'll assist you," Mercie said, her tone leaving no room for argument. "Don't want any more oversights." With that, she turned on her heel and disappeared down the stairwell, her golden hair shimmering in the dim light.

"Percy's sister is mean," Nora said, her voice tinged with an ire Gav had never heard from her before. Her usually bright and cheerful demeanor was clouded by a rare frown, her arms crossed tightly over her chest.

"But oh so pretty!" Ed chimed in, swooning obnoxiously and jabbing his brother in the ribs with a sharp elbow. "Don't you think, brother?"

Leif rolled his eyes, shoving Ed away with a grunt. "Don't drag me into this," he muttered, though a faint smirk tugged at the corner of his mouth.

The evening drew to a close swiftly, as though it had been swallowed by the dark cloud of Percy and Mercie's abrupt departure. One by one, the remaining cadets drifted off to their beds, the promise of the holiday pressing down on them with an eagerness that made it hard to sleep.

As the first light of dawn crept in, cold and unhurried, Gav finally made his way to his cot. The barracks were quiet now, the only sound the soft rustling of blankets and the occasional creak of a bed frame. He lay down, staring at the ceiling, his mind still racing with thoughts of the evening. Despite the heaviness in the air, Gav couldn't help but feel a flicker of hope. Christmas was coming. He loved Christmastime, even if he was far away from home. He closed his eyes, letting the quiet of the barracks lull him into a restless sleep.

When morning broke, the sun shone brightly, its light reflecting off the endless sea of snow like a magnifying glass. Despite the brilliance, the air remained bitingly cold, and the warmth of the sun did little to chase away the chill.

Gav stood at the edge of the courtyard, watching as Nora waved goodbye, her brothers flanking her as they set off for Carlisle. The sight left a hollow feeling in his chest, but he forced a smile, raising a hand in farewell.

"Can I take yer trunk, boy?" Wiglaf's voice broke through Gav's thoughts, pulling him back to the present.

"I got it. Thanks, Wiglaf."

"Aye," Wiglaf said, his keen eyes narrowing as he studied Gav. "Ye'll be seein' them friends o' yours soon enough!"

"I know. You're right."

Wiglaf clapped a hand on Gav's shoulder, his grip firm but reassuring. "Right. Well, we best be off, boy. Snowstorm's a-comin' tonight."

"Is that right?" Gav said, his voice distant, his mind still elsewhere.

"Aye. Ye can tell by the smell. Clouds carry a scent when a storm's brewin' up."

They set off, trudging through the deep snowdrifts that blanketed the landscape. Wiglaf led the way, his massive blade held like a plow, clearing a path. The rhythmic sound of snow crunching underfoot filled the air, punctuated by the occasional grunt as the hulking knight heaved aside icy obstacles.

"It truly be a shame Breca ain't 'round," Wiglaf said. "She'd get us there in no time at all, believe me that, boy."

"Where is she, Wiglaf?"

"Sent her out," Wiglaf replied, pausing to shove a large, icy boulder out of the way. "With some holiday packages fer the family back home. I bet she's cozied up next to Haethcyn as we speak now. Gettin' her belly scratched, no doubt."

Gav's expression softened, but a shadow of guilt crossed his face. "I'm sorry," he said, his voice dripping with regret.

"What fer, boy?"

"You can't go home to be with your family because of me."

"Hogwash!" Wiglaf stopped dead in his tracks. "Gav, I wouldn't be goin' home regardless."

Gav's face softened a little, the tension in his shoulders easing. Wiglaf offered him a warm smile before turning back to the snow, his blade slicing through the drifts once more.

"Besides, boy," Wiglaf continued, his tone lighter now, "I be right excited 'bout spendin' the holiday together. Been meanin' to catch up with ya. Seems like yer doin' well. Made some fine friends, eh?"

"Yeah, I suppose so," Gav said, a small smile tugging at the corners of his mouth.

"Here we are!" Wiglaf announced, his voice filled with triumph. He twisted his body, swinging his sword in a wide arc. A wave of snow erupted upward, crashing down around them and clearing the front patio of his hovel in one swift motion.

"It ain't much ter look at, I know. But she done right by me."

Wiglaf opened the door with perhaps more strength than he intended. The cabin, rough-hewn stone on the outside, concealed an oppressive gloom that reigned within. Dark it was, the only light a grudging, pallid sunlight filtering through the frosted panes that overlooked the snow-blanketed ground.

They shuffled in, boots heavy on the dirty floor. Pots and pans lay scattered, discarded with the careless abandon of a man in a rush. Before them was a long table, scarred and worn, that surely bore witness to countless meals but now stood solitarily, coated grey with filth and grime. Flies, frozen stiff, embalmed in a shroud of dust, clung to its surface like decorations.

"Don't mind the mess, Gav," he said, waving cobwebs out of his face. "There be a room in the back. Set yer trunk down. That'll be yers."

"Wiglaf, I don't mean to sound rude, but it doesn't look like anyone has lived here in a while."

"Aye, boy," he said, clearly irritated.

Gav locked in on the dusty bookcase as he approached the south-facing wall near what would be his room. The dust lay thick on the shelves. But even still, through it all, one book, its spine decorated with dazzling gems, caught Gav's eye. They were familiar to him though he couldn't quite recall why. They lined the ridge of the binding in what he presumed was a purposeful order: ruby, sapphire, citrine, emerald, and deep black garnet. These stones stared back at him, demanding his attention.

"This place is a bloody disaster! That no good, filthy slob!"

"Would you like some help?" Gav said, returning from his room.

"Aye, Gav!" Wiglaf's red face lightened, his smile a little embarrassed. "Aye, I be sorry fer the state of it. Me worthless brother left her in ruin, it seems."

"I didn't know you had a brother!"

Wiglaf didn't say anything but nodded his head solemnly as he continued to tidy up the table.

This was the perfect moment, Gav thought. He had a heap of questions tangled up inside him, all wanting to get out, but he couldn't quite know how to ask them. He wondered if he should just blurt it all out, ask every question at once and be done with it. But the thought made him uneasy. *Would Wiglaf get mad?* He didn't want to seem ungrateful, or worse, like he didn't trust him anymore. All these conflicting feelings gnawed at poor Gav as he turned his head, glancing over his shoulder toward the room where he'd left his trunk, his eyes tracing the old wood around the room as if looking for some kind of sign; as though the letters, sitting in there quiet and still, were giving him some silent nod to go ahead and ask.

"Boy," Wiglaf said. "Would ye carry these over to the kitchen, then?"

"Sure."

"Wulfgar said he left months ago," grumbled Wiglaf, his massive beard nearly brushing the table as he scraped at the grime. "The useless oaf didn't lift a finger to clean a damn thing!"

The brief ember of courage that had previously sparked within Gav's heart then flickered out just as quickly. He let it go, slipping back into the quiet rhythm, working beside Wiglaf to clean the cabin. They moved through the place, wiping away the dust, scrubbing bowls and sweeping corners. When the work was done, Wiglaf vanished into the back room, and after a while, came out with a crate, big and heavy.

"Care to lend a hand, Gav?" He said, pulling out a shimmering red garland, a big smile stretching across his beard.

They set to work, pulling out the decorations one by one from the box. Wiglaf hummed a tune, a soft, familiar thing despite his horrendous pitch, and to Gav's surprise, he recognized it as 'O Tannenbaum.' Without thinking, he joined in, singing. Lavinia, who had been fluttering overhead with garlands of popcorn, twittered the tune too.

Wiglaf took pause, his hands still, and looked at Gav with a kind of amazed joy, as if he'd never expected words to accompany the melody. He began to sing along, his voice stumbling over lyrics he never knew existed, but still trying to follow, matching the rhythm of Gav's voice like a man finding his way in the dark.

By the time they were finished, the cabin looked like a scene pulled from a children's storybook. Sprigs of holly and mistletoe hung in thick festoons, bright against the bare stone walls. Wiglaf had slipped out for a minute, gone into the cold to cut down a tree, and now it stood in the corner, tall and proud, with shiny ornaments strung from every branch like pearls. The room felt full of light and life, like it had been waiting for this, for someone to make it whole again.

The light of day slipped away, leaving the sky awash in the twinkling brilliance of a diamond-studded night. Wiglaf, as jovial as ever, had filled his tankard with mead several times over, his cheeks flushed with the warmth of drink and merriment. Gav, seated across from him, sipped quietly at his warm apple cider, the gentle warmth of it soothing his thoughts.

It was in that moment, as the fire crackled softly between them, that Gav felt it, a small but persistent spark of courage, a twinge that burned brighter in his chest.

"Hey, Wiglaf?" Gav's voice broke.

"Aye, boy?!" Wiglaf replied, his words a little slurred, but good-natured as ever.

"I want to ask you something."

"Anything, lad!"

"It's about my family. My birth family, I mean."

At those words, Wiglaf's face hardened, the playful gleam in his eyes dimming just slightly.

"Obviously, I never really knew them," Gav began, his voice steady but heavy with thought. "Did you?"

"Aye, that I did, boy," Wiglaf said quietly, his eyes falling away for a moment, a shadow passing over his face.

"What were they like?" Gav pressed, leaning forward slightly. "I know it doesn't change anything, and Mom will always be Mom, but she didn't birth me, right? And surely I must've had a father too, and maybe brothers."

The silence stretched between them, broken only by the crackling of the fire as it danced in the hearth. Wiglaf inhaled deeply through his nose, gathering his thoughts, before exhaling in a mighty blast that sent a puff of warm air through his bushy beard.

"Yer mother," he began, his voice softer now, tinged with reverence. "Lady Ragnell, I mean, was a woman of great worth. Like the sea, she was. Fair and beautiful, her love ran deep, wrapt 'round ye like the quiet of a summer dusk. But do not mistake her, for she could be fierce, like a tempest, sinking even the mightiest of ships."

Gav watched Wiglaf with intent eyes as he moved to a nearby bookcase, rummaging through it with purpose before returning to his chair. In his hands, he carried an old photograph, which he handed over to Gav with a slow, deliberate gesture.

Gav held it, studying it for a moment, before speaking softly, almost to himself, "What was her name?"

"Elizabeth," Wiglaf replied, his voice distant as though lost in the past for a brief moment.

In the photograph, Gav's mother stood tall and slender, her green eyes sharp and stunning, cutting through the softness of her chestnut-brown hair that cascaded past her shoulders. A curtain of hair had fallen just shy of her left eye, held back by a simple fringe. Her dress, a rich shade of red, fell with elegant simplicity, neither billowing nor clinging. It had a quiet, angular grace, edged with black fur at the cuffs and hem. She looked like royalty, like a queen, or a princess from some forgotten fairytale.

"She's beautiful," Gav murmured, his fingers tracing the edge of the photograph as his heart swelled. There, in the sharpness of her gaze and the curve of her cheek, he could see himself. "What about my dad?"

Wiglaf's expression shifted, the lightness fading as he paused, his eyes narrowing with something akin to caution. "That be a bit more tangled, lad," he growled, his voice darkening. "Not many pictures of him, and that's all due to... well, the way things be."

"What do you mean, Wiglaf?"

"Just that they be takin' no pictures of black knights."

Black knights, Gav thought. He remembered Nora telling him about the Black Knights. The secret soldiers sent out to carry out top-secret missions for the king. The best of the best. Nora said her brother Gwynn was a black knight. Just like Gav's father, it would seem.

"He passed before yer mother," Wiglaf said softly. "On assignment."

Gav sat there, his fingers wrapped around the green sash, the photograph in his lap as if it held the key to some piece of him he'd never known. The woman in the picture, his mother, felt like a phantom at the edge of his thoughts, a presence that whispered in the stillness of the room. He could almost feel her warmth in the air of Gamalaot, a ghostly echo of something long lost. He didn't understand it, but something deep inside him urged him to hold on to the thread between them, no matter how fragile it seemed.

"Wiglaf?"

"Aye, Gav?"

Gav hesitated, swallowing the lump in his throat. The nervousness tightened in his chest, but he pushed it aside, determined. "What about..." He paused, a sharp breath, then forced the words out. "What about my brother?"

Wiglaf froze. The air between them shifted, thickening. They locked eyes, both wearing the same wary expression, as if some unspoken tension had flared between them, like knives drawn in the midst of a standoff.

"Brother?" Wiglaf's voice was low, a question in itself, though his brows furrowed in confusion.

Gav could see the change in him, the way he shifted uncomfortably in his seat. And then, in the quietest of moments, Wiglaf's words came, slow and cautious.

"I'm not sure I be followin' ye, lad. Ye don't have no brother."

Gav's gaze dropped, the weight of the moment pressing down on him, the quiet thud of disappointment settled in his chest, the air between them felt colder now, sharp with an unspoken truth. *Why would Wiglaf lie to him?* The question hung, unanswered, swirling in the empty space between them. *It made no sense.*

Wiglaf had always been there for him, a steady hand to guide him, a protector, a shield. But now, with the lie looming between them, that image began to crack. And though Gav knew that Wiglaf had always meant well, the anger inside him twisted, stubborn, and dark. The reasons didn't matter; the lie still stung. He couldn't shake the betrayal, that bitter feeling of being deceived, no matter how noble the intent might have been.

"I'm feeling tired," Gav said, his voice despondent. "I'm going to turn in for the night."

Without waiting for a reply, he moved toward his bedroom, each step heavier than the last. He closed the door behind him with a soft click, shutting out the world, and just like that, Christmas Eve came to an end.

Chapter 13
The Fifth House of Gamalaot

It was nine o'clock on Christmas morning, and though the sky stretched clear without a single cloud to break its expanse, the realm of Avalon below seemed covered in shadow. There was no sun, and with its absence, something about the day felt heavy, as if the sun itself had given up its place in the sky. The promise of warmth, of light, was gone, and in its place, a quiet chill.

Gav stirred from his bed, his movements heavy and slow, a weight pressing on his chest. His feet dragged across the floor, each step a labor, each breath a sigh.

"Merry Christmas, Gav!" Wiglaf's voice boomed from the table, cheerful and sunny, like the sun breaking through a stubborn fog.

Gav said nothing. His lips remained sealed, his eyes distant, as though the words had not reached him at all.

"Yes, Merry Christmas indeed," came another voice, smooth and measured.

It was a voice Gav knew well, and it carried a weight that straightened his slouched spine, pulling him upright as though an invisible hand had gripped his shoulders. His body responded before his mind could catch up, standing at attention, rigid and wary.

"At ease, cadet," said Arthur, his tone laced with amusement. He sat at the table, a cup of tea cradled in his hands, steam curling upward like a wisp of smoke. His chuckle was soft, almost imperceptible, but it carried a knowing edge.

"Aye, Gav, take a seat! I made yer plate up! Don't let it go cold now."

"It's quite good," Arthur remarked, his eyes flicking toward Gav as he spoke. He took another sip of his tea, the steam rising up to his nose. "I've never had a better soppes dorre anywhere else, Wiglaf. Truly, you've outdone yourself."

Gav took his seat at the table; a large plate piled high with bread that was toasted to a golden crisp; its surface fragrant with the sweet warmth of spices, a soft note of cinnamon and nutmeg, resting in a shallow pool of creamy custard.

"Ye flatter me, Arthur. Ye be too kind, indeed."

Gav sat quietly at the table, his utensils idly picking and poking at the toasted bread on his plate.

"Gav," Arthur began, his voice calm and measured, "I'm here at Wiglaf's request."

"I've been feelin' mighty rotten 'bout last night," Wiglaf added, his tone uncharacteristically somber.

Gav looked up at the two men, his emerald green eyes softening as he took in their expressions. He could sense the gravity in their faces.

"Wiglaf thought I might be able to better answer some of your questions," Arthur continued. "But Gav, I expect you to, in turn, answer mine. Understand?"

"Yes, sir," Gav said, his voice steady despite the knot of anxiety tightening in his chest. He broke a piece of bread free with his fork, more out of habit than hunger.

"What would you like to know?" Arthur asked, leaning forward slightly, his hands clasped on the table.

Gav hesitated, his eyes flicking to Wiglaf before returning to Arthur.

"He be askin' 'bout his brother," Wiglaf interjected, his voice low.

The two men shared a grim look, their expressions darkening. Arthur sighed, his shoulders slumping slightly as he leaned back in his chair.

"Gav," Arthur said, his tone gentle but probing, "how did you come to know about your brother?"

Gav fidgeted in his seat, his fingers tightening around the fork. "I, well…" he began, his voice faltering. He took a deep breath, steadying himself. "I hope this doesn't sound rude, sir, but I'd like to hear about him first. I've been in the dark ever since I got here. If I can just get some answers first, I promise to tell you everything."

Arthur studied him for a moment, his gaze thoughtful. Then, to Gav's surprise, the man smiled, a warm, approving smile that softened the lines of his face. "You're a fine knight in the making, Gav," Arthur said, his voice filled with genuine admiration.

At this, Wiglaf pushed himself up from the table, the wood creaking under his weight. He shuffled over to the bookshelf, his eyes landing on a dark, imposing book, the one with glittering stones set into its spine, each one glinting with an otherworldly light. Wiglaf lifted the book from the shelf, dust erupting into the air as he blew across the cover.

"In here," Wiglaf said, laying the book on the table with a heavy thud.

A strange pressure emanated from the book, and Gav felt his chest tighten as Arthur reached for it, pulling open the pages. The air grew heavier, the room quieter, as if the very walls were holding their breath.

"Look here, Gav," Arthur said, pointing to a page filled with black-and-white images.

Gav leaned forward, his eyes narrowing as he studied the picture. It was a group of knights, standing together in solemn formation. At the top of the page, bold letters spelled out: *Order of the Midnight Talons*.

"Order of the Midnight Talons," Gav read aloud, his voice tinged with curiosity.

"Aye," Wiglaf said, his tone heavy. "The fifth house of Gamalaot."

"But I thought there were only four houses?" Gav asked, his brow furrowing.

"Aye, four now," Wiglaf replied. "The Talons were, uh, disbanded some years ago."

"Gamalaot was built upon the five houses," Arthur explained, his voice taking on a lecturing tone, as if he were recounting a history lesson. "The five founders of the Round: Sir Siegfried de Charny Lambelle, Gawain the Green, Blue Hand Geoffroi, Godfrey Leonhardt, and Sir Artorias Pendragon. The houses were at first so named to trace the lineage of these chivalrous men, but centuries would pass, families would mix, and the houses would instead represent their ideals."

Gav's eyes remained fixed on the page, his gaze drawn to a tall boy who looked remarkably similar to him. The resemblance was uncanny—the same sharp jawline, the same intense eyes. But where Gav's expression was open and curious, the boy in the photo looked severe and cold.

"And my brother," Gav said, his voice barely above a whisper.

"Mordred Lohot Ragnell," Arthur said, his voice heavy with a mix of disgust and sadness. "Youngest knight made captain in over two centuries."

"Mordred," Gav repeated, the name feeling strange on his tongue. He stared at the photo, at his brother's face. Mordred's eyes looked black and vacant, his expression devoid of warmth. He wasn't smiling. Everything about him seemed severe, from the set of his jaw to the way his black hair fell stiffly to his shoulders, as if even his hair lacked any sense of humor.

"Brilliant swordsman," Arthur added, his tone grudgingly respectful. "Not unlike yourself."

Gav's chest tightened as he studied the image, his mind racing with questions. *What had happened to Mordred? Why had he been erased from Gav's life? And why did Arthur and Wiglaf seem so reluctant to speak of him?*

"Sir," Gav said, his voice trembling as he looked up at Arthur. "What happened to him?"

Wiglaf and Arthur exchanged a glance, their expressions heavy with reluctance. The silence stretched between them, thick and suffocating, until Gav couldn't bear it any longer.

"Please, sir," Gav pleaded, his voice cracking under the weight of his desperation. "I need to know."

Arthur sighed, his shoulders slumping as if the burden of the truth was too much to bear. "Gav," he began, "the Order of the Midnight Talons was formally declared excommunicated after they attacked the Ragnell estate. Mordred, your brother and the man we knew, died during the assault. The assault he led."

Gav's breathing slowed, his mind struggling to process the words. "But that would mean…" he started, his voice trailing off as the realization hit him like a punch to the gut. His entire body stiffened, his hands gripping the edge of the table until his knuckles turned white. "He attacked his family."

"Slaughtered them," Wiglaf added, his voice filled with a fury that made Gav flinch. The big man's hands clenched into fists, his jaw tightening as if the memory alone was enough to ignite his rage.

"But why?!" Gav cried. "Why would he do that?!"

Arthur's gaze softened, but there was no comfort in his eyes—only a deep, unshakable sadness. "I think you know," he said quietly.

Gav's face fell, the color draining from his cheeks as the truth settled over him like a shroud. He did know. It was the reason everyone looked at him with that same foul, loathsome expression. It was the reason he had been treated like an outcast from the moment he arrived at Gamalaot. It was the reason Wiglaf had been tasked with watching over him, the reason Arthur had taken such a keen interest in his training. And it was the reason Mordred had done what he had done.

"The prophecy," Gav whispered, his voice barely audible. He pushed himself up from the chair, his legs trembling beneath him as he took a step back. The room seemed to spin around him, the walls closing in as the weight of the truth pressed down on him.

Arthur and Wiglaf watched him in silence, their faces etched with a combination of pity and regret. Gav felt their eyes on him, but he couldn't meet their gaze. His mind was racing, his thoughts a chaotic whirlwind of fear and disbelief.

"The prophecy," Gav repeated, louder this time, his voice breaking. He turned to Arthur, his eyes wide and pleading. "What does it say? What does it mean for me?"

Arthur hesitated, his jaw tightening as if the words were too painful to speak. But before he could answer, Wiglaf stepped forward, his massive frame blocking Gav's view of the captain.

"Not now, boy," Wiglaf said, his voice firm but not unkind. "Yer not ready fer all that."

"But I need to know!" Gav shouted, his voice cracking with desperation. "If it's about me, if it's why Mordred... why he did what he did, then I have a right to know!"

Wiglaf's expression softened, and he placed a heavy hand on Gav's shoulder. "Aye, ye do," he said, his voice gentle. "But not this day. Not like this. Ye need time to take in what's been said. And we... we need time to figure out how to share the rest with ye."

Gav stepped back, defiant. Without a word, he disappeared into his bedroom for but a moment, the faint sound of rustling papers echoing through the cabin. When Gav returned, his hands were steady, gripping a stack of letters. He flipped through them, his fingers tracing each envelope with purpose until he found the one he was looking for. The one with the prophecy written on it.

"What does it mean?" Gav's voice was quiet but insistent, his tone sharper than before.

"Gav... Where in the world did ye get these?"

But Gav didn't budge. His gaze was fixed, unwavering, as he repeated, "What does it mean?"

Arthur's eyes flicked over the note, his brow furrowing in surprise, his face betraying an emotion Gav had never quite seen before—shock, and perhaps something deeper. He studied the letter with an intensity that spoke volumes.

Gav, unblinking, shifted his focus from Arthur to the letter and then back again, his expression expectant, demanding. The silence stretched between them, yet neither man spoke. The only sound was the low crackling of the fire in the hearth.

Gav's stare lingered, and in that stillness, he could almost hear the words of the letter echoing through his mind, walking step by step alongside Arthur. It was as if they were reading together:

Loke, Gavain, swift and doom-driven, ride thou now as sworn in the hour of thy birth, ride forth to seek him whose coming heralds the unmaking of days. For the Green Knight waits at the world's dim edge, where the last dawn lingers, and the tides of time tremble. Hie thee to the Green Chapel, so commands the Lord Bertilak, when thy knighthood is ripe as the rotting fruit of Yggdrasil, there to take the stroke thou didst deal in an age when the earth was young, to be repaid when the New Year bleeds upon the snow, and the Wheel of Heaven groans toward silence. A boon he grants thee; a life unbroken by the brand of cowardice, yet bound to his own in the weaving of wyrd. With a fell and furious start, he blesses thee with wings of shadow, as the reins of fate twist in his grasp. Thy breath is his breath, thy death his own. So burst forth from the hall-door, his heart like thunder in thy breast, till the sparks of the world's end fly from thy steed's hooves! To what kingdom thou belongest, none now know, for kingdoms crumble, and the stars themselves shall soon be swallowed. Yet ride, ride to thy father's seat, and take the throne ere the final night falls. Thus shalt thou play thy part in the Christmas Game. And when the last candle gutters, when the Green Chapel stands as the final hall of men, then shall all debts be paid, and the horn of doom sound at last.

"Gav," Arthur said, his expression hardening, his usual warmth replaced with a seriousness that made the room feel colder. "Where did you get this?"

"Tell me what it means first," Gav shot back, his voice a fever-pitch, a trace of defiance still lingering.

Arthur's eyes narrowed, and his voice dropped with weight. "Gav, I've been more than fair with you." The familiar ease had left his tone, replaced by something more stern. "Where did you get these letters?"

Gav hesitated, the truth lodged somewhere deep within him, a knot he couldn't quite untangle. "I don't know," he admitted, the words feeling heavy as they left his mouth.

Wiglaf, standing nearby, shot Gav a knowing look. "Come on, boy," he said, his voice soft but still strong. "Ye can trust us, aye."

"I really don't know!" Gav insisted, his frustration rising. "I just started getting these letters, and we've been writing back and forth. That's all."

Arthur's eyes bore into him, his gaze unwavering. "These letters…How did you receive them? Were they delivered to you?"

"Yes," Gav answered, his tone becoming more defensive.

Arthur's eyes tightened; his next question made Gav's stomach drop. "A black raven?"

"Yes… named Titus," Gav replied, his confusion deepening. "But how did you know?"

Arthur leaned back slightly, his face settling into a grim expression. "I see," he murmured, as if piecing together something. "Gav, I believe these letters were sent to you by members of The Midnight Talons. Have they asked you to do anything strange?"

"No! Nothing," Gav answered quickly, shaking his head as if to push away the lingering doubt.

Arthur's face remained unreadable, but there was a quiet urgency behind his next words. "I will need to take them." He rose from his seat, the movement deliberate, final.

"Of course," Gav responded apologetically. "I'm sorry. I didn't know I was doing anything wrong or…"

"Stop, Gav," Arthur interjected, holding up his hand, the gesture cutting off the rest of Gav's sentence. "You haven't done anything wrong." His voice softened slightly, but the gravity remained. "I only wish you had come to me sooner with these."

"Yes, sir," Gav replied, his voice tight with both confusion and unease.

"I don't mean to frighten you, Gav, but if The Midnight Talons have contacted you, it means they are close and watching. Gav, they mean to kill you. You need to keep your wits about you."

Gav's brow furrowed, his heart racing as his mind struggled to process the weight of those words. "But, sir," he stammered, "why do they want me dead exactly? Why does everyone hate me? I know that the prophecy is like some sort of curse, but I don't even understand what it means!"

Arthur paused, as if choosing his words carefully before continuing. "Gav, you're friends with de Boron, correct?"

"Percy? Yes, sir."

"His father is quite the historian, and from what I hear, his son is no slouch either." Arthur's eyes narrowed thoughtfully. "The lot of you—you, de Boron and Edmund—should familiarize yourselves with the *Gamalaot Historia*. Start at the beginning, and all should be made clear."

Gav nodded, though confusion still clouded his thoughts. "Okay," he said, trying not to hide his disappointment. He had hoped for something more concrete, more immediate answers.

A weariness settled upon Arthur's face, a slow erosion of tension that left a ghost of a smile. "Gav," he said, his voice low. "I don't want you to think I'm simply deflecting. To answer your question fully requires much history. Should you come up with more questions after brushing up on the historia, please come find me."

Gav's eyes met his, and though there was still uncertainty, there was a flicker of understanding in Arthur's gaze—a promise that the answers were there, hidden in the past.

"Alright now, moving on, I want you outside, cadet," Arthur barked, his tone brisk.

"Outside, sir?"

"Put on your gear and meet me out front," Arthur replied, already turning to leave.

The door swung shut behind him with a soft thud, leaving Gav and Wiglaf standing in the quiet of the cabin, their faces filled with confusion.

Wiglaf, ever the steady presence, shook his head. "Don't be lookin' to me, boy," he said, a wry grin pulling at his lips. "I haven't the foggiest what Arthur's on about. But best ye follow his lead. The man won't lead ye astray."

Gav looked at the door, still puzzled but feeling a shift within him. The weight of uncertainty had been lifted, at least for the moment, by the fragments of answers he'd been given. Yet, beneath that relief, something stirred, a quiet unease he couldn't ignore. Something felt off, like a knot that tightened every time he tried to push it away. But it was Christmas, and for now, he chose to leave that feeling where it was.

"Catch," Arthur said, throwing a wooden training sword toward the boy.

"You want to spar, sir?"

"Not quite," Arthur said, limbering up his shoulders and neck. "Under normal circumstances, I would teach you this technique further on in your training. It's no secret that you're quite gifted with a blade, Gav. But the Talons are not to be taken lightly. You ought to know some counterattacks should they get the drop on you."

"Alright," Gav said with trepidation. He picked up the training sword and took the position opposite Arthur.

"I want you to do your best to guard and defend against my attacks."

"Yes, sir."

Arthur came at Gav without warning, without a sign, his wooden sword slicing the air in a sharp arc. Gav met each blow with a parry, his hands moving fast, the wood thudding against his own in a steady rhythm. But Arthur did not relent. Again and again, the strikes came, fast and sure, from every angle, a dance of violence that never ended. Gav was pushed back, step by step, his breath quickening as the weight of each strike grew heavier. And in the end, there was no more room to retreat. With one final, decisive blow, Arthur sent Gav's training sword flying from his grasp, leaving him standing, empty-handed, the wooden tip of his blade at his throat.

"What's your next move, Gav?"

"I don't have one, sir. I've lost."

"I see," Arthur said, lowering his blade. "Let's go again. This time, you take the offensive. Do your best to disarm me."

Gav nodded, grabbing the training sword and taking position.

And so he attacked, offering Arthur the same vigorous onslaught he had so unleashed upon him only moments ago. And while Gav's movements were not quite as deft or swift, he did eventually break through, and Arthur's blade went flying. Though he had a suspicion that perhaps Arthur had allowed this to happen. Still, Gav held his blade toward Arthur's face, waiting.

"Continue striking," Arthur instructed.

"But you're unarmed!"

"Strike me, Gav."

He hesitated a moment, but obeyed the command. He swung this blade overhead and brought it down with a heavy slam. Arthur raised his forearm to meet the wooden blade's edge. To Gav's surprise, the blade collided and recoiled as if hitting another.

Arthur smiled, pressing Gav with swings of his arm. It glowed with an ethereal white halo. Gav once more fell into the defensive, raising his blade haphazardly to meet Arthur's strikes. And just when Gav was about at his limit, Arthur jumped back and took an unguarded stance. Gav stared a moment until he realized that Arthur had just walked him back to their starting positions.

"Amazing."

"It's a technique of my own invention," Arthur said. "Should you ever find yourself without a weapon, you can still defend yourself. You might even take victory."

Arthur walked over to his sword and took on a ready position.

"I'm going to come at you, Gav. Should I disarm you, concentrate, and channel all the magic you can into your sword arm. Make a fist and swing as if you're still wielding a blade."

The pair exchanged glancing dints, but of course, Arthur overwhelmed the young cadet, and Gav's training blade went careening into the snow.

"Concentrate," said Arthur, giving Gav but a moment as he swung his blade overhead.

Gav shut his eyes tight, lifting his right arm to greet the blow. A warmth, thick and strange, gathered in his fingertips, though whether it was magic or simply his own mind playing tricks, he couldn't be certain. Still, his arm held firm, and from him, faint threads of white wisping light flittered into the air.

Arthur's blade crashed down upon him.

"Ouch!" Gav cried, pulling his arm away in pain.

Arthur lowered his blade.

"That was good, Gav."

"Good? It didn't work."

"Can you move your arm?"

Gav carefully articulated with his sore arm. He felt the blood pulsing through his veins, but otherwise had a full range of motion.

"Yeah, it just stings."

"If you hadn't been doing it correctly, your arm would be broken," Arthur said with a laugh. "I'm, of course, speaking from personal experience. Keep at it. You'll master it in no time."

Arthur then turned his body to Wiglaf.

"I best be off," he said.

"Aye," said Wiglaf. "If yer ain't busy come this evenin', yer be more than welcome fer supper. After Gav and I catch it."

At that, Gav shot Wiglaf a surprised and concerned look.

"Take care, friend," Arthur said, waving Wiglaf goodbye. "You too, Gav, and Merry Christmas."

"Merry Christmas, sir."

Arthur trudged down the snow-covered road, his figure slowly swallowed by the pale expanse, until he was lost to the distant grey murk.

"Say, Gav," Wiglaf said, placing his massive hand on Gav's shoulder. "I hope ye find it in yer heart to forgive this old fool. I never meant to keep ye in the shadows on this."

Gav hugged the goliath.

"It's alright," he said. "Thank you."

"What say you we go in an open yer presents?"

"Presents?"

"Aye! It's Christmas! Don't tell me yer never celebrated no Christmas before?"

"I have! But you didn't have to get me anything! I didn't get you anything!"

"Your company be bein' the real gift for me, lad!"

They stepped back through the door, the cool air sticking to their coats. Wiglaf reached out, his fingers brushing the edges of a hand-wrapped gift, its paper striped in the colors of Christmas.

"Merry Christmas, Gav," Wiglaf said, handing over the giftbox. "I had a fair bit o' help with that there wrappin'," Wiglaf chuckled, eyeing his massive hands with a sheepish grin. "I ain't exactly famed for me delicate touch."

Gav eased the lid off the box, his fingers respecting the intricate wrapping of it, as if the box itself was just as integral to the gift as what lay inside. He pulled out a sweater, the deep green of it like the earth after a spring rain, the collar and cuffs trimmed in a red so bright it almost seemed to glow in the dimly lit cabin.

"They be yer family house colors, boy. Had 'em made up by the same tailor in town yer mother favored."

He held it up for a moment, running his hands over the woven fabric, as if trying to feel some connection to his family, the warmth of them, before he slipped it over his head.

"I love it, Wiglaf. Thank you!"

"And of course, yer mother sent a little somethin' for ye. Had Breca fetch it. Breca!"

Wiglaf's giant bear roared from outside.

"Aye, ye can squeeze yer way through that door, ye damn bear!"

Wiglaf shuffled over to the door, his gait slow. The door trembled in its frame, groaning under the weight of Breca's growling outside. He disappeared behind it, his broad shoulders vanishing into the snow blind light, and when he came back, he carried with him several plates and dishes.

"Seems we're ready fer the feast! That mother o' yours has laid out a spread fit fer a warrior!"

Gav picked up the card Wiglaf had dropped, carrying the tall tower of pans and dishes to the kitchen.

Gav,

Merry Christmas, dearie. Thought you could use a taste of home. I've made all your favorites...just need a little heat to bring 'em back to life. Now, you take care not to get yourself into trouble, alright? Be good. Be safe. —Love Mom

"That mum of yours be spoilin' us, lad!"

Gav wiped his eyes, his cold, shaking palm brushing away the tears. There was a mix of emotions inside him, like a sky both stormy and clear. He didn't know whether to smile or cry, but in the end, it was love that held him firm; the quiet, enduring warmth of love he always knew at Christmas.

Chapter 14
The Gamalaot Historia

"At attention, Cadets!" Arthur's voice rang out, piercing and clear, carrying a vigor and chipperness unfamiliar to the trainees.

The boys and girls of the Crimson Mane barracks fell into line, their chatter, once lively with tales of holiday adventures and the warmth of shared memories, now quieted to a hush. They stood in formation, their young faces turned toward their captain, their breaths held in anticipation. Arthur paced before them, his boots striking the wooden floor with a steady rhythm, his eyes alight with a fire that seemed to burn brighter with each step.

"The Winter Festival is upon us!" he declared, his voice swelling like a tide. The room erupted in a brief, thunderous applause, a burst of noise that filled the barracks like a sudden storm. Yet, amidst the clamor, a few cadets remained still, Gav among them, their bodies rigid, their eyes locked on Arthur, waiting for the next command, the next word that would shape their day.

Arthur raised a hand, and the room fell silent once more. "For those who are new among us," he began, his tone softening slightly, "let me explain. The Winter Festival is the grand finale of the season, a celebration that ushers in the new year. And at its heart lies the Battle of Camlann, a mock battle between the rival houses, held every winter. This tradition, born from the memory of King Artorias's final stand, is meant to inspire us all. It calls us to rise, to become heroes in our own right, to carry forward the legacy of Gamalaot."

He paused, his gaze sweeping over the cadets, each one standing a little taller under his scrutiny. "The house that defeats the most opponents and holds the center stronghold claims victory. We, the Crimson Manes, have long defended this honor with pride. But," he added, his voice dropping slightly, "I won't lie to you. Wins these past years have been lean for us. We've faced our share of defeats."

The cadets stood firm, their eyes fixed on Arthur, their hearts beating in unison with the rhythm of his words.

"This tradition is also a chance for our senior knights-in-training to lead a full battalion. To command, to strategize, to prove themselves not just as fighters, but as leaders."

A low hum of excitement rippled through the ranks, a restless energy that seemed to vibrate in the air. The cadets' hearts quickened, their breaths coming faster, their hands tightening into fists at their sides. Who would be their leader?

"Daniel von Blumenthal," Arthur called out. He waited, his gaze fixed on the senior cadet, as the young man stepped forward to join him. There was a weight to the moment, a gravity that seemed to press down on the room.

"Sir Daniel," Arthur continued, his tone carrying the solemnity of a knight bestowing a great honor, "upon my recommendation, will command his chosen squad this Saturday at Camlann Field. Sir Daniel."

The boy, still more youth than man, his voice caught somewhere between boyish timidity and the deeper resonance he was striving for, cleared his throat and nodded.

"Right," he began, his words tentative but gaining strength as he spoke. "After conferring with Sir Arthur and observing you all this first semester, I have decided on the following knights to represent us in the Battle of Camlann."

A hush fell over the barracks. The cadets stood rigid, their spines straight, their eyes wide with hope. They were young, but they tried to carry themselves with the same gravitas a soldier might, awaiting their fate. Their breaths were held tight, their hearts pounding in their chests, as they waited for the names that would define their place in this grand tradition.

"Alastair Dunsmore," Daniel announced, his voice cutting through the anticipation. Then, after a pause, another. "Lyonel Vexford." And another. "Galeas Edmund."

Nora's eyes lit up, a spark of pride igniting within her as she turned to glance at her brothers down the line. Ed, ever the boisterous one, was already clapping Gale on the shoulder, his grin wide and uncontainable. Gale, for his part, stood tall, stoic, though the faintest hint of a smile tugged at the corners of his mouth.

"Torian Faelan," Daniel continued, raising his voice to be heard over the growing murmur of excitement. "Armand Ashecomb. And Gavain Ragnell."

At the sound of Gav's name, the room froze, the air thick with surprise. It was a rare thing, this moment of silence, and Gav felt it settle over him like a heavy cloak. He had grown accustomed to the sidelong glances, the whispered words, the quiet disdain that seemed to follow him like a shadow. But then, something unexpected happened.

"Alright, Gav!" Ed's voice broke the silence, loud and full of warmth, as he rushed over to clap Gav on the back, his hands rough but reassuring.

"Fantastic!" Nora chimed in, her voice bright and clear as she grabbed Gav's hand, her grip firm and steady.

And then, slowly, like the first rays of sunlight breaking through a storm, the room began to cheer. The sound started small, a ripple of applause, but it grew, swelling into a wave of support that washed over Gav, lifting him up in a way he had never known.

"Hey, Daniel," Gav called out, his voice carrying a note of uncertainty as he jogged to catch up with the older boy. He slowed to a walk, his boots scuffing against the ground, his hands fidgeting at his sides. "Did you... Did you mean to pick me?"

Daniel stopped and turned, his expression calm but firm. "Of course I did," he replied, his voice steady, leaving no room for doubt.

"Really?" Gav pressed. "You mean Arthur didn't put you up to it or..."

Daniel cut him off with a sharp shake of his head, his eyes narrowing slightly as if to emphasize his point. "I saw your little sparring match with Lambelle," he said, his tone matter-of-fact. "And my brother Tristian says you're the top swordsman in the freshman class." He paused, his gaze locking onto Gav's, and there was something in his eyes—a flicker of respect, perhaps, or maybe just the cold calculation of a commander assessing his tools. "We're going to need that sword arm of yours."

Gav stood there for a moment, the words sinking in, the weight of them settling on his shoulders. It wasn't pity, it wasn't charity—it was recognition. And for the first time in a long while, he felt something stir within him, something that had been buried under layers of doubt and disdain. It was small, fragile, but it was there: a spark of pride.

Gav watched with a quiet smile as Daniel strode off, his face set in a grin as eager as a man ready to fight. He moved toward Arthur and Armand, each of them bearing the same fierce smiles, all of them ravenous to talk of the battle that lay ahead, of the plans they'd formed, and the victory they meant to carve out of it.

"Gav!" Nora called out. She threw her arms around him, pulling him into a firm embrace. "Simply amazing! A first year in the Battle of Camlann! Gav, that's amazing!"

"No love for your dear, beloved brother?" Ed said, hanging off of Gale's shoulders. "That's downright cold, sister."

"Leave her alone," said Gale, laughing slightly. "Looks like we'll be working together, Gav."

"Yeah!"

"Say," Nora said, her voice breaking through the quiet chatter in the room. She glanced around, her sharp eyes scanning the faces of the cadets, a faint crease forming between her brows. "Where's Percy? You talked to him?"

Gav shook his head, his expression blank. "Haven't seen him since before break," he replied, his tone flat, as though the question barely warranted his attention.

"He's over there," Gale interjected, his voice calm and measured. He tilted his head slightly, gesturing toward the far side of the room without turning to look.

Gav and Nora followed his gaze, and there he was. Percy, standing apart from the crowd, his hands moving in a slow, mechanical clap as he offered halfhearted congratulations to the chosen champions. There was nothing overtly rude in his demeanor, but there was a distance to him, a detachment that made it clear his mind was elsewhere.

"You haven't talked to him?" Nora asked, her voice rising slightly, a note of incredulity creeping in. "He didn't say anything to you?"

"No," Gav replied, his tone still even, though a flicker of confusion passed over his face. "Nothing."

"Stupid boys," Nora muttered under her breath, her hands planting firmly on her hips as she exhaled sharply, her annoyance palpable.

"Was he supposed to?" Gav asked.

"Yeah, I told him to," Nora shot back, her tone firm, her eyes narrowing as she met his gaze. "But don't worry. As always, I'll straighten it out." Her lips curved into a small, determined smile, the kind she wore whenever she was already plotting her next move. She gave Gav a reassuring pat on the arm before turning on her heel and striding off, her steps quick and purposeful.

"Cadets!" Arthur's voice rang out a halting command, cutting through the din of excitement. The room fell silent, the cadets snapping back to attention, their faces turning toward their captain. "I, too, share in your enthusiasm," Arthur continued, his tone softening slightly, though his posture remained rigid, his hands clasped behind his back. "But until the day of the battle, your training will resume as usual. Except for our chosen champions, that is." He paused, his gaze sweeping over the select few who had been named. "You fine knights will no doubt need the week to prepare your stratagems. I've already arranged your absences with your instructors."

A collective groan rose from the ranks, a low rumble of discontent that echoed through the barracks. Arthur's expression hardened, his jaw tightening as he raised a hand to silence them. "I understand the frustration that comes with anticipation," he said, his voice growing stern, each word measured and deliberate. "But let us not forget our code of chivalry, cadets." He paused again, his eyes narrowing as he surveyed the room. "I fear I may have led off with too casual a demeanor, so I will be lenient this time. But let's be ever mindful of our decorum. We are knights of Gamalaot, after all. Am I clear, cadets?"

"Yes, sir!" the room responded in unison, their voices ringing out with a force that seemed to shake the very walls.

"Dismissed," Arthur said, his tone final, his hand dropping to his side as he turned on his heel and strode from the room.

Gav lingered for a moment, his eyes scanning the crowd of dispersing students, hoping to catch a glimpse of Percy. But the boy had already slipped into the throng, his figure disappearing among the sea of uniforms and eager faces. Gav sighed, his shoulders slumping slightly as he turned and made his way to the long commons table, where the other champions had gathered. He took a seat, his mind still preoccupied, his thoughts a tangled web of anticipation, doubt, and the faint, lingering hope that perhaps this was another chance to prove himself.

Daniel von Blumenthal stepped forward, taking the position Captain Arthur had just vacated. Behind him, he dragged a rolling chalkboard, its surface already marked with a rough sketch of the battlefield. He stood tall, though his shoulders carried a slight stiffness, as if the weight of command was still an unfamiliar burden. His voice, while earnest, lacked the natural authority that Arthur wielded so effortlessly. Yet, he pressed on, his determination evident in the way he gripped the chalk and squared his jaw.

"I've drawn up here a layout of the field," Daniel began. He gestured to the chalkboard, where lines and symbols mapped out the terrain. "Though the thought is indeed alluring, the battle will prove far more perilous if we rush headlong to seize the center stronghold." He paused, his eyes scanning the faces of the champions gathered around the table. "Those of us who've been around a while remember how this played out last year. Wulfric Woolfmane and The Claws tried to overrun the center stronghold until Garrick Thorne burned it to the ground. His pegasus knights, already in position, turned the tide with one deft strike."

Gav glanced at the others, noting the nods of agreement and the thoughtful expressions. They seemed to trust him, or—at the very least—respected his reasoning. Daniel tapped the chalkboard again, his voice growing firmer as he continued. "The fire left their position wide open, and that's when the Azure Stripes hit them from behind, cutting them down without mercy. That's exactly why we should focus on the southeastern fort instead. It's our best shot. A stronghold we can actually hold. Once we're dug in there, we'll pick our moment to strike the center."

Alastair Dunsmore leaned forward, his brow furrowed. "You want all of us defending this position?" he asked, his tone skeptical. "Shouldn't some of us, say a pair, be out scouting, collecting bodies?"

Before Daniel could respond, Torian Faelan cut in, his voice sharp with impatience. "You shouldn't be questioning him," he snapped. "He's our commander. We simply execute his orders."

"I also don't think downing enemies is a reliable source of points," Gale said, his tone measured. "Unless you're an absolute murderous tank out there, I think the points are likely too spread out between the houses."

Daniel nodded, his expression resolute. "Capturing the center stronghold is the primary objective," he said flatly. "The extra points awarded for routing enemies are really to help decide the runners-up."

Gav, sensing the tension in the room, offered a tentative nod. "Sounds good," he said, his voice quiet but firm. The other champions turned to look at him, their gazes lingering for a moment longer than necessary. He felt the weight of their scrutiny, the unspoken question of whether he truly belonged among them. Yet, he felt no bitterness. In time, he mused, all would find its place—if he could just make himself useful. "How do you plan to take the fort?" he asked, his tone earnest.

Daniel turned back to the chalkboard, his chalk scraping against the surface as he marked a path with a firm, deliberate stroke. "This route is the one we tread," he said, his voice steady. "It is not without its pitfalls; what it may lack in swiftness, it more than compensates in protection." He paused, his eyes meeting Gav's for a brief moment before sweeping over the rest of the group. "We move in staggered pairs, hold the fort, and strike when the moment is right. That is the plan."

For hours, they all sat there, eyes fixed on Daniel as he laid out the finer details of the plan, steady in his words, though his hands fidgeted a bit as he drew his chalk lines. It was just like Torian had said—Daniel was the one who moved the pieces, and they were nothing more than pawns in his game. Whether victory or defeat would be their fate was not theirs to decide, but rested in the hands of their captain and their execution of his will. It was about following the orders, plain and simple, and doing it right. But in that room, there was something else; within that chamber, a strange confidence took root. Gav, perhaps more so than the others, felt it stir within him; an eager hope radiating from the ground and sparking in the air. Confidence. It filled the space, thick. Maybe it was a fool's kind of confidence, the kind that doesn't know the cost of duty yet, but it was there all the same. He could not deny the stirring in his heart, the quiet thrill of conviction that burned brightly within him, undaunted by doubt. And above all, it made him feel something unnamable, beyond the usual anxiety and dread—maybe it was excitement, or maybe hope, whatever it was called, it was something that wouldn't let him sit still.

"Let's plan to meet again tomorrow morning," Daniel said, his voice carrying a note of finality as he straightened his posture and glanced around the table. "Oh, and I almost forgot." He paused, his brow furrowing slightly as if recalling an important detail. "As I said before, I think it wise for us to move in pairs—each with a companion to watch over the other. We'll also be eating dinner together every night this week to build camaraderie." He nodded, as if affirming the plan to himself before continuing. "Now, for the pairs. Let's see..."

He scanned the group, his eyes narrowing in thought. "Dunsmore and Vexford—you two get on well, right?" he asked, his tone casual but firm.

The boys exchanged a glance, their expressions unreadable for a moment before they nodded in unison. "Yeah, we're good," Alastair said, his voice steady, while Lyonel gave a quick, affirmative grunt.

"Edmund and Ragnell," Daniel continued, his gaze shifting to Gale and Gav, "and Faelan and Ashecomb."

Gav and Gale exchanged a look—one of those simple, unspoken glances that Gav had often seen Gale share with his brothers.

"I would suggest spending time with your partner this week," Daniel said firmly, his tone leaving no room for debate. "Could be the difference between us winning or losing." He paused, his eyes sweeping over the group one last time. "Alright, dismissed."

The champions began to rise from the table, their movements slow and deliberate as they processed the plan. Gav lingered for a moment, his mind already turning over the possibilities of the week ahead. He glanced at Gale, who gave him a small, reassuring nod.

"You hungry, Gav?" Gale asked, slinging his bag over his shoulder as he stood. "Just about lunch time."

"Uh, yeah, I could eat," Gav replied, pushing himself up from the table. His stomach growled softly in agreement, and he realized he hadn't eaten breakfast. None of them had.

"Great! We can go over our formations while we eat."

They made their way across the snowy field, their boots crunching against the frozen ground with each step. The air was crisp and cold, biting at their cheeks, but the sun hung high in the sky, casting a pale, wintry light over the campus. The commissary came into view, its windows fogged with warmth, calling to them with a delicious smell that wafted on the breeze. At this, the boys quickened their pace.

Inside, the place was quieter than usual, emptier, the way it gets when most of the cadets are still holed up in class. Gav noticed it right away—the usual buzz of chatter and clatter of trays was muted, replaced by a calm, almost peaceful atmosphere. It felt like the room had more space to breathe, fewer eyes boring holes into him. They settled into their usual spot at the table, not saying much, just waiting for the others.

Soon enough, they came—Leif and Ed, their laughter echoing as they entered, followed by the twins, Bor and Tor, who moved in perfect sync, as always. Gav caught a glimpse of Nora talking to Lucan as they entered the commissary together; she too joined them, sliding into the seat next to Gav. But there was still a seat missing, and no sign of Percy.

"You talk to Percy yet?" Nora asked.

"Haven't had the chance," Gav admitted, his voice low.

"For goodness' sake!" she exclaimed, her voice tinged with exasperation. She shook her head, her hands flailing slightly as if to emphasize her point.

"It's true, sis," Gale chimed in. "We've been busy since this morning."

"Fair enough," she huffed.

"Hey, and since when are you friends with Lucan?" Gav asked, perhaps with a little more snark than intended. "You two looked rather chummy."

Nora's face flushed red, and she quickly looked down at her tray, avoiding his gaze. "Oh," she said, her voice softer now. "Look, he's not really that bad."

"She's got a thing for him, I reckon!" Ed interjected, his voice loud and teasing as he made exaggerated kissing noises across the table. "They were exchanging letters all holiday!"

"It's not like that!" Nora shot back, her face turning an even deeper shade of red. She crossed her arms over her chest, her eyes narrowing at Ed.

"Wait, really?" Gav said, his eyebrows shooting up in surprise.

"Get off it!" Nora slammed her hand on the table, her voice rising. "He's interested in Minnie. Thinks wyverns are pretty cool. Besides, even if I did fancy him, that wouldn't be anyone's business either!"

The table fell quiet, the sudden outburst silencing the usual banter. Leif and Ed snickered to themselves, but they knew when to leave Nora well enough alone. Gale gave her a sympathetic look, while Gav simply stared at his tray, unsure of what to say next. The moment passed, and the conversation slowly picked up again, but the tension lingered, a reminder that even among friends, some lines were best left uncrossed.

"Now you!" Nora said, her voice insistent as she turned to Gav. Her eyes were fixed on him, her expression a mix of determination and frustration. "Let's go. We're settling this now." Before Gav could protest or even ask what she meant, she grabbed him by the arm, her grip firm and urgent, and pulled him along behind her. Without a word, she started toward the door, her steps quick and purposeful, leaving the others at the table to exchange puzzled glances.

They passed through the commissary doors, the cold air hitting them like a wall as they stepped into the snowy courtyard. Gav stumbled slightly, trying to keep up with Nora's brisk pace, but she didn't slow down. Her breath came out in visible puffs, her face set in an annoyed scowl as she marched toward the library. The quiet tension between them grew with each stride, the crunch of snow under their boots the only sound breaking the silence.

Truthfully, Gav was confused. He didn't quite grasp what Nora was playing at with all this talk about needing to speak with Percy. It didn't sit right with him, not knowing what she meant. All he knew was that he hadn't heard a word from Percy since they left for the holiday, and it gnawed at him a bit, not the silence so much, but the big deal Nora made of it. He wanted to ask Nora what she knew, what she wasn't telling him, but the look on her face kept him quiet. She was on a mission, and he was just along for the ride.

Finally, they reached the library, its tall, arched windows glowing warmly against the gray winter sky.

"I bet he's here," she said to herself, pushing the heavy wooden door open. The scent of old books and burning wood greeted them as they stepped inside. The library was quiet, the kind of quiet that felt almost sacred, broken only by the occasional crackle of the fireplace. Gav followed Nora as she made her way through the rows of bookshelves, her eyes scanning the room until they landed on Percy.

"I knew it."

He was set up at his favorite bench nearest to the fireplace, a book open in his lap and a steaming cup of tea resting on the table beside him. His posture was relaxed, his expression calm, but there was something distant about him, as if he were lost in thought. He didn't notice them at first, his gaze fixed on the pages in front of him, but as Nora and Gav approached, he looked up, his eyes widening slightly in surprise.

"You," Nora said, pointing at Percy while simultaneously forcing Gav to sit opposite him at the table. "You need to hash it out."

"Hash what out?" Gav asked, his brow furrowing as he looked between Nora and Percy. "Percy, are you mad at me?"

"No," Percy said curtly, keeping his eyes focused on the book in his hands. His tone was clipped, his posture stiff, and Gav couldn't help but feel a pang of unease.

"Percy!" Nora said, her voice rising in frustration. "Just tell him."

"Tell me what?"

"You're really making me do this?" Percy looked up from his book, his expression a mix of annoyance and resignation as he glared at Nora.

"Yes! You're hurting his feelings!"

"He's fine, Nora. You're projecting."

"Projecting?" Nora repeated, her hands flying to her hips.

"Yes, there isn't anything wrong. You're making it into a whole mess needlessly."

"You haven't said one word to your best friend since returning from holiday," Nora continued, her voice rising. "You didn't even ask him if he had a nice Christmas."

"Did you have a nice Christmas?" Percy said, looking directly at Gav, his tone flat and perfunctory.

"It was alright," Gav replied, his voice hesitant.

"That's good. Mine was quite alright as well." Percy then moved his head, directing his gaze toward Nora. "Happy?"

"No," Nora shouted, slamming her hands on the table. "Just tell him how you're feeling, Percy. You told me this morning that you…"

"Alright," Percy said, exasperatedly closing his book with a loud snap. He set it down on the table and turned to Gav, his expression softening slightly. "I know we haven't talked much lately. I suppose Nora is right somewhat…I should be honest with you. Before the holiday, I was… well, really upset. Mercie and I found that box of letters you'd hidden."

At this, Gav's face fell, and his heart sank.

"I didn't read them. Truthfully, I wasn't all that hurt that you kept them from me; it was the way you'd been sneaking off to write them at odd hours, like it was something I couldn't know. It felt like you were guarding some huge secret I couldn't be trusted with, and that… that hurt my pride a bit."

Gav wanted to express deep regret. He wanted to burst into tears and apologize for it all. But he was frozen.

"I've had time to think," Percy continued. "I'm sure you had your reasons. And I wasn't even going to say anything. I didn't want to make it a fight. I figured I would get over it at some point. But it's been eating at me."

"Percy," Gav started, his voice tinged with guilt. "I didn't…I didn't mean to upset you. I'm sorry."

"It's all alright, Gav," Percy said, his tone gentler, more natural now. "Rationally, I know you didn't know, and that you didn't mean to hurt my feelings, which is why I was intending to keep this to myself."

"You can be mad at me all you want," Nora said flippantly, crossing her arms. "Relationships require effort. Communication and openness. Not to be mean, but you two aren't exactly drowning in friends here. You can't afford not to invest in your relationship."

"Invest in our relationship?" Both Gav and Percy said in unison, snickering as they did. They shared a look, their laughter breaking the tension, and for a moment, it felt like old times again.

"I am sorry," Gav said again, his voice sincere.

"It's alright," Percy replied, his expression softening further. "I was just worried about you. We're friends, Gav. You can trust us."

"Yeah," Gav said, his chest sinking as the weight of Percy's words hit him. "I was being really stupid."

"So wait...letters?" Nora said, her eyes furrowing as she took a seat between the two boys. "What are you guys talking about?"

Gav sighed, running a hand through his hair. "I'm really sorry. To the both of you," he said, splitting his gaze between them. "A couple of months ago, I got a mysterious message delivered to me. It was around the time we learned about familiars. This person, or people...whoever they are, they said they could give me answers, information others wouldn't, but I had to keep it all secret."

"Gav," Nora said, her voice grave. "You have to tell someone."

"I already did," Gav replied. "Both Wiglaf and Arthur know."

Gav explained everything to his friends—the messages, the revelations about his brother Mordred, the disbanded Order of the Midnight Talons, and the prophecy that seemed to loom over him like a shadow. He told them about the attack on the Ragnell estate, the role Mordred had played, and the heavy burden of knowing that his own family had been torn apart by a prophecy he still didn't fully understand. And lastly, he told them of the book Arthur had recommended they read.

"I know exactly the story to which Arthur is referring, and you do too," Percy said, his voice tinged with excitement as he sprang from his seat. He hurried to a nearby shelf, his fingers skimming the spines of countless books before landing on a hefty tome. He heaved it off the shelf, the weight of it evident as he carried it back to the table. The book landed with a loud thud, sending a cloud of dust into the air.

"He wants us to read this whole thing?" Nora exclaimed, her eyes widening as she took in the size of the book.

"It's really a great read," Percy said sincerely, brushing the dust off the cover. "But the abstract should suffice."

Nora shot him an inquisitive look, one that she shared with Gav.

"The introduction section," Percy clarified, his tone slightly exasperated. "Should provide a sufficient enough summary."

Nora rolled her eyes but leaned forward, resting her chin on her hands as Percy flipped open the book. He cleared his throat, his eyes scanning the page before he began to read aloud:

In the elder days, before the realm of Avalon took its name, the world was whole—a vast and untamed land where the stars themselves were young. It was an age of primordial power, when the earth bleated under the rule of Bertilak the Green, a being who wore tyranny like a crown. His dominion stretched from the deepest seas to the stony roots of the mountains, enforced not by law but by the whims of a creature who saw mortals as playthings. To him, their suffering was art; their wars, a diverting spectacle.

Bertilak's cruelty was not without purpose. He had once been a force of creation, a shaper of realms, but time and solitude had twisted his heart. He gifted humanity magic not to uplift, but to corrupt—a glittering poison that turned kin against kin. Villages that might have united instead burned, their people wielding spells like knives against one another, all while Bertilak watched from the shadows, laughing.

Yet every shadow must meet its light. Merlin the White, Bertilak's twin in power but his opposite in spirit, walked among mortals not as a god but as a wanderer. Where Bertilak saw chaos, Merlin saw potential; where his brother reveled in dominion, Merlin sought only to understand. For centuries, their battles raged—not only with spell and blade, but with visions of what the world could be. Bertilak fought to preserve his game; Merlin, to break the board entirely.

The turning point came when Merlin allied with a mortal king: Artorias Pendragon, a warrior whose courage mirrored Merlin's compassion. Together, they shattered Bertilak's throne and cast him into the abyss. But victory demanded sacrifice. To prevent such tyranny from rising anew, Merlin divided the world. With a whisper, he spun The Veil, a living boundary between two realms: Avalon, a land of enchantment, where magic pooled like dew and Artorias ruled in peace. And Logres, a realm of iron and fire, where humanity's ingenuity flourished, unshackled from magic's temptations.

The Veil was a covenant; a promise that neither realm would encroach upon the other. And with its making, Merlin vanished. Some say he retreated somewhere within Avalon to rest; others, that he bound his soul to The Veil itself, becoming its silent guardian.

But Bertilak was never truly gone. "The Green does not die; it sleeps." Every few centuries, the earth trembles with his return—a blight on crops, a whisper in the hearts of the greedy, a knight bearing emeralds demanding fealty. Each time, the descendants of Artorias's Round Table rise to meet him, their swords bright with Merlin's lingering grace. They are the keepers of the balance, the proof that light endures.

And so the cycle ever continues: the shadow, the light, and the fragile world between.

"I didn't realize this is what you meant. I know this story! It's a children's series," Nora said, her voice tinged with surprise and a hint of nostalgia. "I remember my dad reading to us as little kids. King Artorias, Lancelot, and Merlin... we had so many great books about their adventures."

"It's a famous story," Percy said, nodding. "But it's also considered highly speculative. The two dragons, Merlin and Bertilak, likely existed, but who's to say they fought in this manner exactly?"

"So it's not real?" Nora asked, her brow furrowing.

"Not quite what I said," Percy replied, adjusting his glasses. "I'm simply suggesting that these writers are perhaps filling in the gaps a little too liberally, framing the story as 'good vs evil.'"

Gav studied his friends' faces, not really listening to much of what they were saying. His mind was elsewhere, consumed by the weight of the prophecy. Yet, in that moment, it was as Arthur had said, some of the prophecy had begun to unfold. He felt a strange sense of inevitability, as if the threads of fate were tightening around him. And though it wasn't all completely clear, what he did know, with a certainty that hung heavy in the air, was that he was tied to this Bertilak in some way. And something about Gav being in Gamalaot now, whether people knew the prophecy or not, had stirred a restless unease among the people. The whispers, the sidelong glances, the tension in the air—it all made sense now, though it offered little comfort.

Time moved by quickly, as if the weight of this newfound discovery, with all its baggage, had swept the rest of the day along in a rush. Before they could catch their breath, the evening had crept up on them, and they found themselves standing in the mess hall, ready for dinner.

Gav drew in a deep breath, letting it out slowly. The air around him was dense with the scent of roasting chicken, saffron, and a dozen other spices he couldn't quite name. His stomach rumbled. There was something different about this view of the mess hall, sitting at the champions' table. He missed Percy and Nora beside him, but Gale's presence made it easier to bear.

"Oh, yeah!" Gale boomed, bits of chicken and onion flying from his mouth, a wild enthusiasm in his voice. "This has got to be the best part of the winter festival!"

From beside him, Torian hummed a quiet agreement, carefully blowing on his meat skewer. "So many flavors and seasonings! Beats the braised hogget we usually get."

"Hey, I like the hogget!" Armand shouted, grinning as he bit into his skewer. "Festival meals are just extra special 'cause we don't get them every day."

The warm smells curled through every corner of the hall, mingling with the hum of laughter and conversation. It was a festival for the senses, and though Gav's heart ached with the absence of his friends, he couldn't bring himself to complain. There was too much joy in the air, too much happiness bubbling up around him for that. The entire commissary seemed to buzz with it.

Gav looked out and saw Nora and Lucan talking once more, standing next to the buffet line.

"Jealous?" Gale said, hitting Gav with his elbow.

"What?" Gav said, his cheeks blushing. "No, just curious. I didn't know they were friends."

"Came about rather suddenly."

"Is that so?"

"Yeah. He started writing her letters during the holiday. She spent so much of her time reading them and writing back. Very giddy, she was. Downright sickening." Gale winked and chuckled at this.

"I see," Gav looked at them, talking with a liveliness. He felt suspicious. He hadn't known Lucan to be personable or pleasant. Gav couldn't help but wonder if he had some kind of ulterior motive.

Chapter 15
The Battle of Camlann

The sun sat high in the sky, bright and shimmering, watching as the whole of Gamalaot's Knight Academy poured onto Camlann Field. Today was the day. A day that carried the weight of tradition; a powerful tradition, the mock battle marked the beginning of each new year, and the energy in the packed stands was palpable. Last year's victors, the Gilded Wings, were a formidable force, but Nora and Percy had their hopes pinned on the Crimson Manes, and on Gav. They both knew, with a silent certainty, that this wasn't just a game for him. This was Gav's chance to prove himself. A chance to find acceptance, to finally fit in, and to belong in a world that had, until now, kept him at a distance.

"Champions! Assemble!" said King Uther Pendragon, smiling at them.

The grey-haired king gazed upon the young cadets with a quiet pride. It was evident in the very posture of his frame and the cadence of his voice that he held a deep, abiding affection for this ancient rite.

The young knights stood gathered in solemn formation, their figures clad in gleaming armor, each piece enchanted. The weight of the metal was not just physical; it carried the gravity of tradition, of an ancient rite passed down through generations. Every detail of their attire was deliberate, from the etchings on their breastplates to the polished hilts of their swords. They weren't solely champions; they were like actors in a grand performance, each one with a part to play and a costume to wear, as though the battlefield was a stage and they, the players, were bound to their roles by fate itself. And as such, the battlefield, too, had been prepared with the utmost care. The very soil beneath their feet had been consecrated, blessed, and woven into the magic that hung like a shroud in the air.

"Make your houses proud," said King Uther. He then led the champions out onto the battlefield, escorting each squadron to their starting positions.

Camlann stretched before them, vast and open, framed by towering stands that pierced the sky like grand obelisks around the arena. The air buzzed with an electric fervor as the crowd, eager and alive, filled the stands to capacity. The noise was deafening, a swell of voices rising in a unified roar.

The people were restless with anticipation, their eyes fixed on the young knights who stood at attention in their positions on the field. Flags and banners fluttered in the wind, their vibrant colors flashing like bursts of flame against the backdrop of the bright, sunlit sky. The crowd's energy was contagious, rippling through the stands like a living thing. Children sat upon the shoulders of their fathers, their bright faces alight with wonder, while the old men, stooped with age, acted years younger with their canes raised high. The women, adorning their finest raiments, waved scarves and handkerchiefs in the air, their movements as free and unrestrained as the wind.

Each spectator, each soul that gathered in that moment, was united by the promise of spectacle, of the clash of steel and the merriment of the Winter Festival.

And then, a single horn sounded, piercing through the clamor of the crowd, commanding attention, signaling that the moment had come. The noise, the chaos, the fervor—everything paused, suspended.

Everything was silent, save for the rustling of banners in the wind. All eyes turned to the knights, their bodies poised and ready, hearts racing.

They all waited on the command of the Archbishop, who presided in the center of the field, his figure draped in the regal robes, deep dark blues that reflected the cosmos. His eyes were steady, unwavering as he surveyed everyone with a look of both paternal pride and a hint of something greater, something none of them understood. He raised his hands to the sky, and a hushed silence fell over the crowd.

Then, with a voice that seemed to shake the very heavens, he began his incantation. Words that no mortal tongue could or should speak poured from his lips—ancient, powerful, and terrifying in their resonance. As his voice reached its peak, the ground trembled beneath their feet, the wind howling in response, and the very fabric of reality bent and twisted under the strain of the spell.

The field was now sealed—protected by a barrier of primordial magic, a shield that would hold against all.

"Let the game begin!" he shouted with glee.

The crowd erupted into cheering, and the band of horns began to sound.

"Gav, stay close to me," Gale said, his voice tight with nerves.

"Right."

This was the first time Gav had ever worn the full armor, chainmail, and all. It hung on him, heavy—heavier than he'd expected. His movements, awkward and clumsy, felt unnatural, but he kept stride with Gale as best he could.

"Watch out!" Gav cried, pulling on Gale's tunic.

Gale recoiled back, narrowly avoiding an arrow that flew at him. Both boys turned to see a figure standing there, holding a bow and quiver, a grimace on his face as he realized he had missed by a hair.

"That was close," Gale said, laughing nervously. "Thanks, Gav."

"Sure, but…"

Before Gav could finish his thought, he witnessed it; the first point was scored. The boy, clutching the bow in his hands, never saw it coming—didn't have time to brace. With a swift, sure motion, another cadet, draped in his golden tunic, sliced through the air with his blade, tagging him cleanly. He'd been struck. And just like that, he seemed to unravel, to dissolve, as if the very substance of him had been snatched by the wind. The boy, the bow—both vanished, leaving nothing behind. Only that fleeting moment, when they dissolved into blue wisps of light and vanished into the empty air, remained as the sole testament that he had been there.

"We've got to keep moving," Gale said urgently, pushing Gav along.

"What happened to him? Is he..."

"He's fine," Gale said flatly. "It's us you should be worried about."

"Okay."

Gav was uneasy. The boy died. He had seen it. Sliced through. But something about the way Gale spoke made him question what he'd seen. Gale was a friend he trusted, had always trusted, but this? This was a sight that rattled Gav in a way he couldn't shake. He'd never come across anything like it, and it stuck with him. He figured, though, it was just one of those things, something he'd have to find a way to bear if he were to be a true knight.

They rounded the corner, their steps heavy as they secured the perimeter of their assigned post. Gav's heart hammered in his chest, each beat louder than the last. The plans they had so carefully laid out were coming unraveled. It seemed that The Gilded Wings had chosen to strike the same stronghold they had been targeting, throwing a wrench into their strategy. But to Gav, it didn't add up. The stronghold was so far away from where they had begun, an odd choice for the enemy to target. Did they somehow know their plans?

And then, out of nowhere, the trap was sprung. Gale had taken the hit square on the wrist from some incoming blade. His hand vanished into nothing. No blood, no pain, just a useless nub remained on the end of his arm.

"Gale," Gav cried.

"Behind you!" Gale shouted.

In a moment of perfect synchrony, they moved as one. Gale, with a swift motion, reached out with his good arm to impale the soldier who had been eyeing Gav. At the same time, Gav surged forward, his body a blur, to rend the knight who had been the first to attack his friend. They called out in unison as they struck, a battle cry ringing through the air. And just like that, it was over. Gale had outmaneuvered the boy, just as Gav had done with his opponent. The two collapsed to the earth, gasping for breath, as a soft, ethereal blue light encircled them, swirling upward toward the sky.

"Are you alright?" Gav asked, rushing to Gale.

"I'm fine, Gav," said Gale, frustrated. "Damn. They got my good hand. I'll be totally useless as a lefty."

Just as Gale attempted to push himself to his feet, he stumbled and fell again.

"Oh, brilliant," he groaned, "they got my heel, too." He glanced down, and sure enough, there was a small, empty patch of blue where a chunk of his heel had once been.

"Lavinia," Gav called, his voice low and steady, summoning his familiar from the unseen plane. And from the aether, a small red bird burst forth, swift as a spark, its wings a crimson blur, rushing to Gav's shoulder as she sang a bright tune. Gav's hands moved with purpose, digging through his rucksack, fingers brushing against tools and supplies. He pulled out a scrap of parchment and scrawled his message in hurried, jagged lines. "This needs to get to Blumenthal. You hear me?" His voice was firm, but there was a softness in it, too.

Lavinia chirped once, sharp and clear, a sound that carried both understanding and resolve. Then she was gone, a flash of red against the vast, blue sky.

"Gav," Gale said, his voice quiet but heavy. "He's gonna tell you to leave me."

"I won't do that." Gav's words were simple, but they carried in them the weight of a promise, the kind that men make when at war.

"It's okay, Gav. Really. It's just a game. And I'm not in any pain." Gale's smile was thin.

"It's not right," Gav said, his voice firm. "We stick together."

"You're taking quickly to the knighthood," Gale said, his smile widening just a touch. "Alright then, I've got an idea. You're not going to like it. But it's the best I can offer, unless you've got something better."

Gale laid out his plan, and as predicted, Gav protested at every turn, his voice rising and falling like the wind before a storm. But in the end, the pull of the game, the hunger to win, was too strong to deny. With a sigh that seemed to carry the weight of the world, Gav relented. He helped Gale to his feet, his hands steady but his heart heavy. Under his breath, he muttered an incantation, soft and low, and the wind stirred in response, coming to their aid. Gale, meanwhile, lit the fuse on his smoke bomb, the spark catching with a hiss, and tucked the smoldering thing into his waistband. Together, with Gale leaning on Gav's shoulder, they moved forward, shrouded in the thickening smoke, their steps deliberate and sure as they made their way toward the center stronghold, hidden from sight.

"I feel bad about leaving our post."

"The plan has fallen apart, Gav," Gale replied, his tone calm but firm. He spoke with the ease of someone who had learned, through hard lessons, that plans often do.

"I know," Gav said, his voice tightening, the doubt creeping in. "But what about being a good knight? Following orders, seeing it through, all of that? Isn't that what we're supposed to do?"

Gale turned to him, his eyes steady, his face resolute. "Gav, there's a danger in blind loyalty," he said, his words measured. "We haven't broken rank on purpose. You'll understand as you get older. It's called situational awareness. We're not doing anything wrong here, not really."

For a moment, Gav fell silent, the words settling over him, heavy but comforting. He nodded, slowly at first, then with more certainty. He placed his trust in Gale, as he always had, and for a moment, he almost forgot the years separating them, the difference in their experience. Gale never made him feel that distance, never let it hang over his head. To him, they were equals, bound by something deeper than rank. Friendship perhaps.

"Stop. Right here," Gale commanded, hurling the smokescreen as far as he could into the distance. "You go inside. Take the stronghold. Just remember, once you do, they'll be coming for you."

Gav gave a sharp nod, carefully propping Gale up against the outside wall before slipping quietly through one of the stronghold's windows, disappearing within it. Gale smiled to himself with a flicker of satisfaction before he raised his spear above his head. With a sudden, crackling burst, a bolt of magic shot skyward, slicing through the air like a flare. "Come and get me," he murmured, his voice resolute, like a challenge cast into the wind.

Gav moved through the narrow stone corridor, his boots hard against the worn floor. The stronghold itself wasn't much—a few winding hallways that fed into a single, wide chamber. He walked with care, the words Gale had imparted to him ringing continuously in his mind. To claim the hold, he needed to light the beacon. He wasn't sure how it worked, or what would happen when he did, but something told him the answer would reveal itself when the time was right, and he'd know what to do when he got there.

As Gav rounded the corner of the hallway, the space around him trembled. A deep, bone-rattling explosion shook the air from the other side of the wall. He winced. Gale had done it. Just as planned. Gav breathed in, reminding himself it was all just a game—nothing more. There was no pain. There was no death. And that Gale had actually been eager, almost too eager, to spring his trap, hoping to rack up as many points as he could in the process. And so Gav pushed the thought aside, forcing his mind back on the mission as he pressed deeper into the hold.

The main chamber lay before him, eerily quiet, and at the far end, an altar stood. Upon it was some kind of device—almost shaped like a flagpole stand, though curiously empty, as if waiting for something to be planted there. Gav moved closer, each step measured, his eyes flicking nervously over his shoulder as he did. When he reached the strange contraption, he paused, studying it with both suspicion and curiosity. It looked simple enough, almost like it didn't demand anything from him, like it had no purpose but to exist. Without thinking, he laid a hand on it.

That was all it took. The air bubbled around him for a moment, and then a brilliant red light erupted from the device, soaring upward in a blinding column, the color of his order, beautiful and bright. It punched through the ceiling, streaking toward the sky and passing through any barrier in its path.

And then, as if someone had sounded an alarm, a sharp, incessant chirping filled the room, growing louder and closer with each passing second. It came at him, relentless and shrill, echoing off the walls as if it were alive, charging straight for him. Gav's entire body jumped, turning rigid.

"Lavinia?"

It was her. His familiar had returned, bringing with her a warning before the danger could claim him. It was thanks to her that Gav spun around just in time, feeling the cold flecks of frost graze his cheek as a jagged spike of ice hurtled past him. He ducked low, and another pointed ice spike narrowly missed the edge of his shoulder.

"Lucan!" Gav exclaimed, running to a nearby stone column, evading an onslaught of ice along the way.

"I'm glad it's you," he said, his voice calm, almost pleased. "I've been dreaming of our rematch. This time, though, you won't have the old man to save you."

"That's funny," Gav said. "I distinctly remember you being the one needing saving."

A surge of flame erupted, crashing into the stone column with a deafening roar. The fire spilled over the edges, curling like wild serpents, its heat licking at Gav's arms, threatening to burn him away to nothing.

Lucan crept further into the room, each step measured, ever vigilant, remaining fixated on Gav, ready to strike the moment he dared to show himself. With a slow, deliberate motion, Lucan reached out for the device. His fingers brushed against it, and in that instant, the air seemed to shift. The beacon pulsed once, twice, then flickered to life, its hue changing from the fierce red of The Crimson Manes to the deep, unyielding blue of the wine-dark sea— the same color as Lucan's order, The Azure Stripes.

"You can't win, Gav," Lucan sneered, his voice cold as he sent another fiery blast crashing into the pillar that stood between them, pinning him down further.

Gav's gaze flickered toward another column across the room. He knew it was within reach, but he had to focus. He shut his eyes, feeling the pulse of the magic rise from the earth beneath him, pooling into his legs, his feet. He could feel it. Now. With a breath sharp as a prayer, Gav launched himself from his position, the force of the leap carrying him like the wind, fast and sure.

Lucan's retaliation came quickly—a shard of ice, jagged and merciless, cut through the air, aiming to slow him, to break his stride. But Gav wasn't running—not really. His body was floating like a feather in the breeze, but fast and precise like a missile, he was airborne, sailing from pillar to pillar with a grace that would've seemed unnatural if not for the magic thrumming beneath him.

In the blink of an eye, he landed. Safe for the moment, but further from the altar. Further from his goal.

"Face me, you coward!" Lucan bellowed, his voice echoing off the stone walls, a confident fury burning in his eyes. He unleashed another torrent of fire, the flames lunging at Gav, hungry, followed then by jagged shards of ice that sliced through the air, cold and sharp as death itself. Each attack alternated between them, each strike a promise of destruction.

Gav found himself cornered, stuck. Lucan was unrelenting, pinning him down. But Gav then reminded himself that he had bested Lucan once before. The boy may have been a force of nature with his magic, but Gav was quicker; quicker with his feet, quicker with a blade. That was his advantage.

And so his eyes poured over the room, tracing walls, from the back to the front. *There—that could work.* It wasn't much, but it was enough of a plan to make his move. His mind set, Gav sank into a crouch, the pulse of magic thrumming through his veins, matching the drumbeat in his chest. The air was thick with tension, but in it, he found his focus. This next move would be decisive. He would either win or lose trying.

With a sudden burst of magical wind energy, Gav propelled himself forward, leaping from his crouch, aiming for the wall opposite the altar. The world blurred as he darted across the room, narrowly dodging the searing flame and icy shards that Lucan hurled in his direction. He moved like a shadow, swift and fluid, but there was something more to it now—something calculated.

Just as Lucan's gaze sharpened on him, ready to unleash another spell, Gav made his move. With a powerful kick, he pushed off that opposite wall, sending himself hurtling through the air straight at Lucan. The move was sudden, unexpected, and for a moment, it seemed to catch Lucan off guard.

Flinching, Lucan attempted to evade him, but Gav was already past him, slicing through the air like a windstorm. He wasn't the target.

In that same fluid motion, Gav reached the beacon. His fingers brushed it, and with a twist, he activated it. The room spilled over with a warm crimson color. But Gav spent no time noticing. Without hesitation, he kicked off the altar, propelling himself back toward Lucan, his body a blur of motion, his arms holding tight to his blade. This was it. He was ready to strike. This time, there would be no questions about who had won.

Gav clenched his eyes shut, bracing for the clash—the moment when he would strike down upon Lucan, claiming victory as his own.

But there was no grand explosion, no earth-shaking collision. Instead, there was only silence, a stillness that seemed to stretch on forever. The seconds blurred together, too quick to grasp. And when Gav finally opened his eyes, he found himself seated on a bench—a bench inside the tent where, only hours ago, his fellow champions of the Crimson Manes had donned their gear and prepared for the day. His gaze swept around, meeting the faces of his comrades, their expressions a combination of astonishment and triumph.

Then, a roar from outside the tent—the sound of a thousand voices, maybe more, crashing together in deafening applause. The cheers spilled into the tent, overwhelming, echoing like a storm. The faces around him lit up, and before Gav could fully make sense of it, they were lifting him from the bench, hoisting him high onto their shoulders, shouting praises in his ears.

"You did it, Gav!"

"Fantastic!"

"Absolutely brilliant!"

They carried him through the tent's flaps and out into the wild celebration, their joy contagious. Gav then felt a surge of happiness, but underneath it was a thin thread of confusion. *What exactly had happened? And how did he get here?* The roaring of happiness pushed those questions aside, letting the cheers wash over him.

"Gav," cried Nora, rushing to him. "Gav, that was incredible!"

Gav smiled politely at her, opening his mouth to ask how she knew about his victory or whether it had truly been as incredible as it felt. But before the words could form, he saw it. At first, he thought his eyes were playing tricks on him, but no—there they were. Enormous, floating glasses, multiple ones, suspended in midair like the eyes of some colossal beast. They were showing the battle—his battle with Lucan—playing in vivid detail for the crowd.

Gav watched in awe as the scene unfolded before him. He saw himself racing toward Lucan, the clash of their forms, and then—everything went still. He

170

saw it now, in perfect clarity. When they collided, it wasn't with a crash, but with a shimmering burst of blue, like an ethereal light swallowing them whole. They had both struck each other at the same time, their final blows meeting in the same instant. Furthermore, in that moment, at the heart of the battlefield, they were the last two knights standing. And though they had technically tied for the final blow dealt, the beacon was red at the moment of impact. The Crimson Manes controlled the center stronghold. Gav had done it. He had won the Battle of Camlann for his order.

The crowd erupted, a wave of cheers crashing down upon him, louder and more overwhelming than anything he had ever felt. In that moment, all the disdain and suspicion that had followed him like a plague seemed to vanish. He cried. Not out of sorrow, but out of happiness, out of relief. He didn't know if this moment of acceptance would last—if the whispers of hatred would return—but for now, it didn't matter. He let the tears fall, savoring the warmth of the crowd, and allowed himself to be fully present in the joy of the moment. They saw him now. Saw him for him and not as some cursed child or foul omen. He was one of them; a knight of Gamalaot.

Chapter 16
A Lesson in Etiquette

Weeks had passed since the Winter Festival had come to its end, and the snow, once a thing of beauty, had turned into nothing more than a nuisance. What had been soft and beautiful now lay in muddy patches, melting away in the thaw. The world outside was a slurry of wet earth and slush, the pristine white giving way to the dreariness of spring's reluctant arrival. It seemed only fitting; a natural correction for a season of indulgence, for the revelry and celebration that had painted the winter in such brilliant colors. The pathways, once lined with snowdrifts, now bore the marks of a world ready to move on.

And so life, as it always does, pressed forward, slow and steady. The Academy, that ever steadfast fortress of order, returned to its rhythm, its halls once more filled with the murmur of lessons and the shuffle of boots on stone.

Gav sat down at the long table in the commissary, the dull, familiar buzz of the morning settling over them. Percy was beside him, as usual, while Gale slouched across the way, his eyes scanning for more sausage. Ed and Leif, true to their nature, were locked in some petty tussle over the last of the bread, their fingers swatting and grabbing like animals over a scrap of meat. The only seat unoccupied, the only space left empty, was where Nora should've been.

"Anyone seen her?" Gav asked.

"She's probably off with her boyfriend," Ed said, lips curling into a mock kiss.

"She says they're just friends," Percy replied, his voice flat.

It was curious that Lucan was also missing from the commissary. Not a trace of him anywhere. In fact, the table where the Azure Stripes usually sat, filling the hall with their rowdy chatter, sat eerily empty this morning. Only a handful of cadets were drinking their tea quietly. Gav gave a small shrug, the weight of it barely enough to move his shoulders. He didn't give it much more thought.

What truly caught Gav's attention, though, wasn't the absence of the usual faces but the unexpected presence of so many more at his own table. Ever since the Battle of Camlann, it seemed the air around him had changed—lighter, or perhaps just less burdened with suspicion. The knights at the academy, once distant and cold to him, now seemed to regard him with something different. Less hostility. More curiosity, even warmth. They greeted him in the corridors, their nods not just polite, but genuine. He noticed it more and more—those glances, those quiet acknowledgements, the feeling of kind eyes following him across the room.

Like now, for instance. Across from him, seated a few feet over, sat one of the first-year Crimson Manes; a young girl named Vivian Blaiddyd, if he remembered correctly. She wasn't even trying to hide it, the way her eyes lingered on him, a longing in her gaze. The way she watched him, so openly and so awkwardly, was almost enough to make Gav shift in his seat. But he didn't. Instead, he met her eyes briefly, then looked away, pretending he hadn't noticed her prolonged staring.

Vivian seemed like a decent enough girl, Gav thought, though he hadn't known her long enough to say much more than that. His second term had just begun after the winter break, and with it came a slate of new classes. Among them was Etiquette, a subject that, for reasons not so convincingly explained, was part of the curriculum. Vivian found herself in that same class.

A knot of unease began to tighten in Gav's chest. He sat at one of the small circular tables in the tea room, the usual setting for their lessons. Vivian sat across from him, her smile bright as ever, while Sir Bagdemagus carried on with his tedious lecture about the proper use of cutlery—fork in the left hand, knife in the right, the edge of the knife always facing the plate. And while the rest of the boys in the room were barely keeping their eyes open in the face of Sir Bagdemagus's monotonous voice, Gav's attention was drawn to the empty seat beside him. Nora was missing again. First breakfast, now class. She was meant to be here, and it wasn't like her to simply skip out on class. Something felt off.

"Mister Badge," called out Bor, his voice carrying a certain bluntness. "Why do we gotta bother with any of this?"

"Yeah," Tor chimed in, his twin brother, his thick fingers clumsily pushing the tiny forks and spoons around the table. "Can't see Sir Wiglaf doing none of this nonsense, right, Bor?"

"You said it, Tor."

"Boys," Sir Bagdemagus said, his thick, meticulously groomed mustache twitching as he scowled. "First, it's Sir Bagdemagus to you. Pet names are for those who share a more personal connection. And second, this is no trivial matter! A knight must be strong of body, yes, but he must also be rich in spirit and in humor. Proper etiquette is not a mere luxury; it's a cornerstone of our chivalric code."

Almost as if on cue, the sharp crack of a plate shattering echoed through the hall. It was clearly an accident, and the twins shot quick, apologetic glances, but it didn't do much to soften the fury in Sir Bagdemagus. His face turned crimson, and the veins in his forehead swelled, pulsing with the kind of hot frustration that could almost be seen steaming in the air around him. He had hoped to be rid of these boys this semester, but they had unfortunately failed Etiquette in the first term and needed now to make it up in the second.

"I know some of you might not see the worth in etiquette, not when swinging a sword feels more…visceral," he said, the last words slipping out in barely above a whisper. "But take a look at Gautere here."

All eyes shifted to Hubert, who sat with a teacup cradled in his hands, his movements deliberate, almost ceremonial, as he sipped. There was a quiet grace to him, a stillness that seemed to command the room without effort.

"Gautere would make a fine dignitary, a liaison, even," Bagdemagus continued. "And mark my words, it's not at the cost of his skill with a blade or wand."

Hubert said nothing, his face a mask of calm, but inside, the warmth of the compliment spread through him like sunlight breaking through a storm.

Sir Bagdemagus pressed on with his lecture, his gaze deliberately passing over the more unruly cadets in the back of the room. Gav leaned in toward Bor and Tor, who were still bent over, their hands fumbling with the shattered remnants of the plate.

"Either of you seen Nora?"

The twins exchanged a glance, a faint worry passing between them, before they turned their eyes back to Gav. "No, we haven't. Is everything alright?"

"I don't know," Gav muttered, his voice distant.

"Hey Gav," Vivian's voice floated across the table, soft but insistent

He turned to her, his gaze catching the faint blush that had risen to her cheeks, the way her lips curved into a smile that seemed both shy and eager. There was a nervous energy about her, a kind of trembling anticipation that made her words come out in a whisper, low and halting.

"Do you think you could help me with my stances later?" she asked, her voice tinged with embarrassment but also a kind of giddy hope. She laughed then, a small, self-conscious sound that seemed to escape her before she could stop it.

Huh?" Gav said, his voice rough, distracted. He shook his head slightly, as if to clear it. "Yeah, I can do that."

But even as he spoke, his thoughts were elsewhere, tangled in a knot of worry that had settled deep in his chest. *Where was Nora?* The question ate at him, persistent and unrelenting. Something felt off, wrong in a way he couldn't quite name. It was like a shadow at the edge of his vision, always there but never clear enough to grasp. He wanted to do something, to act, but the truth was, he didn't know what to do. And so he sat there, his mind adrift, caught between the warmth of Vivian's smile and the cold, creeping dread that something was amiss.

The bell rang, signaling the end of class, and Gav felt a gentle but insistent pull at his sleeve. Vivian had come up beside him, her hand gripping his arm, drawing herself close as they made their way out of the hall and toward the open fields beyond.

"I really appreciate you helping me," she said, her voice light and bright, like the sun breaking through clouds.

But Gav, still tangled in the fog of his thoughts, moved in a kind of daze, his mind sluggish and distant.

They walked together toward the training mound, the earth beneath their feet soft and wet. The wooden swords were lined in a neat row on the rack. Gav reached for one, his fingers wrapping around the cracked wood, and tossed it to Vivian with a quick flick of his wrist. It sailed through the air, but her hands weren't quick enough, and the training blade slipped from her grasp, thudding softly onto the grass.

"Sorry," Gav called out.

"No, that's on me," she replied, a faint blush coloring her cheeks. "I'm a little clumsy."

"So, uh, what exactly do you need help with?" Gav asked, his voice drifting as he tried to focus.

"The Knight Kneeler," she said.

Gav nodded, setting his feet firm in the dirt. He stood with his feet shoulder-width apart, his left foot just a little ahead of the right—steady and planted. He raised the sword above his shoulder in one smooth, practiced motion, his arms bending naturally, hands steady, the tip of the blade poised with purpose.

"The power of the swing comes from rotating the hips," he said, his voice steady and calm. "When you make the cut, you turn your hips slightly toward the target, generating the force with your whole body, not just your arms."

He mimed the motion slowly, showing her each part of the movement, then in a flash, he did it fast—one seamless swing.

Vivian couldn't help but smile. She didn't say a word, but her gaze lingered, bright and warm. The way she looked at him spoke louder than any words could, her eyes shining with an enduring admiration. He was something else; so effortless, so sure, so cool.

"Now you try."

Vivian hesitated for a moment, then planted her feet in a stance that was more awkward than deliberate, almost as if she were asking for him to come over and correct her. She tilted her head and gave him a playful, almost teasing look.

"Like this?" she asked, knowing the stance she'd taken was all wrong.

"Not quite," Gav said, stepping closer to correct her stance, but before he could reach her, a sharp, piercing yell cut through the air.

"Ragnell!"

Gav's head snapped around, his gaze shooting toward the source. Lucan was striding toward him, his face twisted in fury, and there, struggling in his grip, was Lilah, the girl from Lucan's house, the one always hanging around him. Her arm was trapped in his hand, his fingers digging into her skin, dragging her forward with a force that made it clear he wasn't in the mood for questions.

With a savage motion, Lucan threw Lilah to the ground, her body hitting the wet grass with a dull thud, just before Gav's feet.

"Tell him!" Lucan barked, his voice sharp with a venomous edge, his eyes never leaving Lilah as if they could burn through her.

Gav's pulse quickened, a knot forming in his stomach. He knelt down slightly, his gaze never leaving Lucan's furious face.

"Lucan, what's the matter?"

"Tell him!" Lucan repeated, his words like a command, his glare fixed like a blade, aimed squarely at the girl on the ground.

"She's gone," Lilah said, her voice breaking, the desperation clear as tears welled in her eyes. "They took her."

Gav opened his mouth, the question on the tip of his tongue—*who?*—but the words caught in his throat. The look on her face, the one of frantic fear, and the cold, venomous anger burning in Lucan's eyes, twisted something deep inside him. The nagging feeling that had followed him all morning suddenly clicked into place.

It was Nora.

His heart sank, the realization settling like a weight in his chest.

"I just thought they'd prank her or something," Lilah said, her voice trembling, a sob choking off her words. "I didn't know that they wanted to hurt her. We were just jealous!" She shot a look at Vivian, who feigned a shocked and surprised look.

"What do you mean by 'they'?" Gav asked, the question almost slipping out before he could catch it.

"I got these letters and…they wore masks like birds," Lilah stammered, her eyes wide with fear. "They were covered in black feathers."

Lucan's eyes flicked over to Gav, searching his face. For a moment, nothing seemed to register—until Gav's expression shifted, his face going pale, a look of horrific recognition spreading across him like wildfire.

"Gav, they want you. They said you need to go where it all started."

Gav's breath caught in his chest, the weight of those words sinking deep into his bones.

"Why did you wait so long to tell anyone?!" Lucan roared, his anger snapping through the air like a whip.

"I'm sorry!" Lilah cried, her voice breaking, hands pressed to her face, her sobs pained. "I'm so sorry."

Lucan turned to Gav, his face suddenly urgent, his tone softer now. "Gav, do you know what she's talking about?"

Gav's nod was slow, heavy with the burden of something dark.

The pair exchanged a look—nothing more needed to be said. Without a word, they turned, rushing forward into certain peril, their hearts set on one thing: saving Nora.

Chapter 17
Return to House Ragnell

The light was fading quickly, the sky deepening into shadows as Gav and Lucan sprinted through the streets of Gamalaot castle town. They ran, driven by nothing but instinct, their feet pounding the earth with a frantic urgency.

Lucan kept pace, barely aware of the path beneath him, his mind consumed by panic. This was the road to his family's estate, and it stretched out before them, a familiar route he had walked countless times. But it wasn't the Lambelle estate that would be their final destination.

No, their focus was on the ruin across the street—Gav's old family home. What had once been a proud manor now lay in ashes, a blackened husk of what it had been, reduced to scattered rubble. The remnants of a past Gav had only just begun to uncover.

"Here," Gav said, his voice quiet, yet certain, though he couldn't have said how he knew. It was as if the place itself had called to him, even before his thoughts had fully caught up. Ever since Christmas, with Wiglaf and that conversation with Arthur, a nagging feeling had taken root in him; a quiet certainty that, one day, he would find himself here. And now, standing before the ruin of his family's legacy, he knew he was right. This was where it began.

Night had settled in, the darkness thick and all-encompassing. Yet within Gav and Lucan, a fire burned brightly—a fierce, unwavering flame that cast a light more vivid than the shadows around them. Even still, it wasn't enough to fully dispel the heavy sense of foreboding that hung in the air. Fear lingered, creeping at the edges of their hearts, and for a moment, they paused.

They didn't speak a word, but in that brief silence, they steadied themselves, each drawing strength from the other. The resolve between them grew, unspoken but undeniable. With a single, shared understanding, they stepped forward—side by side, in perfect synchrony. Each knew, without a doubt, that no matter what lay ahead, they were in this together.

Some of the stone archways and hallways still stood, stubborn against time, but the ground was choked with charred, fragile wood. The seasons of rain and snow had done little to heal the wounds of this place; the decay seemed almost alive, lingering in the air, thick and oppressive, as though the very walls held on to the death that had once claimed it.

Gav and Lucan moved cautiously through the crumbling halls, their footsteps light, wary of the fragile pieces beneath them. Each turn, each step felt like a puzzle, until they finally emerged into the courtyard.

There was Nora, kneeling on the cold, broken stone. Her head hung low, her form motionless, either unconscious or asleep. Above her, a towering figure loomed, draped in a cloak of black feathers that seemed to absorb the weak moonlight, casting an eerie shadow over everything. The figure was still; its presence filled the space with an unsettling weight, as though it were waiting for something, or someone.

"Nora!" Gav's voice rang out, urgent and raw, as he sprinted toward her.

Lucan was right behind him, his movements swift. But as they closed the distance, Lucan's focus shifted. Without breaking his stride, he thrust his hand forward, a spike of ice shooting from his palm, hurtling toward the cloaked figure with deadly precision.

But the ice never reached its target. It didn't even strike the wall behind him. In a flash—quicker than a blink—the cloaked figure moved. It was impossible to see what he had done. Maybe he had melted the ice with magic, or perhaps deflected it with a wave of his blade. Whatever it was, it happened so fast that they couldn't make sense of it. All they knew was that Lucan's attack had failed, dissipating into nothingness before it could even land. The figure stood there, still as ever, unfazed and unreadable.

Then he lunged. He moved like a force of nature, fluid and deadly, like a bird of prey swooping down upon them. Gav and Lucan drew their swords, the metal meeting the weight of his strikes with a sharp crack. It was unreal—the way he moved with such deliberate, focused aggression, each strike heavier than the last.

The man shifted between them effortlessly, his movements like a dance of violence. Neither Gav nor Lucan could find solid ground. Their feet slipped on the loose earth, their hands struggling to control the flow of battle. He was everywhere, keeping them on the back foot, and with every blow, it became clearer—he had the upper hand on both of them.

Lavinia descended from the heavens like a fiery comet, her form a streak of burning light against the night sky. She plunged downward, swift and furious, as though Gav himself had called her to strike. But before she could meet her target, the harsh cry of a raven shattered the air, shrill and commanding. In an instant, her flight was broken, and she fell, her flame extinguished by the dark, unyielding grip of the bird's talons. There she lay, crumpled and still, the weight of the creature pressing her into the dirt. But just then, out of the shadows, pounced a white lion cub—Lucan's familiar. The raven released Lavinia, launching itself toward the cub, pecking out one of their eyes. The cub whimpered in pain, scurrying away to safety, but only once Lavinia had flown off.

The shadowy assailant holding his own against the boys was relentless. He pressed forward with a renitent fury, each strike coming harder, faster, and more powerful than the last. Lucan stumbled, his footing giving way under the assault, and finally fell to the ground.

The man then shifted his focus, zeroing in on Gav with terrifying precision. He swung with a force that made the air crackle, each blow striking with such power that Gav could feel the weight of it in his bones. His sword groaned under the pressure, and Gav struggled to hold his ground, the feeling of it threatening to snap the weapon in two. Every strike was a storm, and Gav was caught in its heart, fighting not just to block but to survive the crushing onslaught.

And then, as Gav had feared, his sword, Galatine, the precious arm Morholt had made for him, shattered in his hands, the fractured blade breaking apart with a sickening crack. For a fleeting moment, he stood vulnerable, but instinct kicked in. With a rush of reflex, Gav gathered every ounce of his strength, focusing all his energy into his arm like Arthur taught him. He raised it just in time.

The cloaked man's next blow came crashing down, but instead of meeting flesh, it collided with a brilliant alabaster light that now radiated from Gav's forearm. The strike was repelled with a force that sent a shockwave through the air. Gav smirked, his gaze locking onto the man's surprised face.

With newfound power coursing through him, Gav took the offensive, swinging his glowing arm like a blade. The weight of the battle shifted in that instant. For the first time, Gav held the advantage. His strikes were precise, forceful, each one pushing the cloaked figure back.

Lucan, recovering too, joined in the assault, hurling firebolts and spikes of ice, his magic biting into the dark figure's defenses. Together, they pressed him, not giving him a moment's respite.

Finally, the pressure proved too much. With a sickening crack, the figure's obsidian mask shattered, falling into two pieces on the ground. What lay beneath stunned them both. The face that was revealed was one they never could have expected—a face they both recognized, yet couldn't quite believe.

The man's face, now exposed, struck a chilling resemblance to Gav's own. Strong cheeks, a pronounced nose—the features were unmistakable. Lucan blinked in disbelief, marveling at the eerie similarity, his mind struggling to connect the dots. But for Gav, the recognition was instantaneous, and horror flooded his chest.

He knew that face. He had seen it before, in Wiglaf's cottage, photographed into the pages of a book, a name that haunted him in the dark corners of his thoughts.

This man before them, this terrifying creature cloaked in darkness, was no stranger. He was Mordred Lohot Ragnell—Gav's brother.

The realization hit Gav like a physical blow, his heart hammering in his chest, the weight of it almost unbearable. *How had it come to this? How had the brother he never knew become the monster standing before him? Arthur and Wiglaf had said Mordred had died. More lies. More deceit. It was a tangled web of half-truths and veiled secrets that choked the air around him. Why couldn't anyone just be honest? Why did they all insist on hiding the truth from him, leaving him to stumble in the dark?*

The frustration pumped through Gav's body. His heart raced, pounding hard against his ribs, blood roaring in his ears.

Without thinking, without control, Gav exploded. The anger ripped through him like fire, uncontrolled and furious. He lunged at his brother, desperately swinging with reckless abandon, striking at him, at nothing, and at everything. His wild eyes locked onto Mordred's visage. He moved like something feral now, consumed by the chaos within, his body moving on pure instinct, blind to everything else.

"Gav!" Lucan cried, his voice strained as he moved forward, reaching out, trying to pull him from the storm of anger that consumed him.

But Gav, lost to his rage, was a whirlwind—wild, untamed. Every strike came from a place of pain, of frustration, a desperate need to shatter the lies and the truths that had been withheld from him. His fists flew, but Mordred—calm, almost detached—dodged each swing effortlessly, his movements acute and precise. The composure in his stance was a stark contrast to Gav's fury, and it gave him an edge.

As Gav's movements grew wilder, more unhinged, Mordred saw his chance. In a fluid motion, he sidestepped one of Gav's blows, then, without warning, used the momentum against him. With a swift kick, a quick push, he sent Gav stumbling backward, his backside colliding with the hard ground.

Lucan steadied him, lifting him to his feet, and there they stood, side by side—Gav and Lucan, their shoulders set and strong. They faced Mordred, their eyes locked, feeling the weight of the world pressing upon them.

Mordred's gaze settled on Lucan, heavy and appraising, like a man weighing the worth of a blade. "You're well trained," he said. "You remind me of myself, in another time, another life."

Lucan's jaw tightened, his eyes hard as flint. "Just let her go," he said, the words clipped and sharp. "She's done nothing to you."

"True enough," he conceded. "It's not her I'm after. It's your friend there."

Lucan's eyes flicked toward Gav, and for a moment, something dark and unspoken passed across his face—a flicker of disdain, or perhaps something deeper, more corrosive. "We're not friends," he said, the words cold and final.

"Smart," Mordred said, nodding slowly. "Then you see it too. He's a threat to everything we know, everything we hold dear. You know it as well as I do." His voice was calm, almost gentle. "Help me end this. Help me, and I'll let her go. We can save our way of life, our home, and the people we love. Isn't that worth something?"

"You killed our family!" Gav shouted, his words trembling with fury and grief. "Why? Just to get to me? Was that it? They were your family, too!"

Mordred turned to him, his face a mask of disgust, regret, or perhaps a strong combination of both. "They wanted to protect you," he said, the words sharp, cutting. "You. A blight on this world. They were willing to shield you! You! The very thing that would destroy us all." He paused, his voice dropping lower, heavier, and unkempt. "I did what I had to. Even though it tore me apart inside, I did what was necessary. What a knight must do to protect his kingdom." Mordred's gaze shifted back to Lucan, sharp, like the edge of a blade pressed against the skin. "You know this! You know it, you can feel it. He will destroy us all—everything we are, everything we hold dear. This isn't just about you or me. It's about all of us. Help me. Help me save Gamalaot."

Lucan's eyes lingered on Gav, and for a fleeting moment, it seemed as though the weight of Mordred's words had resonated with him, impressing upon him that perhaps he was right. But then his jaw tightened, and his gaze hardened, and what came out of his mouth next struck Gav.

"A knight doesn't kill the innocent," Lucan said, his voice steady. "A knight doesn't turn his back on his king or his kingdom. Even when the order doesn't make sense, even when it chafes against your own will, you're not meant to question. You're a tool, nothing more. You carry out the will of your lord. That's the oath. That's the duty."

Mordred's face twisted, his lips curling into a sneer. "Blind fool," he spat, the words incisive and venomous. "Blindly following commands, like a dog on a leash. I overestimated you. Maybe we're not as alike as I thought."

Lucan's stance shifted, his feet planted firmly, his body coiling like a spring. "Good," he said, his voice final, raising his blade, ready.

Mordred surged forward, his form dissolving into a shadowy blur, as though the very air around him had turned to smoke. He moved like a specter, swift and ethereal, a ghostly figure shrouded in darkness. In an instant, he was upon Lucan, a tempest of feathers and steel, his movements too fast to follow, too precise to evade.

His strikes were relentless and merciless, each one a flash of silver and pain. Lucan's left side was engulfed in the onslaught, the blade ripping through flesh and bone.

Lucan's cry tore through the still night air, visceral and angry, a sound of pure agony. He crumpled to the ground, his body folding in on itself, his left arm cradled against his chest. Blood seeped through his fingers, dark and glistening, the limb twisted and broken.

Mordred's gaze shifted, caustic and predatory, locking onto Gav. In an instant, he was moving again, his form dissolving into a swirling mass of black smoke that devoured any light in his path. He surged forward, a dark tempest hurtling toward Gav with terrifying speed.

Gav braced himself, his arm still glowing with a faint, otherworldly light, a desperate shield against the onslaught. He swung and parried, each movement frantic, each block a struggle to hold back the tide of Mordred's fury. But it was clear—painfully clear—that he was outmatched. Every strike from Mordred landed with the force of a hammer, sending a painful jolt into Gav's bones, driving him further back, his footing slipping, his defenses crumbling.

Sweat dripped from Gav's brow, his breath coming in ragged gasps as he fought to keep the shadowy figure at bay. He knew, deep down, that this was a battle he couldn't win. Mordred was relentless, a force of nature, and it was only a matter of time before the darkness would swallow him whole. Yet still, Gav stood his ground, his jaw clenched, his eyes blazing with a stubborn will of fire. He would fight until the end, even if it meant certain death.

Just then, voices rang out, sharp and commanding, cutting through the chaos. Arthur led the charge, his presence like the sun breaking through a storm. Beside him strode Wiglaf, steadfast and stalwart, King Uther with his regal bearing, Lady Guinevere with her quiet strength, and Miss Morrigan, her eyes alight with a fierce determination. Even the Archbishop hurried into the fray, his robes billowing like the wings of some great and powerful dragon.

"Mordred!" Arthur's voice boomed, echoing off the cracked stones of the courtyard. "Enough of this madness! It ends here!"

But before the knights of Gamalaot could close the distance, shadows stirred at the edges of the courtyard. From the darkness, figures emerged, cloaked in feathers that shimmered in the moonlight—the Midnight Talons. They moved with a predatory grace, their blades gleaming as they surged forward to intercept Arthur and his companions.

The clash was immediate, the courtyard erupting into a cacophony of steel meeting steel, the sharp, metallic ring of swords colliding. Each knight found themselves locked in combat, their movements a blur of skill and desperation. Arthur's blade flashed like lightning, meeting the strike of a Talon with a force that sent sparks flying. Wiglaf fought with the might of a bear, his every move a broad swing of his colossal blade. Lady Guinevere and Miss Morrigan moved like shadows themselves, their strikes swift and deadly, while King Uther and the Archbishop stood side by side, their figures resolute against the swirling chaos of the courtyard. Before them loomed the mage, her presence as ominous as a black storm cloud, ready to burst. Her hands moved with an eerie grace, fingers twisting through the air like the threads of some invisible tapestry. Around her, objects trembled and lifted—stones, shards of metal, even the very air seemed to bend to her will. She was a tempest given form, her telekinetic power a force of nature unleashed.

"You go on," the Archbishop said, his voice steady. "I can handle her." With that, he unleashed flares of magic from his fingers, each one colliding with hers in a brilliant explosion of energy.

King Uther gave a solemn nod to his old friend, a wordless thanks that carried the weight of many years. Without hesitation, he pressed forward, moving swiftly toward Mordred and Gav, where Arthur awaited.

As father and son—Arthur and Uther—joined the fray, their swords meeting Mordred's strikes with strength, each blow countered and parried. But despite the beautiful, coordinated attacks, Mordred still managed to fend them off.

Arthur's voice rose, cutting through the air like his very blade. "Relent!" he bellowed, the weight of his fury twisting his words. "You've done enough, Mordred. More than enough. This ends now!" His movements, once measured and sure, began to falter, just barely, but it was enough. Mordred's eyes gleamed with a predator's instinct, seizing the moment with cold precision. With a swift, merciless kick, he sent Arthur sprawling, and in one fluid motion, his sword found its mark—a cruel, calculated thrust where the armor yielded, piercing the king's flesh beneath. The blade sank deep, and Arthur's breath caught, his eyes widening as the light within his father's face dimmed, fading like the last ember of a dying fire. King Uther fell, his life spilling out onto the ground.

"No!" Arthur's cry tore through the air as he surged forward, his heart pounding like a war drum. But Mordred was relentless, a storm of vengeance and rage. He descended upon Gav like a shadow, pinning him to the earth with a force that brooked no resistance. The dagger gleamed in his hand, its tip hovering above

Gav's chest, trembling for the briefest of moments as Mordred's gaze locked with his brother's. In that fleeting instant, something flickered in Mordred's eyes—a flicker of recognition, of kinship, of the boy he once was. But the hatred, scathing and unyielding, roared louder, drowning out the whisper of memory. With a grim resolve, he drove the dagger down, piercing flesh, aiming for the heart. Or so he believed.

When Mordred looked again, his face twisted into a mask of horrified realization. The truth, bare and undeniable, stared back at him from Gav's eyes. But before the words could form on his lips, before the weight of his actions could fully settle, the world tilted. Mordred's head tumbled from his shoulders, hitting the ground with a sickening thud, his body collapsing in a heap.

Arthur stood above him, his sword dripping with the blood of his once-friend. Tears streamed down his face, a torrent of grief for Gav, for his father, for the shattered bonds that could never be mended. In that single, brutal stroke, Arthur had ended Mordred's life, his pain, and the cycle of vengeance that had consumed them all.

Mordred's fall was a signal, rippling through the ranks of the Talons like a cold wind. They moved as one, their loyalty bound not to the man who lay broken but to the mage who now rose above the chaos. She descended like a wraith, her form gliding over the blood-soaked ground until she reached Mordred's lifeless head. With a tenderness that seemed out of place amidst the carnage, she cradled it in her hands, her fingers brushing against his pale, still features. For a moment, she lingered, her eyes shadowed with grief. Then, with a whisper of power, she dissolved into wisps of smoke, vanishing as though she had never been.

The Talons followed suit, retreating in silence, their movements coordinated and deft. And then, there was nothing but the stillness, the heavy, suffocating quiet that follows the storm. The air clung to the scent of iron and ash, and the ground bore the scars of yet another tragedy. House Ragnell, already steeped in sorrow, now carried the weight of more loss, another chapter of blood and betrayal etched into its history.

Chapter 18

A Good King

The fog hung low and heavy, a somber shroud of gray that seemed to mourn alongside the people of Gamalaot. They came in their multitudes, lining the cobbled streets, their faces etched with the weight of loss as King Uther was borne to his rest. The priests, robed in their solemn vestments, led the procession with voices that rose and fell in ancient prayers and psalms, their words weaving through the air threads of grief. The king's body, cradled by their hands, moved slowly through the heart of the town, past the homes and hearths he had once ruled, toward the cold embrace of the sepulcher behind the castle. There, in the shadow of stone, the kings before him lay in their eternal silence, waiting to welcome him to their ranks.

The knights of Gamalaot stood as sentinels, their armor dulled by the damp air, their eyes fixed on the procession as it wound its way to the tomb. They watched as the great door was sealed, a final, echoing thud that seemed to reverberate through the very bones of the earth. And then, as if the heavens themselves could no longer hold back their sorrow, a fine mist began to fall—soft, almost tender, like the tears of gods weeping for the passing of a good king. The people turned, their steps heavy, and made their way back to the castle courtyard, the mist clinging to their cloaks and hair.

The courtyard was a sea of bodies, crowded and still. Knights in their polished mail stood shoulder to shoulder with nobles draped in somber finery, while dignitaries and common folk alike pressed into the space, their faces drawn and their hearts burdened. King Uther had been a man who could touch the lives of all, from the highest lord to the lowliest farmer, and now, in death, he had brought them together as equals. For this moment, the divisions of rank and station melted away, leaving only a shared grief, a collective mourning for a man who had been as much a part of their lives as the earth beneath their feet.

Gav stood among his fellow cadets, their young frames stiff and formal in their black uniforms, the pendants of the four orders of Gamalaot glinting faintly against the dull light. He felt the weight of the day pressing down on him, a strange, hollow ache in his chest. Then, suddenly, a firm hand struck his back, jolting him from his thoughts. It was Wiglaf, his face solemn but his eyes steady, offering a nod that carried solidarity, a quiet acknowledgment of the loss they all bore, and Gav felt a flicker of gratitude amidst the heaviness.

"Greetings," Arthur called out, his voice steady but carrying the weight of the crown that now rested upon his brow—the same crown his father had worn, its gold gleaming faintly against the gray sky. He stood tall on the castle balcony, his gaze sweeping over the multitude below, a vast and silent sea of faces turned upward, waiting. As his words echoed across the courtyard, the crowd began to move, a slow and deliberate ripple, as one by one, they bowed. Knights, nobles, and common folk alike bent their heads, a wave of reverence rolling through the throng, a gesture of respect not just for the new king, but for the memory of the one who had come before. Arthur watched them, his heart heavy yet resolute, knowing the burden he now carried and the legacy he must uphold.

"My father was a good king," Arthur began, his voice carrying over the hushed crowd, each word measured. "One of the best in Gamalaot's long and storied history. And now, as I take this crown, I do so with trepidation, with a sadness lodged deep within my spirit, for I know he had more to give—more wisdom, more strength, more love for this land and its people. I cannot promise to be as good a king as he was. I cannot promise to walk in his footsteps or wear his mantle as he did. But what I can do—what I must do—is act in a manner that honors his legacy. I ask not for your blind faith, but for your trust, as I give you my sincere oath: I will serve you, the people of Gamalaot, as your king, with all that I am and all that I have."

The crowd stood in silence for a moment, the weight of his words settling over them. Then, as if stirred by a single breath, their voices rose in unison, strong and clear, piercing the misty air:

"Long live King Arthur!"

It was not a cheer, nor a celebration, but an affirmation, a solemn acceptance of the oath he had offered. They bowed again, not just to the crown, but to the man who now bore it, and to the promise he had made—a promise to honor the past while stepping into the uncertain light of the future.

The day had been declared a solemn respite, classes canceled in honor of the former king's passing. The castle grounds, usually alive with the chatter and bustle of students, now lay quiet, save for the soft rustle of leaves and the distant murmur of the lake. Gav, Nora, and Percy had found their way to a tree near the water's edge, its branches drooping low as if in mourning. They stood together, their silence speaking louder than words, each lost in their own thoughts yet bound by the shared weight of the day.

Nearby, their familiars moved about, socializing. Minnie, her plump lizard body waddling with an almost comical determination, darted around Lavinia, who hopped gracefully just out of reach. Both creatures had taken to using Orf, Percy's sturdy hound, as their makeshift playground, leaping and scampering across his broad back. Orf, for his part, bore it with a resigned patience, though his drooping ears and the occasional low grumble betrayed his annoyance. Minnie, in particular, seemed to be testing the limits of his tolerance, her round form growing ever larger by the day.

Gav glanced over at the scene, a faint smile tugging at the corner of his mouth despite the heaviness in his chest. It was a small, fleeting moment of lightness in an otherwise gray day, a reminder that life, in all its messy persistence, would go on.

"Aye, Gav," Wiglaf said as he strode up to the group, his voice lacking its usual gruff warmth.. "Percy. Nora."

"Hi, Wiglaf," they replied in unison, their voices blending into a single greeting.

Wiglaf's eyes settled on Nora, and he gave a nod of approval. "I'm pleased to see ye standin' strong once more, Miss Edmund. I feared for ye for a time."

Nora shrugged, her fingers brushing against the bandage wrapped around her arm. "I wasn't all that hurt," she said, her tone light but her eyes flickering with a deeper sadness. "It's Lucan you should be checking on. He took the worst of it."

"Aye," Wiglaf agreed, his expression sobering. "He's still in the healer's care. He'll be back on his feet soon enough, but the lad needs his rest, that much is certain. Can't rush the healing of a warrior."

Percy shifted uncomfortably, his gaze dropping to the ground. "I'm really sorry I wasn't there," he muttered, his voice thick with embarrassment.

"No," Nora and Gav protested immediately, their words overlapping.

"Percy, it's good you weren't," Nora said firmly, her eyes locking onto his. "It was… it was horrible. And I only saw part of it. You don't need to feel bad about missing it."

Gav nodded in agreement, his voice steady. "We know you would've been there if you could've. That's what matters."

Wiglaf clapped a heavy hand on Percy's shoulder, his grin returning, though it was tempered with a seriousness that didn't often show itself. "Aye, lad. There'll be many a chance to prove yer mettle. Mark me words! This life's got no shortage of trouble, alas. Yer time will come."

Percy looked up, his cheeks still flushed but his shoulders a little straighter. The weight of his guilt seemed to ease, if only slightly, as the others' words settled over him.

"Say, Gav," Wiglaf said, his voice lowering as his gaze shifted toward the distance. "The Archbishop asked me to come and get ya. He'd like a word."

Gav followed Wiglaf's line of sight, his eyes landing on the old Archbishop standing some ways off. The man was bent slightly at the waist, his long fingers plucking berries from a bush with a quiet, almost meditative focus. He popped one into his mouth, chewing slowly, his expression calm, almost serene. It struck Gav as odd—this was the day of King Uther's funeral, after all, and the Archbishop had been a close friend of the late king. Yet here he was, picking berries, seemingly untroubled. Maybe this was his way of coping, Gav thought. A quiet defiance against the weight of grief. No one else seemed to find it strange, so Gav pushed the thought aside.

He turned back to his friends, uncertainty flickering across his face. Nora and Percy exchanged a glance, then nodded at him.

"Go on," Nora said softly, her voice carrying a note of reassurance. "We'll be here."

"Best not to keep him waiting," Percy said, offering a smile.

Gav hesitated for a moment longer, then nodded. With a final glance at his friends, he turned and made his way toward the Archbishop, his footsteps crunching softly against the gravel path. The air felt heavier with each step, the weight of the day pressing down on him once more. Whatever the Archbishop wanted, Gav had a feeling it wasn't about berries.

Wiglaf's solid presence at his side was a small but steady comfort as Gav approached. The last time Gav had spoken to the old man, it had been when he was punished for fighting with Lucan. Even then, the Archbishop was an enigma, neither warm nor cold, his demeanor as difficult to decipher as the ancient texts he often studied. He was undeniably powerful, a figure of reverence and authority, but there was something about him that always left Gav feeling off-balance.

"Hello, Gav," the Archbishop said, his voice carrying a gentle warmth as he turned to face them. "And Sir Wiglaf."

Both Gav and Wiglaf bowed deeply, their movements synchronized. The Archbishop chuckled softly, the sound like the rustle of dry leaves in the wind. "Wiglaf's formalities are rubbing off, I see," he remarked, his eyes crinkling at the corners.

The old man's gaze drifted upward, settling on the gray mist that hung low in the sky, veiling the world in a soft, mournful light. "It's a nice day for your funeral, friend," he said quietly, almost to himself, as though addressing the late king directly. There was a wistfulness in his tone, a quiet acceptance of the natural order of things, but also a hint of something deeper—perhaps a private grief, a sorrow he carried alone.

"Gav, you seem to have taken to Avalon quite nicely. Have you enjoyed it? Quite magical, especially compared to America, right? Though I must say, there's a certain magic beyond The Veil as well."

Gav blinked, caught off guard by the question. He hesitated for a moment, then nodded.

"It's… different, sir. In a good way. Everything here feels alive in a way I never noticed back home. But I guess that's the magic, isn't it?"

The Archbishop's smile deepened, his eyes twinkling with a knowing light. "Indeed, it is. Avalon has a way of making you see the world anew. But tell me, have you ever wondered about the magic you left behind? The kind that doesn't come from spells?"

"I… I suppose I haven't thought much about it, sir."

The old man chuckled softly, his gaze drifting as if lost in memory. "That's the thing about magic, Gav. It's not always where you expect it to be. Sometimes it's in the mundane, the ordinary. Sometimes it's in the people, the places, the moments you take for granted."

Gav shifted uncomfortably, feeling the weight of the Archbishop's words but not quite understanding their full meaning. "Have you been to America, sir?"

"I've seen the world over several times," he said. "It sounds more impressive than it is. When you're as old as I am, it sort of just happens. You wake up one day and realize you've walked more paths than you can count, seen more wonders than you can remember. But the true magic, Gav, isn't in the places you've been or the things you've seen. It's in the connections you make, the lives you touch, the legacy you leave behind."

Gav nodded slowly, though he wasn't entirely sure he understood why he wanted to tell him this now.

"Is that all, sir?"

"Not quite," the Archbishop replied, turning to face him fully. His expression was calm, but there was a weight to his words that made Gav's stomach tighten. "If you would, please walk with me to my office. Wiglaf, I would appreciate your company as well."

"Aye, sir."

The three of them began to make their way toward the castle, their footsteps crunching softly against the cobblestone path. The mist had thickened, wrapping around them like a shroud. As they walked, Gav's mind raced, trying to anticipate what the Archbishop might say next.

"Gav, I am sorry to say this, but I fear you are stuck here for the time being."

"Say again, sir?"

The Archbishop glanced at him, his expression somber. "At the end of the term, I am afraid I cannot let you return home for the summer season. It's too dangerous."

"The Talons?" Gav asked nervously, his voice barely above a whisper.

"Correct," he replied. "Their reach is long, and their intentions are clear. Until we can ensure your safety, it's best you remain within the protection of Gamalaot."

Gav's mind spun, a whirlwind of frustration and fear. He had been counting on the summer break, on the chance to see his mom, and Tommy, to return to some semblance of normalcy—or at least what passed for normalcy in his life now. But the Archbishop's words left no room for argument.

"Sir?"

"Yes, Gav?"

"My brother… Mordred. He didn't kill me. He tried to, but he didn't go through with it. He looked scared, or sad. I don't understand why he spared me."

The Archbishop stroked his long beard, his eyes distant as though searching for the right words. "I think," he said slowly, "he perhaps understood, in that moment, that he couldn't kill you."

Gav frowned, his confusion deepening. "Even after everything he'd already done?"

The Archbishop's gaze softened, and he gave a small, almost sad smile. "People can be surprising, Gav. Even those who seem lost to darkness can find a flicker of light, if only for a moment. Mordred's actions that day… they may have been driven by something deeper than hate. Perhaps regret. Perhaps love. Or acceptance. It's hard to say."

Gav fell silent, his thoughts churning. He wanted to believe there was still something good in Mordred, something worth saving. But the memory of his brother's blade, the coldness in his eyes, made it hard to hold onto that hope.

As they reached the castle doors, the Archbishop paused and placed a hand on Gav's shoulder. "For now, focus on what's in front of you. Your training, your friends, your place here." He then turned. "Wiglaf," he said, his voice carrying a note of solemnity as they walked through the castle's grand halls, "I understand you and Gav got on well during Christmas. Would you be willing to watch over him, to act as his guardian while he remains here?"

Wiglaf's chest puffed out with pride, his shoulders squaring as he met the Archbishop's gaze. "I'll guard him as if he were my own blood, sir. On that, I swear me oath."

"Good," the Archbishop said with a smile, nodding in a way that showed no surprise. "I had a feeling you'd say as much."

Gav glanced between the two men, a warmth blooming in his chest. Wiglaf's promise felt like a shield, a reassurance that he wouldn't have to face whatever was coming alone. Still, the weight of the situation ate at him, and he couldn't help but feel a pang of guilt. He didn't want to be a burden.

The Archbishop led them up a winding staircase, the stone steps worn smooth by centuries of use. The air grew cooler as they ascended, the faint scent of old parchment and incense growing stronger with each step. Finally, they reached a heavy wooden door, its surface carved with intricate patterns of vines and runes. The Archbishop pushed it open, revealing his office—a room filled with towering bookshelves, flickering candles, and a large, ornate desk cluttered with scrolls and trinkets.

"Come in," the Archbishop said, gesturing for them to enter. "Wiglaf, would you mind waiting outside for a moment? Stand guard. I would like no interruptions."

Gav stepped inside, his eyes darting around the room, taking in the strange combination of order and chaos. Wiglaf waited beyond the door frame, his presence disappearing as the door closed with a soft click, sealing them in the quiet, dimly lit room.

"Do you know what it means to scry, Gav?"

"I've heard the term before, sir," Gav said, hesitating, his brow furrowing as he searched his memory. "But I really don't know what it means."

The Archbishop smiled faintly, a glimmer of amusement in his eyes. "Come over here, Gav. I'd like to show you something."

Gav stepped forward, his curiosity piqued. As he approached the desk, something extraordinary happened. A large bronze mirror, its frame intricately carved with symbols and runes, seemed to rise from the shadows, floating gently toward them as if summoned by an unseen force. The glass at its center shimmered, not solid but fluid, rippling like the surface of a pond disturbed by a gentle breeze.

"Whoa," Gav gasped, his eyes widening as he stared at the mirror, mesmerized by its otherworldly movement. He reached out instinctively, his fingers hovering just above the surface, afraid to touch it but drawn to its strange, liquid beauty.

The Archbishop watched him closely, his expression unreadable. "Scrying," he said, his voice both far away and measured, "is the art of seeing beyond the veil of your current perception. It is a way to glimpse what lies hidden—be it in the past, the present, the future, or in the depths of the soul. This mirror is a tool, a conduit for such visions."

Gav's hand trembled slightly as he finally let his fingertips brush the surface of the mirror. The liquid glass rippled at his touch, sending tiny waves radiating outward. It felt cool, almost alive, and for a moment, he thought he saw something flicker within its depths—a shadow, a shape, something just out of reach.

"What... what am I supposed to see?"

"Well," the Archbishop leaned forward, his gaze fixed on the mirror's surface. "That depends," he said. "Sometimes, the mirror shows us what we need to see. Is there something you need to see, Gav?"

"Just put the boy on!" shouted a familiar voice, sharp and full of energy.

Gav froze, a rising in his chest. "Mom?" he shouted, his voice trembling as he stared into the mirror.

There she was, her face filling the shimmering surface, her eyes wide with worry and relief. She looked exactly as he remembered her—her hair slightly tousled, her expression fierce yet tender.

"You've gotten so big," she gushed, her voice cracking with emotion. Then her eyes narrowed, her motherly instincts kicking in. "What's with that bruise on your cheek? What are they doing to you out there?! Marius? Are you there? Answer me!"

Gav couldn't help but laugh, the sound bubbling up from deep within him. It was so like his mom to jump straight to fretting over him, even in the middle of what should have been a magical, awe-inspiring moment. He glanced over his shoulder, noticing the Archbishop slipping quietly out of the room, a wry smile playing on his lips as he disappeared through the door.

"He's gone, Mom," Gav said, still chuckling.

"Oh, that man!" she huffed, her hands on her hips. "Always so mysterious, so dramatic. Couldn't even stick around to say hello?"

Gav shook his head, tears streaming down his cheeks now. He hadn't realized how much he'd missed her voice, her presence, until this moment. Even her nagging, her over-the-top concern, was like a melody he hadn't heard in far too long.

"I'm fine, Mom," he said, his voice thick with emotion. "Really. It's just... It's been a lot. But I'm okay."

The Archbishop closed the door softly behind him, latching it with care to give Gav the privacy he needed to catch up with his mother. He stood in the dimly lit hallway with Wiglaf, the two men exchanging a look that was far graver than the one they had worn in Gav's presence.

"Master La Faye?" Wiglaf began, his voice low and hesitant, as though he were reluctant to voice the question but knew he must.

"What is it, old friend?"

"The other night, at the old Ragnell hall... was that...?"

"Morgana?" the Archbishop interrupted, his voice steady but tinged with a quiet sadness. "Yes, it was."

Wiglaf exhaled sharply, his shoulders sagging under the weight of the confirmation. "So she's commandin' The Talons now, is she?"

"It would seem that way," the Archbishop said, his gaze distant, as though he were seeing not the hallway around them but the shadowed past.

"She's always been, uh, fearsome."

"She was prodigious," the Archbishop said gravely. "She will make a terrible adversary."

The two men stood in silence for a while, their faces bore the same pained expression, a silent lament for the state of things, for the loss of what once was, and the uncertainty of what lay ahead.

But then, from behind the closed door, a burst of muffled laughter broke through the heavy silence. Gav's laughter, pure and unrestrained, penetrated the door and echoed in the hallway. It was a sound so full of life, so full of hope, that it seemed to cut through the gloom like a ray of sunlight piercing a storm cloud.

The pair of men exchanged a glance, their grim expressions softening slightly. For a moment, the weight of their worries seemed to lift, replaced by a quiet, shared resolve.

"He's come a long way, that one," Wiglaf said, his voice quieter now, almost tender.

"He has," the Archbishop agreed. "But he still has much to learn. Much to face. The Talons won't wait. And the prophecy... It's already set too many on edge. The boy is going to need all the help he can get."

"Aye, that he will."

"He will need friends. Allies. Strength. Skill. And time—though I fear time is the most precious, and is the one thing we cannot give him."

Wiglaf's jaw tightened, his hand instinctively resting on the hilt of his sword. "We'll do all we can. I'll see to it."

The Archbishop placed a hand on Wiglaf's shoulder, his touch warm and reassuring. "I know you will, old friend."

Another burst of laughter drifted from the office, pulling them both back from the edge of their grim thoughts. The sound was a reminder—a reminder of why they fought, why they endured. Gav was more than just a boy caught in the crossfire of a prophecy. More than anything, he was a beacon, a spark of hope in a world that seemed increasingly shrouded in shadow.

Even if he didn't know it yet.